Second Draft of My Life

Also by Sara Lewis

The Answer Is Yes

But I Love You Anyway

Heart Conditions

Trying to Smile and Other Stories

Second Draft of My Life

A NOVEL

Sara Lewis

ATRIA BOOKS
New York London Toronto Sydney Singapore

LEW

ATRIA BOOKS, a division of Simon & Schuster Inc.
1230 Avenue of the Americas, New York, NY 10020

Library of Congress Cataloging-in-Publication Data

Lewis, Sarah.
Second draft of my life: a novel/Sarah Lewis.
p. cm.
1. First grade (Education)—Fiction. 2. Fiction—Authorship—Fiction.
3. Women teachers—Fiction. I. Title.

PS3562.E9745 S43 2002
813'.54—dc21

2002017083

ISBN: 0-7434-3669-5

First Atria Books hardcover printing May 2002

10 9 8 7 6 5 4 3 2 1

Printed in the U.S.A.

To Richard Abate and Emily Bestler
with oceans of gratitude.

Acknowledgments

I would like to thank my excellent friends, Binnie Kirshenbaum and Niels Aaboe, for reading drafts (numbers 7 and 10, I think) of *Second Draft of My Life* and for giving me feedback and crucial moral support. Thanks, you guys!

1

My old life ended at the South Coast Book Awards. I was the author of five critically acclaimed novels that no one had ever heard of. I was attending the awards ceremony because I was nominated in the Mainstream Fiction category for my most recent novel, *My Self-Portrait of Someone Else.* Sometimes people's lives change forever when they win something huge; mine changed because I lost something small.

It wasn't just this awards ceremony that made me want to chuck everything and start over from scratch. If my life had been a novel, readers would have seen the foreshadowing in any number of incidents that led up to that evening. What happened at the South Coast Book Awards wasn't the worst moment of my writing career; it was simply the last, the event that jerked my former existence to a final, screeching halt.

At the ceremony, I was sitting at a table with a group of writers of how-to computer books. They all knew each other. The event took place in a hotel meeting room. You may not think of southern California as a place where a lot of writers live. Most of the time, it seemed to me that I was living in a land of software engineers and biotech specialists. But once a year, I found myself in a room packed with writers of every physical description, ethnic group, interest area, and income level. Of course, many of them wrote about computers and biotechnology, but still, the room was so filled with writers that the waiters could hardly squeeze between the tables. Small talk nearly drowned out the Easy Classics tape. I didn't have a date for the evening. My boyfriend, Andrew, a software engineer, never came with me to these events. He said he wouldn't know what to talk about in a roomful of writers. I tried to explain that he would have more in common with most of the attendees than I would, but he was unconvinced. He asked me, "Why would I want to pay thirty dollars to eat a bad dinner, make polite conversation with people I don't care about, and listen to a bunch of boring speeches?" I didn't have a good answer for him, so I went alone.

"Who are you again?" a woman asked me, shouting over the noise of the crowd, as we waited for our drinks to arrive. I had already introduced myself a few minutes earlier.

"Charlotte Dearborn," I said again. "I'm a novelist."

"A novice?" a man across the table shouted, cupping a hand behind one ear. "We've all got to start somewhere!" He smiled magnanimously. Everyone nodded in agreement.

"Starting out is the hardest part," a young woman across from me said. "When I first started—"

"No," I said, shaking my head. "I said I write *novels.* The one I'm nominated for is my *fifth,* and it's called *My Self-Portrait of*—"

"Self-published first novel!" said a heavy man with a frizzy gray pony tail. "More power to ya!"

I shook my head. "It's published by Collard & Stanton. You know, in New York? It's about a portrait artist who—"

I didn't continue because just then a waiter brought rolls, and everyone leaned forward to peer into the basket and see what kind.

I participated in this kind of event in the hope that the press coverage it generated might sell a few more copies of my books. However, there had been no media at all at last year's event. After winning the highest honor of the evening, I hadn't even ended up with my name in the San Diego newspaper. I was hoping that this year there would be some press. Now I put dressing on my salad and stayed out of the conversation at my table, which was about computers and people I didn't know.

After dessert, there was a rambling speech by a local television chef about the vast and varied writing community in our area, how fortunate we all were to live here. Then the awards presentation began. There were a lot of categories—cookbooks, children's picture books, self-published poetry, eight different categories for books having to do with computers. Everyone at my table either won an award or was the date of someone who did. I clapped for each of them. As they returned to the table, I admired their plaques and congratulated them.

"And now," said Jim Shaw, after what seemed like hours, "we've reached the very last category and one of my own special favorites." I sat up straighter and felt for my lipstick in my purse. Almost home, I thought. Jim said, "It's the horror fiction category."

"What?" I said loudly.

Jim continued. "I've been reading scary stories since I was six years old. I love 'em. We're blessed with a thriving community of excellent horror writers from historical to sci-fi. So it gives me great pleasure to announce the three nominees in this category. They are Aaron Garner for *Never-Ending Nightmare,* Bonnie Chernoff for *Screaming Bloody Murder,* and Cheryl Dearborn for *Self-Portrait of Myself.*" He began to open the envelope. He did this slowly to heighten the drama.

"Oh, no!" I said. I turned to the man on my left. "They got my title wrong, my name wrong, and my category wrong!" The man looked annoyed that I was talking during the presentation. I went on. "This is a *mistake!* I'm supposed to be in mainstream fiction!" I turned to the woman on my right. "This is not—I can't—what should I do?"

A couple of people at my table turned to me, smiling tolerantly, even though I was making noise and distracting them.

"And the winners are," said Jim, pulling the paper from the envelope, "in third place, Charlotte DiBone for *Soft Portrait.*"

The people at my table smiled and clapped. I walked to the front of the room, took my award certificate, walked back through the tables, out of the room, down the stairs to the lobby, and out the door to the parking lot. I dropped the certificate in a trash can and drove home.

Of course, it wasn't the awards ceremony that made me decide to give up writing. When you lose a war, it probably doesn't end with the explosion of a big bomb or the death of an important general. While such a singular event may directly precede your walking out of your bunker with your arms raised, a white flag held high in one hand, defeat happens by degrees. And so it was with my career as a novelist. The award I didn't win was simply the last of a series of defeating events.

2

The next morning, a Saturday, I prepared myself to tell Andrew that I was quitting writing. I made coffee for both of us. He was sitting at one of his computers in our bedroom. "Thanks," he said, taking the cup I handed him. Then when I didn't walk away, he looked up. "What?" he said, and then looked back at the screen.

"I'm not going to write anymore," I said slowly and clearly so there would be no mistake about the seriousness of my decision. "No more novels. No more short stories, essays, book reviews, articles. I am quitting. As of right now. I'm finished with writing. Forever."

I thought he was going to say how disappointed he was in me, how I was letting us both down by giving up my dream. I was ready with a long list of reasons.

Andrew turned in his chair and said, "Good idea!" He turned back to his work.

"Oh," I said.

"Whatever you do, I'm sure it will bring in more money than writing," he said.

You'd think that I'd be relieved not to encounter opposition. In fact, his quick, easy agreement made my skin prickle with anger. The hair on the back of my neck stood up, as if I were an animal preparing for attack. "Andrew," I said. I had the same feeling I sometimes had when I wrote, when my character was about to say something important. I was curious myself to find out what it was. I said, "We've been living together for four years. Are we ever going to get married?"

Oh! I thought, hearing my own words. *That.*

"What?" Andrew said, a flush coming into his cheeks as though I'd caught him pilfering office supplies or digging into a special dessert I'd made for guests. In the next second, he straightened, as if he were about to say something to turn the tables and make *me* feel guilty. "I thought we agreed not to discuss—"

"*Are* we?" I said with an insistence that surprised me even more than the original question. "Do you love me enough to stay with me, to buy a house together, get a bird feeder for the backyard and some pets and a joint savings account and to—well, just, are we ever going to promise to be together forever?" Now that I'd started this, I needed to know, right now, this minute, what was going to be true for the rest of my life.

He scratched his head. He looked at the computer screen. He typed three characters. Then he looked up at me. "No," he said, "I don't think so. I could be wrong, I guess, but why do you always have to—it's not like marriage is this—"

"Stop," I said. I held my hand up, a traffic cop. "I do not want to hear any of that speech ever again!"

I grabbed my keys and my purse and walked out the front door.

* * *

As soon as I walked into The Book Club, an independent bookstore in a shopping center near the ocean, a loud voice rang out. "Charlotte Dearborn! My favorite author!" This was my twin sister, Emily, the owner of the bookstore, who was behind the cash register, ringing up a sale. When I came closer, she peered at my face. "Charlotte?" she said. "Are you OK?"

"Fine," I said, letting her know that this was something I wasn't going to talk about in front of her customer.

Emily slid a store bookmark into the woman's new book, while I craned my neck to see what it was—*Nine Lives: Miraculous Cat Tales.* I knew the author. It was a skinny little book, her first, still available only in hardcover, but over a million copies were in print. Emily put the book in a bag and handed it to her customer. "Now, before you go," she said, lowering her voice conspiratorially, "let me show you something." She came around the counter and led the way to a special display of my books right up by the front door. "These are the most wonderful novels you'll ever read in your life. *And,"* she put her hand on the customer's arm, "I'd like you to meet the *author,* Charlotte Dearborn."

"How do you do," said the customer, giving me a brief nod. She was an older woman with long, perfect acrylic nails painted the delicate pink of the inside of a baby's ear. She said, "I've got enough books right now." She was backing out the front door, tightly gripping her cat book.

"They make great gifts!" Emily said. "Especially signed!"

"No, thank you," the woman said, leaving the store.

"Have a nice day!" Emily and I called after her in unison.

"I've planted the seed," Emily said. "Next time she comes in, she'll buy one of your books. At least one." She fussed with my display, which she had decorated with a small African violet plant, a blue and white teapot, and some knitting-in-progress.

These were objects that my sister considered cozy, at once old-fashioned and contemporary, the very essence of what people would be pursuing when they chose one of my books, she believed. None of the other piles of books received such adornment. The small shop couldn't spare the space, but I got special treatment.

Two years earlier, one of the book superstores had moved in directly across the street from Emily's shopping center, threatening the precarious niche she had carved out for herself with book groups and tourists and longtime neighborhood residents, dramatically cutting into her business. "You've got to give me credit for choosing a good location," she said when she finally stopped crying about the big new store. "I mean these guys don't just plop an outlet down at random. It has to be *right.* They research the location. They have people for that. And think about it—I found it twelve years before they did! All by myself!"

Emily almost never sat down at work. If you wanted to have a conversation with her, you had to follow her around the place while she straightened, rearranged, dusted, tended her books, her shelves, her recommendation cards. Every couple of minutes, she would grab a book off the shelf and start reading it out loud to you, some poignant metaphor or descriptive detail that she loved, a paragraph she said was worth the whole price of the book. "Listen to that! Now if I had written that, I would consider myself satisfied. I'd tell myself that I had made a valuable contribution to the world and never give myself a hard time again!"

"So, tell me," Emily said to me, now pinching a dead bloom off the violet plant. "How was the awards ceremony last night? Did you mention the store in your acceptance speech?"

"Emily, listen. It was a turning point. They got the title wrong. They got my name wrong. And I came in *third.* I spent the evening trying to explain what I did to computer people who don't even read fiction, and I came in *last* in the wrong category! I was in horror. I've never even *read* a horror novel, let alone written one. They never announced mainstream fiction, which was what I entered. Em, I can't do this anymore. I'm done."

"You're absolutely right. Don't even enter your next book. It's not worth it."

"I mean, I'm finished with writing," I said. "I'm quitting right now."

"Oh, right!" she said. "Charlotte, don't be ridiculous. It's what you do! It's who you are! What are you talking about?"

"No," I said. "I'm dead serious. I'm quitting. Starting today, I am no longer a writer. I have to make a decent living. I'm tired of scraping by. I'm tired of trying to explain myself. I'm sick of waiting for something to happen. I am giving up. I quit." Emily took a breath to say something, but I went on. "That's not all. I'm breaking up with Andrew. The relationship is going nowhere."

She just looked at me silently for a long time. "Charlotte," she said finally. She took a breath. I knew what she was going to say. She was going to give me a whole string of examples of writers who had not been immediately successful, then had finally broken into the big time with movie deals and runaway best-sellers that took their publishers by surprise. I even knew the examples she was going to give, people whose first three, four, even five books went completely unnoticed, authors whose names were now practically synonymous with success. She was going to say that Andrew would come around eventually, that he really did love me, even though he didn't always act like it, that people have to be allowed their own time to make a commitment. When you have an identical twin, her thinking is never a surprise.

Emily opened her arms wide, then threw them around me in a tight squeeze. "Thank God!" she said. "I am so proud of you!" She let me go, backed up, smiling. "I know this was a really hard decision that you didn't want to make, but I'm so proud that you are brave enough, flexible enough to switch your focus and move on."

"What?" I said. "I didn't plan to do this. It's just that at the ceremony last night, all the hope I had left just, well, evaporated. And then this morning, Andrew—I mean it just hit me that he doesn't have the dream for us that I hoped he would. He's another dead end, like my books. I can work on it, hope, pray, visualize, fight for the rest of my life, and neither one of them, the writing or Andrew, is ever, ever going to give me what I need. Or want." I looked at Emily, smiling at me. "I thought you were going to say—"

"You are doing the right thing. Andrew doesn't deserve you, Charlotte. And the writing, well, you gave it your best shot. You really did. You put everything you had into it and then some. I've never seen anybody work so hard as you have on your novels. I know it must hurt to have to do this, but it's right." She put her hands on her hips. "So. What's next?"

I took a deep breath. "I'm going to become an elementary school teacher. After all, I have my California teaching credential."

"Who would've thought?" Emily said. "How about that? When we got those credentials, we sneered at the idea. But you know, I think it's a good idea. You'll be a wonderful teacher."

I said, "I hope so. I wouldn't be doing it if I didn't think I could make a contribution. Now with reduced class size, there are a lot of jobs. And people with some life experience are supposed to be pretty hirable. At least, that's what I've read. I just want a steady income and a benefits package. I can't tell you how good it will feel to have checks come in on a regular basis."

Emily said, "And we offer discounts to students and teachers!"

"Somehow, I expected you to have a harder time with this."

Emily put her hand on my shoulder. "Are you kidding? You are my hero! Look at you! You're leaving everything familiar behind and striding off into new territory."

"Right. I am the perfect role model. A forty-two-year-old spinster with a failed career," I said. "And I feel like I've just leapt off a cliff into the wild, blue yonder."

"A leap of faith! Perfect image!" Emily said.

"I don't know about *that,"* I said. "Faith in what? I mean—"

"In *you.* In Charlotte Dearborn!"

"Oh, no, I sure don't have any—" Suddenly the enormity of what I had decided to do hit me, and my eyes filled with tears.

A customer walked in, a man in a hat and shorts. "Do you have maps?"

"Don't I wish," I said under my breath.

"Yes, we do," Emily said. "Let me show you."

"Emily," I said. "I'm going to sweep the floor."

"Thanks," Emily called to me from the map rack. "It needs it."

I went in the back room and wiped my tears on my sleeve. I took a deep breath. I said, "It's OK. It's OK. Everything is going to be *OK."* I got the broom and dustpan from the closet. I swept hard, briskly swiping over areas that didn't even seem dusty. By the time the floor was finished, I felt a little better. I helped in the store for the rest of the day, staying away from home as long as possible.

I had dinner with Emily and her family. Then her husband, Brad, took their three kids to the movies. Emily and I went back to the house where I had been living with Andrew. He was at a party to celebrate the sale of a software program he had helped to create, so Emily and I started packing my things into boxes.

Monday morning I called my agent in New York. I was dreading his reaction to my decision. Howard and I had worked together for years. I considered him a close friend, though we had never actually met in person. A long time ago, after he read one of my short stories in a magazine, he wrote to me, suggesting that I write a novel. He said he would represent me. So we had been together since my first book was just a tiny shred of an idea. He had encouraged me, talked me through developing it, waited while it germinated, grew, blossomed, and flourished into a real-live book. The *New York Times* called that book "at once a funny and heartbreaking read that heralds the arrival of a fresh, intelligent voice." And Howard had shared in my joy and excitement at the promise of early success. He was just starting his own agency then; we were both beginners. "Together," we used to say to each another, "you and me." And, "It's a partnership. Whatever progress we make benefits us both."

I knew I was going to be letting him down by what I had to say. We had a history; he was one of my best friends, though, as I say, we had never met.

"Howard," I said, "I have something to tell you."

"Oh, boy," he groaned. "Go ahead. Shoot. But remember, I'm very sensitive."

"I don't really know how to tell you this."

"What? Wait! If it's short stories or poetry, I don't want to hear about it. I just couldn't take it today!"

"No. Listen. It's not that. I'm quitting," I said. "I'm not writing any more books. I'm finished. After all these years, all this work, no one has heard of me. I don't make enough money. I've tried everything I can think of to make this work. I'm going to do something else."

I cringed, bracing myself for what he was going to say. How could I do this to him, after all our years together? How could I leave him alone after all we'd been through together? Why now? He would tell me the pieces were about to click into place, that people were about to catch on, wake up, and find me. As a matter of fact, he had just heard that Oprah was planning to devote an entire program—

In New York, Howard sighed. "I don't blame you. Geez, I'd do the same thing if I were you, only I would have done it eight or ten years ago. Charlotte, I admire your perseverance. I really do. But there's perseverance, and then there's a death wish. I'm glad you see that. Get out of this cesspool of a business. Drop everything and run as fast and as far as you can. I'd do it myself if I weren't making so much goddamn money."

"Oh, well, I thought you were going to say—"

"You know you've always been my favorite."

"Thanks. Are you sure you don't say that to all your—"

"Do I still get chocolates for Christmas?" he wanted to know.

"Sure, Howard. Of course. You're still one of my best friends. This doesn't change—"

"Charlotte, I've got movie people on another line. Do you want to hold or are you done?"

"Oh. Well, I guess I'm done. Thanks for your support and, um, you know, understanding."

"Always and forever. You're my special one. Bye, Charlotte."

"Bye."

I hung up and called Jordan, my editor. She was a lot younger than I was, maybe twenty-five or twenty-six. We had not been working together very long. I hadn't met her either. Her three predecessors had been let go, casualties of the shrinking publishing industry. One was writing greeting cards now; another was doing gift books for a big, commercial house; and the other had opened a diet-center franchise on Long Island.

"Jordan," I said, coming straight out with it, "I have something to tell you. I'm not going to write any more books. I'm not even going to promote the ones I have out. I'm quitting. I'm sorry. I just can't do this anymore."

I got ready for Jordan to tell me that she, personally, was a big fan of mine, as were most of the staff, that she was sure the next book was going to be my chance to break out, that if I gave up now, I'd never know what might have happened.

"So, what are you going to do instead?" Jordan was eating something.

I took a deep breath. "I'm going to teach elementary school."

Now she would tell me I wasn't going to make any money teaching.

Jordan said, "That sounds great! I love kids. So I guess I should get in touch with Howard if anything comes up?"

"Right," I said.

"Well, congratulations! And good luck!" she said cheerfully and then hung up.

3

Emily and I were shoving my new couch into place under a window. We had brought it to my new apartment in her van. It was just a love seat, so with the car seats folded down, it fit. Getting it up the stairs of the building wasn't too hard either, and this way I didn't have to pay for delivery. "Do you think it's too flowery?" I asked Emily.

"I keep telling you, I think it's beautiful," she said. "That creamy background is perfect. You can pick up any of those flower colors—red, blue, green—with curtains, throw pillows, accessories. And it looks brand-new! Really. I'm going to get *my* next couch at Floor Samples Plus."

"There's the smudge, though" I said, rubbing my hand over the gray streak at the side of one arm.

"Put a pillow over that," Emily said. "Make it a solid, and that will tone down the flowers."

"So you do think they need to be toned down. Oh, no! I've made a mistake. What was I thinking? It's this crazy mass of flowers coming at you from every direction. Busy! Overpowering!" I put my hands over my eyes.

"Charlotte," Emily said.

My sister put both her hands on my shoulders. I let my hands drop as she looked into my face. Looking at my twin sister was not like looking into a mirror, the way people sometimes think. It was like looking at an "after" picture of myself. I was the "before" picture—before the diet, the therapy, the haircut and makeover, the exercise program, falling in love, the attainment of inner peace, take your pick—and my sister was the "after" picture.

"Listen to me," Emily said. "Your couch is fine. It's a beautiful couch. I love it! Every time I buy something big, I feel like I've made a mistake. You just have to get used to it. Your new apartment is *great.* It's going to be so good here. I *know* it is. It's the start of a great new chapter, or a whole new book, even."

"Well, I don't know about that. Maybe it's a second draft." I forced a smile. "You're right. It's going to be great. And I like the couch. I do. I think."

"I would have told you if it were too busy. And the apartment is clean and full of light. Convenient. You're going to be really happy here."

"I already am," I said. I smiled better. "I like my new life."

"That's the spirit," she said. "Now, are you sure you don't want to come over for dinner?"

"No, thanks. I'll have dinner here. At my *new* table. That you gave me. From your garage."

"I'm glad we found a spot for it. I think it looks cute there."

"Very." I nodded, and we both looked at the table. When Emily and her husband had just Janie, their first child, Emily and I had bought this little, round table at a garage sale and painted it white. For a while, she had used it for her kitchen table. By the time her third child was born, they needed a bigger table. So this one became an art/homework table for her kids' playroom. Then when they moved into their new house last year, the table had somehow ended up unused in the garage. My sister had scraped off almost every trace of crayon, paint, and glue before she brought the table to me the day before, my first day in my new place.

Now Emily got her keys out of her pocket and picked up her purse. "I have to get going. I'm worried Brad might've forgotten to give the kids lunch." She hugged me. "Call me later."

"OK," I said. "And listen. You know what? Besides just changing my job, something else is going to happen."

"I'm sure a lot of things—" she started to say.

"I'm going to meet someone," I interrupted.

"Oh, great, Charlotte. I'm glad you're feeling positive."

"No, I mean, The One. This is it. It's going to happen soon."

"How can you know that? I don't think you should put so much pressure on—"

"No, it's not that I'm *hoping* it will happen. I *know.* It's like outlining a plot for a novel. You know there are certain things that are going to happen. You just don't necessarily know *how.*"

"OK, well," Emily said, turning toward the door, "I hope you're right. I just don't want you to be disappointed if it doesn't happen."

Not wanting me to be disappointed was a major occupation for Emily. She worried about the fact that I wasn't married, that I didn't have kids, that I didn't own a house, that not enough people had bought my books. Emily tried every way she could to make up for these things. She had welcomed each of my boyfriends as instant family members. She included me in every one of her own family's activities, from holiday dinners to buying school shoes. She promoted my books by putting up displays in her store, sending copies and writing letters to Oprah, writing customer reviews for Amazon.com, anything she could think of. I really appreciated my twin sister's efforts. Occasionally though, like now, when I had just broken up with someone and was forced to rethink my life, I wanted to feel that she didn't have to work so hard for me. I wished I had the kind of life that she could ignore, that didn't need any help.

"Disappointment is not even a possibility," I said. "I am going to meet that special one. It's going to happen. There's no way to stop it. The way I figure it, most adults in the world are married and have regular jobs. How hard can it be?"

Emily smiled. "I'm glad you're so optimistic!" She hugged me. Still smiling, she went out my new front door.

I went to the window and watched her get into her van. She bent her head sideways and looked up at me through the windshield. She waved. I knew she would, just as she knew I would be standing there, looking down, waiting for her to wave to me. I waved back, smiling. She backed her car out of its spot. I waved again, for good measure, though she wasn't looking at me anymore. She turned right and drove off down the road.

I sat on one of my moving boxes. The top of it squished in until I hit something solid. *The second draft of my life,* I said to myself. That was a good thing, I guess. A fresh start, a new beginning. Of course, I had been hoping that the first draft was going to work. But I was on the right path now. Really. I was.

4

I was looking forward to working with people, for a change, instead of being by myself most of the time. When I pictured myself eating lunch with a group of talkative teachers or standing in front of a roomful of children, I felt a buzz of happiness and anticipation. I was eager to do the work of teaching, in part because, unlike writing novels, the lessons were already there: A curriculum of reading, writing, and math already existed; you just added your own bulletin boards and folder decorations. There were even packages of this stuff you could buy without creating anything of your own. It wasn't like writing fiction, where you had to dream it all up out of thin air.

To prepare for my new career, I removed all the files that contained my books from my computer. Two of them were already published, so there really wasn't any good reason for having them taking up valuable memory. The only unpublished piece that I had to take off was the novel I had been working on when I decided to quit. I thought I was about halfway through the writing of it, approximately halfway to the point where I would give it to Howard for comments, go over it one more time, and smooth out the rough spots before letting him offer it to a publisher for sale. I had never abandoned a novel at this stage before. The main character was a teacher, ironically enough. Her name was Janet Greenhill, *Miss* Greenhill.

I wasn't going to finish that book. It always took a long time to get the characters up and walking around. If I told you how long, you'd be shocked. You'd wonder why anybody ever wanted to write a novel if you have to spend that long feeling as though you weren't getting anywhere. But once I finally got my characters, the payoff was that they came to seem like my good friends. But Miss Greenhill wasn't there yet. There was something wrong. She had this distant feel. I never quite warmed up to her. I'm not sure why. Even though this would have been my sixth novel, it was my slowest and most painful to get going. It doesn't seem fair, does it? Writing novels should get easier and easier, like Rollerblading or playing the harmonica. Occasionally a book or a part of a book would just seem to pop out of me easily, and I'd think, Now I've got the hang of this. I'd think writing would be easier now for the rest of my life. But then the very next thing might be the slowest, most halting process yet. Like snowflakes and children, no two novels are alike, and you just never knew how it was going to go.

The long, hard work is not even the worst of it. The nastiest part of writing is that you don't know until the thing is practically on the store shelves if it's ever going to turn into anything you can use. It's practically the last second before the thing starts to resemble a book.

So not finishing this particular novel wasn't like moving and leaving my best friends behind. It was more like being told that a hard test I hadn't studied for was canceled. Maybe there just wasn't enough to Miss Greenhill and her story to sustain a novel. Sometimes book ideas just didn't work. The night before I was to start school, I selected the document on my computer, copied it, transferred it to a Zip disk, trashed the original, labeled the Zip disk, put it into a small plastic box, and turned off my computer. Elated, I ate a whole pint of coffee ice cream to celebrate.

To update my teaching credential, I had to take fifteen units of classes on health, special education, and computers. Meanwhile I signed on as a sub in the school district where I now lived. It was a suburban neighborhood where most of the parents worked for computer and biotech companies. Apparently there was a shortage of subs, so once you got into the system, you could work every day if you wanted to. I got a phone call at five one morning. A school near my new apartment needed a sixth-grade teacher. The regular teacher had had knee surgery the night before after some kind of accident, and he would be out for a couple of weeks.

The sixth-graders were more challenging than I had expected. They seemed to talk all day during class and even interrupted me while I was speaking, blurting out answers, and even random comments on completely unrelated topics, without raising their hands. The first day, two boys got into a fistfight during PE. The next day, one by one, ten kids raised their hands and asked to go to the bathroom. Then they had a mass coughing fit. I ignored these pranks, of course, but it shook me to try to explain converting fractions to decimals over the sound of thirty-one children coughing.

The teacher, Rick Barnstable, had left detailed instructions along with his phone number, in case I had questions. I waited until he got back from the hospital and then gave him a full twenty-four hours at home before I dialed his number during recess. "The kids want to know if they're allowed to work on their research reports during library time," I said.

Mr. Barnstable said, "Only if they finish everything Ms. Scott has for them."

"Oh, right, sure," I said. "That's what I told them. Also, for the math test, are you including the stuff in the blue boxes? Or just sections 6.1 through 6.4?"

"All of it," he said. "The whole chapter. There are extra practice problems in the green math bin under the windows. Anyone who's having trouble should take home those packets."

I said, "I'll tell them that again. And, um, what do you do about the, uh, when the kids are throwing things in the classroom—small harmless stuff like erasers and tortilla chips, not dangerous or anything—or, let's say, using four-letter words in their essays?"

"What?" he almost shouted.

"Oh, it isn't everyone. It's just about six or eight, maybe twelve, kids."

"The use of obscene language is a violation of the school conduct code, and you send those students to the principal's office. When they come back, you tell them I expect a five-paragraph essay about why this kind of language is unacceptable at school. I want it on my desk the day I return, no later. Tell them that throwing anything in the classroom is an automatic detention." He sounded shocked and hurt. Then he said, "This is an age when kids really try to test the boundaries. You have to be pretty firm about setting limits. Are you going to be able to handle them until I come back? It will be another couple of weeks at least."

"Oh, yeah," I said. "No problem. Really." To be honest, I had tried not to think about how many more days it would be. I was trying to just survive one at a time. Sometimes I was trying to make it through a morning or a spelling lesson or a single paragraph in reading.

"Don't be afraid to speak up if this is too much for you. They can find another sub, I'm sure."

"Really, I can handle it," I said firmly. "I can be really tough, *mean,* practically."

"If you say so. And can I ask you for a big favor?" he said. "When the research reports come in, do you think you could bring them to me? I want to look at them myself, and I won't be able to drive for a while. I just live a mile from school on Camino Cielo."

"Sure," I said. "No problem. That's the way I go home anyway."

"Great. Thanks a lot. See you Friday then."

"Feel better!" I said.

At the end of the week, I called Rick Barnstable to let him know I was coming over with the reports. When I rang the doorbell, he yelled to me to come around to the backyard. He was in shorts and an old T-shirt, his recovering knee propped on a pillow.

"So, how are they?" he asked, taking the papers, squinting up at me from his lawn chair.

I said, "Pretty good. Most of them are five pages or more. They've all got bibliographies with at least five sources, the way you wanted."

"I meant the kids," he said.

"Oh!" I said. "The kids! Yeah. Well, much better! Everything's under control! Really. It's going *great,*" I said. I hoped my voice sounded confident.

"Did Stephanie finish the book I gave her? Is Nathan getting to school on time?"

I tried not to look at his swollen knee, which seemed to be held together by tape and a blue splint. Instead, I looked at his face.

He seemed to be about my age, and he had greenish-blue eyes with minuscule dots of yellow, brown hair with some gray coming in, one eyebrow a couple of shades darker than the other, and a rather large nose. While no single feature struck me as particularly attractive, something about the way it all worked together made me want to tell him anything he wanted to know.

It took an hour and a half to answer all his questions about which children had to be separated for talking, who asked what about the math homework, whose feelings were hurt at recess. After that, he called me every night for two weeks for a summary of the day's events and to advise me about flare-ups of bad behavior.

I found out that he was divorced, with two daughters in high school, that he had originally wanted to be an actor, got a teaching job right out of college as a temporary position, and stayed because he loved it. When he wasn't teaching or with his daughters, he surfed. The knee problem had nothing to do with surfing, though. He was just rolling his garbage can out to the street when he somehow twisted his knee stepping off the curb. After two and a half weeks' recovery, he was well enough to teach again.

I went to the district office to formally apply for a position. I put down Rick's school as my first choice. Rick was in my plan about my new life. We had chemistry. On the application, I said I was especially interested in teaching in the lower grades, which I was sure must be easier than dealing with children on the brink of adolescence. I subbed all through the spring, in the four elementary schools in the district where I lived.

During the summer, while I was waiting to get hired, I had taken an intensive course on teaching reading and math in the elementary grades. Now I was up-to-date on phonics versus whole-language issues, chunking, journal writing, strategies and games for teaching math facts, the works. I hadn't taught any actual children yet, besides my student teaching back in my twenties and a few months of subbing, but otherwise I was fully prepared to teach school.

Ten days before Labor Day, I got a call from the school district office. There was an opening for a first-grade teacher in the school where I had subbed for Rick Barnstable. "Our numbers are up again this year. There's so much building over that way," the superintendent said. "Anyhow, the job is yours if you want it."

"I do," I said. "I'll take it."

"Fine. We'll need you down here to fill out some paperwork, and then you can start setting up your room."

"Thank you!" I said.

I called my sister. She said, "Congratulations! Let's go out to dinner and celebrate! I'll get Brad to come home early and watch the kids—or, wait, we could all go! Do you want to go to that wood-fired pizza place down by the beach? I hear they have really good—"

"Could we do this some other time? I don't think I want to go tonight. I mean, if that's OK with you."

"Oh," she said. "Oh, sure. Why? Did you have something else—"

"You know that guy I subbed for? I'm going to call him. I'm going to ask him out."

"That's a great idea! Listen to you! This is exactly what you needed."

"You're not disappointed that I don't want to—"

"We'll do that some other night! I think it's a great idea. Call him right now before you think about it too much. I'm hanging up. Call me back and tell me what he says."

"I will."

Rick answered on the first ring. I said, "This is Charlotte Dearborn. I subbed for you a few months ago."

"Sure, of course. How are you?"

"Very well, thanks. I just got a job. I'm going to be teaching first grade at your school."

"Congratulations!"

"Thank you."

"At our school, huh? I heard they were hiring some new people in the lower grades."

"Yeah, so, I just have to fill out the papers and start setting up my room."

"You're on your way."

"I'm really happy about it. I would have subbed some more if I had to, but this is much better."

"I almost taught first grade once. When I was new in this district, my second year, it looked like we were going to drop a sixth-grade class. They were going to give me a first-grade class, so I moved everything to a different room, bought all this first-grade stuff, put away my sixth-grade stuff. Then three days before school opened the numbers changed. I had to move back again."

"What a pain," I said.

"I was glad, though. I'm pretty comfortable in sixth grade. But now that I think about it, I still have a bunch of stuff that you could have. First-grade materials that I never used."

"You do?"

"Yeah. Brand-new. I've got a whole box of flash cards, and I think there are some early readers in there, some calendar and weather stuff, and, I don't know, good materials that I don't need. Do you want it?"

"Oh, you're kidding. That's very generous of you. That would really help. I have nothing, of course. Thanks, yeah, I could really use it."

"It would help me, too," he said. "I have too many boxes of stuff I don't need."

I said, "I have to go to the district office and get my paperwork started. But after that, would you like to meet somewhere and maybe get some dinner?"

"Tonight?"

"If it's not too—"

"Not at all. What about that wood-fired pizza place?"

"Over by the beach? Sure."

"I hear it's good."

"Great. I'll meet you there around six."

We finished and hung up. Amazing, I thought. My new relationship might start even before my new job. If I had known it would be so simple, I would have made this move a long time ago.

I called Emily back. "It was easy. Really. I hardly had to do anything. He had this box of first-grade stuff he wanted to unload on someone, and it just—"

"When it's right, it happens easily and naturally. You don't have to scheme. It just—"

"Happens. I was thinking the same thing."

"Call me when you get home. Even if it's late. I don't care if you wake me up."

"OK."

I pulled into the restaurant parking lot right behind Rick, who had an old green pickup. He came over to my car carrying a cardboard box. "I'll just put this right into your trunk."

"Great!" I said. "Thanks."

He put the box down in my trunk and lifted the flaps to show me some of the things inside it. "Here's this felt calendar thing. You put the number for the date here. See all these black numbers? Then you have these felt things for weather. Here's a sun, a cloud, a rain cloud, and I guess this is supposed to be wind. Here are some snowflakes. You won't get much use out of those. See this? I think this is cool. It's a 'Helping Hands' chart. You decide what jobs you're going to have in your room, and then you have hands with kids' names on them. You assign the jobs, and then, each week, you put up a hand for the kid who has the job. You can buy new hands each year. And, oh! I like these, too. They're flash cards for practicing sight words. By the end of the year, the kids are supposed to know a certain number of words by sight. The pictures are on the back. See? Dog. Ball. House."

"That looks great. Thank you so much."

"Sure." He closed the flaps on the box. "I'm glad you can use it."

I closed the trunk. "Of course I can. I'm starting from scratch."

"You'll love it. Teaching is great."

We went inside and got seated right away because it was still early. We ordered.

"I can't wait for school to start," Rick said as the waitress walked away. He tapped a knife against the table. "I'm going to try to organize a theater field trip this year. I know some people who will get us into a rehearsal. Some of the actors will be able to talk to the kids about the process of putting a play together. Then, if I can organize it, I'm going to try to get them into a performance of the same play. You know, so we can see how things develop into a finished product. We might put on a play of our own. Yeah, maybe I'll do that!"

The waitress brought our drinks and left again.

He looked at me. "So," he said, "you're going to teach first grade."

"Yes," I said. "I'm really looking forward to it."

He nodded. "You'll like it. I've been reading sixth-grade books all summer, and I think I've found some that my kids are really going to like. There are so many new ones coming out all the time. It's really hard to keep up. You have to get a nice little library started in your room."

I said, "Sure, yeah, I'll try to. It's a lot—there's so much to—"

"Don't worry! You'll be all settled before you know it! Or do you think you'll miss writing? Your friends and—"

"No. I am really relieved to be starting something new. Really. You can't imagine how disappointing it can be to—"

Our food arrived. We were sharing a portobello mushroom pizza and a large Caesar salad.

"This looks good," Rick said to the waitress. "Thank you."

He was going to ask me about my writing as soon as she left the table. She put down some extra napkins and a piece of pizza on each of our plates. With some people, I wouldn't have wanted to talk about it. I would feel protective about my books and a little defensive about giving up. But with Rick, I would be honest and wouldn't mind letting him know how hard it had been to give up on my dream.

The waitress left. Rick took a bite of pizza. "Mmm," he said. He didn't ask me anything about my books.

We ate.

"Sometimes you get these kids in your class that you don't think you'll be able to stand every day for the whole school year," Rick said. "Then one day, you'll look at that kid and just want to hug him or her. You love 'em all after a while. It's the greatest thing. In some ways, it's like being a parent. Even when they're complete brats, they're *your* brats and you're crazy about them."

I smiled at him. "Your kids must love you, too," I said.

"We develop a strong bond."

When we were finished, the waitress asked us if we wanted dessert. We both said, "No, thank you" at the same time.

Rick added, "Not for me."

The waitress put the check down between us.

I picked it up. "I've got this," I said. "You gave me all those supplies."

"Thank you," he said.

I wanted to pay, of course, because of all the expensive stuff he gave me, but I guess I was a little disappointed that he didn't say, "No, no! You're still technically unemployed!" and put up a little fight. It would have seemed more like a date if we had at least split the check. Once I'd paid, the evening seemed to have been no more than a simple exchange related to work: one box of teaching supplies traded for one dinner. I already had a sinking feeling by the time we were walking to our cars.

"Thanks for the stuff!" I said as I unlocked my car.

"Thanks for dinner!" he called from his truck.

I didn't have to worry about waking Emily up; it wasn't even dark yet when I got home. "He talked about school a lot," I told my sister. "Like, the whole time. I mean, it wasn't, you know, romantic at all; it wasn't even very personal. He just talked about the kids he's taught and his plans for next year. I don't think he—we never even—I don't know."

"So, you mean, no kissing or anything?"

"Ha!" I said. "Not even close. To me, it was just this side of a date, but he obviously didn't see it that way. Maybe, to him, it was just something he did to help someone out. I'm the only one aware of the chemistry. And if only one person feels the chemistry, then it really isn't chemistry, is it?"

"I don't agree. If any chemistry is detected by anyone, then it exists. You wait. Something will happen."

My sister is very optimistic.

The school gave me two sets of book shelves. On these, I put the fifty or so paperback easy readers that my sister's kids had outgrown. In my car, this had seemed like a lot of books. On the shelves, they didn't look like anywhere near enough. I put up

Rick's felt calendar and Helping Hands chart. I bought some bulletin board decorations, and more easy readers. I made name tags to stick on the desks.

I saw Rick twice before school started. The first time was in the hallway near the office. As he passed me, he said, "Hi. How's it going?" and kept walking. The second time he was in the staff work room. I was looking for markers. He came in and said, "Hey, two more days!" and took a package of paper and went out.

I told Emily that she had been wrong about Rick.

"Oh," she said. "You know what that means, don't you?"

"No. What?"

"Now the path is clear for the right person to find you!"

"I see," I said.

5

The first day of school, I wore my red and yellow Hawaiian shirt and a pair of white painter's pants with my red high-top sneakers. I can remember that I felt happy, excited about the adventure I was about to begin. But looking back, I can see that I got off to a bad start.

From my classroom, a so-called portable that had been set out on the blacktop alongside the main school building fourteen years earlier, I saw a crowd of parents. Many were holding video cameras. I hadn't counted on being video-taped on my first day of teaching, but there wasn't any way around it. I heard the first bell. I wished I had time to go to the bathroom once more before facing the kids and the cameras, but I didn't. I ran my tongue over my teeth to check for poppy seeds from my bagel earlier. I tucked in my shirt and straightened my belt. I took a deep breath and opened the door. I came out smiling.

I stood at the head of the line of children. "Hi, guys," I said. No answer. "OK!" I said in a loud voice. "I'm ready for first grade to start! How about you?"

Still no answer.

"Well!" I said, clasping both hands together. "We have a lot of exciting things to do today. So let's give our parents a big wave." I waved and a couple of children limply followed my example. "And let's tell them, 'Have a great day!' "

"Have a great day," a few of my new students repeated grimly.

One very small girl burst into tears and ran out of the line to her mother, a small woman wearing a peach-colored sweat suit. I waited. The mother didn't look at me. The little girl's name was Katie, I remembered from Open House a few days ago. I said to the boy who was first in line, "Would you like to be my line leader and take the boys and girls inside?"

He shook his head hard. His lips trembled. "I don't want—"

"Fine," I said quickly, "you don't have to. We'll all stay right here for a minute." I went to the little girl who was crying. I put out my hand. "Come on, honey. We're going to have fun today!"

"No!" she cried.

Some of the parents with cameras were taping this. I tried to peel her fingers loose from her mother's pants, which was useless without her mother's cooperation. Some of the other kids were getting out of line and going back to their parents. Under my breath, conspiratorially, I said to Katie's mother, "What do you want to do?"

She looked horrified. "*You're* the teacher," she said.

Realizing that I had no ally, no one at all to team up with in hard times, I said in a false, bright tone, "All right, we're going inside. Katie, we'd love it if you'd join us!"

I went back to the head of the line. Katie and her mother went to the end of the line. Several parents, seeing that Katie's mother was going inside, stood next to their own unhappy children. As I led the line, now much larger than a few minutes ago, into the classroom, I saw the teacher next door to me, Marilyn, and *her* first-grade class waving good-bye to all their parents. Marilyn had been teaching first grade for over thirty years. For the first day of school, she was wearing dangling yellow pencil earrings and a denim dress with colored number buttons. The top button was a yellow 1. The second button was a green 2; then there was a blue 3 and a red 4. A few years before, Marilyn had won a Distinguished Teacher award. Her picture was in the office above a framed plaque. As my students and their parents entered my classroom, Marilyn gave me a puzzled look. But she didn't offer any helpful suggestions.

Eight parents joined us inside. I said, "Boys and girls, please find your seats. You'll see your name at the upper right-hand corner of your desk. That's right, Seth. Now sit down in your chair. Good. Please hang your backpacks on the backs of your chairs. That's it. We'll just wait until everybody's settled. Ryan H., good, that's your spot. Amanda, oh, I guess, Katie's mom is going to help you. Fine, there you go. Everybody's found the right desk. Great. Now, boys and girls, moms and dads, welcome to first grade! I think this would be a very good time to thank our parents for helping us get started. And now we are going to say good-bye." I tried to sound firm, but I heard my voice wobble a little with nerves. My lips were sticking to my teeth, and my heart was racing.

A father and two mothers moved toward the door. Two more mothers were whispering good-bye to their children. A father gave his daughter a kiss and waved to me as he started to back out toward the door. I waved back, smiling at him with gratitude. The children watched from their seats as seven or eight parents left the room.

Katie's mother squatted down on the floor and held her daughter tight. All the children were looking at the two of them. "Now, boys and girls, we're going to see if anyone is absent on the first day of school. Do we have any empty desks?"

The children looked around. "No," some of them said. Several heads were shaking. Some of them looked back at Katie and her mother.

"Good. No one is absent. Now, how many of you will be buying hot lunch today? Raise your hands, please." A few hands went up, and I counted them. "Tomorrow we'll start having one of you do the lunch count, but for today—"

"How come *her* mom gets to stay?" a girl named Patience wanted to know, "and *my* mom had to go to work?"

"Yeah, no fair!" said one of the boys.

Katie's mother looked at me. "Katie, I have a job for you," I said. "Would you and your mom take this attendance sheet to the ladies in the office? It says that no one is absent today and that four students will be having hot lunch. When you come back, we'll be sitting on the carpet over here. OK? Can you do that for me?"

Katie nodded. Her mother nodded.

"Fine. I know you can." While they were out of the room, Katie's mother could say good-bye to her privately and Katie could rejoin the class alone. I congratulated myself on finding a way out of this predicament that allowed all three of us to save face. I continued with the rest of the class. "Now, boys and girls, we're going to read a story about the first day of school. Let's all leave our desks for now and come and sit down on the blue carpet. Excellent. Make sure you give your neighbor room."

"What neighbor?" Seth wanted to know. "My neighbor is in sixth grade, and he—"

"When I say neighbor, I'm talking about the person sitting next to you."

"Oh. Hey, teacher, he pushed!"

"I'm sure it was an accident. Who remembers my name?"

"Mrs. Dear!" Seth yelled.

"Ms. Dearborn," I said. "Good. Now. I think you're going to like this story. And you want to know something? Look at this. I can read upside down." I held a book open in my lap to read to them. "If you want to be a first-grade teacher, just learn to read upside down, and you'll find a job"—I snapped my fingers—"like that!" The children sitting on the floor in front of me opened their eyes a little wider, but they did not laugh. "Just kidding," I said. "It was a joke." It was going to take some time to get to know my audience.

"Hey, teacher!" one of the girls said. Her name was Amanda, I remembered. "We forgot to say the Pledge."

"Oops. When Katie gets back we'll do that. OK?"

The door opened. Katie and her mother walked in together.

There was an anxious silence in the room. A small crowd of pinched faces looked up at me, waiting.

"Her mom still didn't go," said a small voice.

"It's time for the Pledge," I said. "Let's all stand up and face the flag."

We pledged. Then all the children and Katie's mother sat down on the carpet again. I got to use a chair. Maybe Katie's mom was just going to slip out quietly during the story.

I had chosen a book called *Edie and Fred's First Day of School,* by Timothy Weeks. Edie was some kind of beetle and Fred was a fly. In the illustration I was looking down at right now, a bunch of insects painted in wild colors were lined up outside their classroom, just as the children in front of me were a few minutes earlier. A purple girl ant looked suspiciously at a blue boy grasshopper, wearing glasses. On the next page, the teacher came out. The teacher was a different kind of beetle, lime green and orange, with six hairy legs. She was wearing a crown.

I read the text: " 'Good morning, boys and girls,' said Mrs. Beetleman. 'Good morning, Mrs. Beetleman,' said the children. 'Welcome to first grade!' Mrs. Beetleman said with a smile.

" 'Where's the bathroom?' said Fred."

The children in my class laughed. Seth stood up and walked to the back of the room.

"Seth," I said.

"*What?* I'm getting a drink! I can get a drink if I want to!"

"I'm afraid not, Seth. Not when we're listening to a story."

"I don't like that book," he said.

"Seth, come back to the carpet and sit down. You may get a drink when we're finished reading and discussing the book."

Seth went to the drinking fountain and took a long, slurpy drink. The children watched him, then looked back at me. I glared at Seth as he walked back to his seat. Seth smiled. Katie's mother was looking at me. I almost expected her to say something like, "You blew that, didn't you?" I went on with the book.

When I finished, I said, "Raise your hand if you can tell me how you think the class felt on the first day of school?"

"Good!" Seth shouted.

"Bad!" said Amanda.

I said, "When I see a quiet hand, I'll call on someone."

Amanda and Seth raised their hands.

"Seth?" I said.

"They felt *good!*"

I said, "You think so? What do you think, Amanda?"

"That guy wanted to know where the bathroom was." There was another round of laughter; two girls covered their mouths and giggled behind their hands.

I said, "Yes, you're right. Do you think maybe they were a little nervous about finding their way around their school? And about what kinds of things they were going to do in first grade? I think so. Do you agree with me, Ryan J.?"

"One of the bugs cried because he lost his lunch. He was a cry-baby."

"Insects!" said Seth fiercely. "They were *insects,* not bugs!"

"Raise your hand if you'd like to make a comment, please, Seth."

"It's true," Seth insisted. "They weren't bugs!"

"You're correct," I said. "They were all insects. We're very close to you, Seth, so we can hear you, even when you speak to us quietly."

I stood up and put the book in the shelf. "Boys and girls, I thought you might like to find out more about our school, too, so we're going to take a tour."

Seth yelled, "I already was here in kindergarten!"

I said, "Seth, try to remember not to call out." Seth raised his hand. I went on. "Even though some of you went to kindergarten here, we have four students who are new to our school. And you'll be having some classes you didn't have last year. We'll meet our computer teacher and our music teacher. Now I want you to line up *quietly* at the door."

When they were standing in a wiggly line at the door, I said, "I have a name tag for each of you. This is so our other teachers who don't know you can read your names." The name tags were the characters from the book that I'd just read, grasshoppers, beetles, ants, and flies. I had photocopied them at 500 percent, colored them with pastels, laminated them, and hung them on a piece of yellow yarn. They were identical to the set of name tags I'd put on the students' desks. The class was divided into four groups, corresponding to the creatures on their name tags.

There was a lot of excitement over the name tags. "I'm a ant. Are you?"

"I got the guy who had to go to the bathroom." Laughter. "I like him. He's my favorite."

"I got the guy who forgot his lunch."

"Is this the girl with the sister in third grade or the one who got her shirt wet at the drinking fountain?"

Seth said, "I want a different one. I don't like this guy." He tried to hand his name tag to me.

"Put that on, please, Seth. That's the one you get."

"No way! I want the fly with the glasses. He's cool. This guy is a dork."

More laughter.

"I'm waiting."

Seth took his name tag off.

"Put it on," said Ryan H. "You're going to get in trouble."

Katie's mother looked at me in disapproval. I looked right back at her. *Why don't you leave?* I tried to communicate with her telepathically. Amanda said, "You might get a detention. My brother's friend got a detention one time, and he—"

"There's no detentions in first grade!" said Ryan J.

"Boys and girls," I said sharply. "I'm waiting until it's *quiet!* Then we're going to leave the classroom. Hands down at your sides, please." I held my first two fingers up in a peace sign, known at this school as "the quiet sign." Several children did the same. I had to wait a long time, and even then, two of the girls were still talking about pierced ears. I had a hot, churning feeling of annoyance in my stomach.

We stopped first outside the bathrooms, waiting several minutes while two girls and a boy used the facilities. We paused again at the drinking fountain. Then we went to the front office, where I introduced the school secretary and the receptionist.

"Boys and girls, let's say good morning to Mrs. Chavez and Mrs. Roland."

The class chanted, "Good morning, Mrs. Chavez! Good morning, Mrs. Roland!"

We visited the computer lab, the media center, and the first-grade lunch tables. Then we walked back to the classroom. Katie's mother was at the end of the line. This would have been another good time for her to head for her car. She followed the class inside.

Back in the room, I said, "Go quietly to your seats. Boys and girls, does anyone have any questions?"

"Are you married?" Seth asked.

"You didn't raise your hand," said Amanda. "She's not going to answer your question until you raise your hand."

Seth raised his hand and at the same time said, "Are you married?"

"No, I'm not, Seth. Does anybody have questions about our school?"

"I know," said Patience. "She's divorced. My mom and dad are divorced. My mom has a different last name. It used to be her name before she got married."

"As a matter of fact," I said, "I've never been married."

"How come?"

I didn't say, "I don't understand it myself. Do I unconsciously place barriers in my own path? Or is it a question of luck, timing, or fate?"

I said, "I know you're all curious about me, and I'm curious about you, too. We'll get to know each other a little better each day."

"Do you have a boyfriend?"

"Does anyone have any questions *about our school?* Let's stick to that topic. What is a topic? A topic means what we're talking about right now. We were talking about—"

"How old are you?" Grace wanted to know.

"Not appropriate!" Amanda announced, folding her arms across her chest.

I said, "It's usually not a good idea to ask adults how old they are. But as it happens, I don't mind telling you that I'm forty-two." I turned around and wrote a big four and a big two on the board and looked around for my pointer. "Eyes up here, please. Now, look at the number line above the chalkboard. Does everyone see the number forty-two?"

"I don't!" Seth yelled.

"It's way, way down over there! All the way over by the flag!"

I got my pointer and put it on the number 1. "All right, then. Let's count together to forty-two." I was getting the hang of this now. A simple question about my age could be made into a math lesson. "Ready, begin. One, two, three . . ."

Lunch would have been a good time for Katie's mother to break away. But when I went outside to bring in my line after lunch recess, they were both at the end of it, holding hands.

I led the line inside. The children were noisy and still active after the long recess. They took a long time getting into their seats. I held up my fingers in a peace sign. Two girls held up their fingers, but they kept talking. I waited, a threatening scowl on my face. It was wasted, though, because no one looked at me except Katie's mother, and she wasn't one of the ones who was talking.

"Boys and girls!" I said too loudly. "This is *not* the way we behave in first grade! I expect you to be much quieter from now on! Thank you. Now, who is our pencil passer?" I looked at the Helping Hands board, saw a cardboard hand with Seth's name on it in the pocket marked "pencils." "Seth, please pass out these pencils. I have a September journal for each of you. Paper passer? Patience, that's you this week. Just listen to all these 'P' words, boys and girls! *P*atience, *p*lease *p*ass out *p*aper." I bore down on the beginning *p* sounds. "Please give one of these sheets to everybody."

Patience, a very small girl with long, blonde hair, was happy to be passing out September journals. These were a few sheets of lined first-grade writing paper stapled together with a blue construction-paper cover.

In their journals, I had the children copy the date from the board. I said, "Now I want you to think about the story we read this morning."

"What story?" Seth wanted to know.

"About the bugs," Amanda reminded him.

"THEY WERE INSECTS," he bellowed straight into her face.

Amanda started to cry.

I put down the chalk I was holding and walked over to them. "Seth, I want you to apologize to Amanda."

"What'd *I* do?"

"Tell me. What did you do?"

Seth smiled, glancing around at the class. "Yelled in her face?"

"Exactly."

"That didn't hurt her."

"Seth, you may apologize now and sit down quietly or go talk to Mr. Dean, the principal."

There was a gasp from some of the class. Seth started to cry. But he didn't just cloud over and let a few tears tumble down his cheeks. He opened his mouth wide, and a tremendous roar came out.

I had a headache. For the first time all day, there was no talking in the room. "Seth, what will it be?"

"Apologize," he bellowed, his face wet and red.

A drop of his saliva landed on my cheek. "All right," I said, "I'm waiting."

"Sorry," he grunted in the direction of the pencil sharpener.

"Look at Amanda and tell her what you're sorry for."

"For screaming at you," he sobbed.

"Amanda, look at Seth and say, 'I accept your apology.' "

"No," said Amanda. "I want to go home!" She sniffled into the pocket of my pants.

"Amanda, turn around and look at Seth."

She kept her face against me but looked at Seth. "I assept your apology."

"Now, both of you, return to your seats."

Katie's mom was looking at me. She looked very large perched on a first-grade chair next to her daughter.

My headache was starting to pound, and I had to go to the bathroom.

"We're all going to write in our journals," I said.

There was a clamor of protest. "I don't know what to write!"

"Can we just write our names?"

"I'm just going to draw a picture."

"I don't want to do this."

I said, "We're all going to write at least one sentence. I'll help you. If you don't know what to start with, I'm going to write a starter sentence on the board. Then you may add sentences of your own. As many as you want. If you don't know how to spell a word, give it your best try with the letters you do know and then I'll help you with it later. There is absolutely *no talking* during journal time."

"What if we have to ax you a question and—"

"What if we have to go to the bathroom?" Seth said. He had already recovered.

The children laughed. I had an urge to pick Seth up and deposit him outside the classroom door. "Seth," I said, "I'm giving you a warning. The next time you interrupt me—"

"Hey, no fair! I wasn't the only one who interrupted!"

I pressed my lips together. My head throbbed. "You will stay quiet until the end of the day or you will owe me five minutes of recess time tomorrow morning."

Seth looked stung. His face reddened, and his mouth trembled.

I picked up a piece of chalk. "I'm going to write two sentences on the board. You may copy one or both of them onto your paper. Or you may begin with your own sentence."

"I only know how to write my name!"

"Can we just draw a picture?"

On the board, I wrote:

We read a story about insects. It was the first day of school.

I wrote some words on the board to get them started: *boy, bathroom, teacher, insect, lunch, crying,* and so on. "It's fine to copy what I wrote," I said.

After journal time, even some of the children looked tired. I had them all sit on the carpet again and read another story, not as good as the one about the insects but part of the first-grade curriculum. It was about making friends and sharing. Amanda fell asleep sitting up. When I reached the end of the story, which, in my opinion, should have been cut by about half, some of the children were snickering and pointing at Amanda. I got up and stood next to her. "Boys and girls," I whispered, "get up quietly and go to your seats." I laid Amanda down on the carpet.

Several minutes before the 2:30 dismissal bell, a big crowd of parents had gathered. "Boys and girls, put away everything that is on your desks. Put on your backpacks. Push your chairs in." A few kids ran for the door. "Anna, Grace, Ryan J., I did not say to line up. Go back to your desks. I will dismiss you by table. The first table that is standing quietly with their desks cleared, backpacks on, chairs pushed in will line up first."

The children scurried back to their desks.

"I see that the Grasshopper table looks ready. Grasshoppers may line up quietly by the door. Now Beetles may line up. Good, now Ants and Flies may line up. Boys and girls, we had a great first day!" I smiled, my face muscles straining from fatigue. "I'll see you all tomorrow. If you see your parent, you may go. If you're going to the bus or to Aftercare, please follow me."

"Amanda's still asleep!" Seth shouted right in front of me.

I had already forgotten about Amanda. "I'm aware of that, Seth. I'll take care of Amanda." I scanned the crowd of parents. "Is there someone here to pick up Amanda?" I asked the group.

There was no answer.

"She rides the bus!" Seth yelled.

I should have known that; I had a chart. Under Amanda's name there was a yellow construction-paper bus that I had cut out myself. "So she does."

This would have been a perfect time for Katie's mother to step forward and offer me some help. But she was standing in line with the walkers, holding Katie's hand.

"Parent pick-ups, if you see your parent, you may go." Half the class went out, including Katie and her mother.

Ryan J. went out and came back. "She's not there," he said, clouding over. "She didn't come!" Tears started to spill down his cheeks.

"Ryan J., your mother is not here *yet,* but she's coming. Now, will you come with me to the bus lines? Thank you. Wait right here while I get Amanda."

I went to the carpet. "Amanda," I whispered, "Amanda, honey." I shook her shoulder. She turned over and made herself more comfortable. "Sweetheart, time to wake up and go home."

The kids I had lined up by the door were beginning to crowd around me. Grace squeaked, "We're going to miss the bus!"

"I have to get the bus or I can't get home!" William said in panic.

I looked up at them. Two were already crying. Several more looked on the verge.

Somehow I managed to lift heavy, limp Amanda from the floor and stand up. I put her over my shoulder, sack-of-potatoes style. "OK, bus riders, let's go." I took off in front of my line at a brisk walk. Ryan J. was trotting along beside me. "I want to hold your hand," he said.

I said, "My hands are pretty busy right now. Grab my belt loop."

"OK," he said. Then as we walked, he pulled it right off. "Hey, teacher? What should I do with this?"

"Stick it in my pocket right there by your hand. Thanks."

He held my shirt, running along beside me.

The buses were already loading, and the kids panicked and started to run. "Walk!" I bellowed. I guess my voice went right into Amanda's head, because she started to wake up. Some of the kids knew which bus she went on. I made sure she was awake before I put her on the ground.

"Is it time to go home?" she said, seeing the bus. "Oh, good. Do I have my backpack?" Ryan J. put it on her shoulders.

As soon as all the buses were loaded, they closed the doors and took off, already behind schedule. I looked around to make sure I didn't have any leftovers. There was just Ryan J., squinting up at me.

I sighed, relieved.

"*Now* can I hold your hand?" said Ryan J.

"Yes, you may."

Ryan J. and I walked back to the classroom. His hand was warm and wet. I could feel a couple of warts near his thumb. I hoped his mother would be there soon, so I could finally get to the bathroom. Then I'd go to the nurse's office for some aspirin or something. But Ryan J.'s mother wasn't there yet. "Ryan J., why don't we file these papers in the take-home folders until your mother gets here?"

He looked anxiously out the window. "OK," he said.

At 2:50, Ryan J.'s mother appeared in workout clothes.

"Hey, bud," she said to Ryan.

He put one last picture into a file, then got his backpack and shuffled over to her without making eye contact.

"You didn't have to watch him," Ryan J.'s mother said to me. "He would have been fine on the playground."

"I wouldn't allow an unsupervised first-grader to play on the playground," I said.

"Oh." She drew her head back as if a bad smell had just hit her in the face. She turned to her son. "Good day, kid?" she asked Ryan. He didn't answer.

"Great day!" I said. "We were very busy. I don't know about Ryan J., but I'm *tired.*"

"Me too," Ryan J. nodded. "I want to go home. See you tomorrow, Mrs. D."

"See you tomorrow."

I walked fast to the faculty bathroom. I couldn't believe I was going to have to do all this again the next day.

6

A long time ago, when my first novel, *P.S. Will You Marry Me?,* had just come out, Howard called me to say that someone was interested in the film rights. "Someone big," Howard said. "Someone good. Someone you are really going to *like.*" It was Perris Tremont, the actor/producer/director who had adapted a series of American short stories as classy, one-hour dramas starring big-name actors for HBO. I drove up to Los Angeles and met Perris for lunch, and he introduced me to his sister, an actress I liked, who was to play the lead in the movie of my book. I wrote the screenplay and got ready for my life to change.

Perris didn't have any money of his own to spend, or at least not much that he was willing to give to me, so I got very little cash from selling him the option on my book and screenplay. Eight hundred and fifty dollars, if you want the exact figure. That's $1,000 minus Howard's commission. But the option money is hardly the point when you're working on a film deal. Howard explained this to me.

"Repeat after me," he said. "Production bonus."

"Production bonus?"

"Very good."

"What's a production bonus?"

"Those are the magic words you want in your contract. They mean that, even though your option sale may be modest, you will get a large number of dollars when somebody actually starts making the film."

"I see."

"Once you get somebody to throw some real dough into this, you'll get paid what you deserve."

Unfortunately, I didn't get that far. Perris stuck with it, off and on, for a couple of years before he got worn out looking for backing. Howard tried, too, with some film contacts of his own. Even I tried. I stopped hearing from Perris around the time he took a role in a big-budget action film. He played a toy action figure that comes to life and develops a mind of its own. He must have gotten a personal trainer and contact lenses, and changed his hair color for that film because I didn't even recognize him when he came on the screen. He has made eight sequels since then. In between, he produced and directed small-budget, tasteful films that won prizes at Cannes and the Sundance Film Festival. He never got around to my book again, though. I think he'd remember me if, say, we stood in line together at the post office. Come to think of it, maybe he wouldn't. I was twenty-six the last time he saw me. In any case, he'd apparently moved away from the idea of making a film of my book. Most movie options don't result in actual films. It's no reflection at all on the writer's work if the movie doesn't get made. It's really just a matter of luck.

On Friday, I didn't go straight home after school because that was where I always started reviewing what happened that day in my class. On Tuesday, I had called a friend in New York, another writer, and cried. She said, "Is it as bad as proofreading legal briefs all night, five nights a week?" I said yes, but she didn't believe me. On Wednesday, I just sat on the floor and ate a whole bag of Doritos and cried by myself. Then I fell asleep for an hour and a half with my head resting back on my flowery couch. Thursday, I had been so tired from struggling to control my kids and straining to accomplish something that I had gone to bed before nine o'clock. Now as the weekend stretched out before me, I tried to delay facing myself at home by stopping off at the grocery store first. Unfortunately, my delaying tactic made me buy things that I didn't need. I got four bags of Halloween candy without asking anyone how many trick-or-treaters I could expect in my complex. And it wasn't even October yet. To offset the candy, not that I planned to eat it or anything, I bought some low-fat, low-calorie meal replacement drinks. Maybe this weekend was the time I was going to get started taking off the extra weight.

After the first day, things had gotten worse in my class, instead of better. Seth had become louder and less cooperative. Three of my kids had gotten into a fight in the classroom on Tuesday. A mother had come by after school on Wednesday to tell me that her child was gifted and wasn't being challenged; another mother told me Thursday that her child was feeling stressed by the overdemanding curriculum. Katie hadn't returned after the first day. Her mother had withdrawn her from the school and enrolled her in a private school a couple of miles away. Now, driving home with my groceries, I felt achy and tender, as if I had lifted loads of bricks in the hot sun all week.

I parked my car next to the stairs to my apartment. I got out, opened the trunk, and put a grocery bag on the sidewalk. I was setting my second bag down when I heard a crash. A man got out of a dark blue car that had just backed into mine, walked around, looked at his car, and bent to look at mine. Then there was the oddly delayed sound of glass hitting the pavement.

The man said, "Sorry, I was just—"

"Backing up fast with no lights on!" I said. "That's all!"

As soon as he walked closer to me, I realized I knew him. From a long time ago, I recognized this man, though at first I couldn't place him. High school, that was it. But he looked different now, less hair, more weight. The name took a few seconds longer to come to me. He was Dave Conklin. He had been in my eleventh-grade English class. With the name, a lot of other details came back. He had glasses then, and he had worn hiking boots every day, even with shorts. The desks in the classroom had been arranged in a semicircle, and Dave was directly across from me. He used to stare at me for the whole class. Sometimes when my sister and I went to the library or the movies or Taco Bell, Dave showed up right after we did. It seemed, for a while, that he was following me. I hadn't thought about him in years.

"Oh. Did I forget to put my lights on?" Dave looked back at his car, an older model, that was either maroon or brown. I couldn't tell in the dark. The motor was still running. "I guess I did. I'm really sorry. I just walked by a minute ago. You weren't parked here."

"Things change, you know," I said.

"It isn't even a parking space, so I guess I wasn't expecting anyone to be parked there."

We both looked down at the red curb where my car was parked.

I said, "I was just unloading my groceries here before I parked for the night. My space is all the way over by the pool, and I—"

"I understand. I would have done the same thing. Let's see what kind of damage we've got here."

We both looked. The front of my car was smashed in on the passenger side. The side window was on the ground in pieces.

"Whoops," he said, "I guess it's going to need some work." It was Dave all right. I recognized his voice, his bitten fingernails as he touched my car's mangled side.

"Well, I guess *so!*" I said. I ran my hand over the pushed-in place.

"Are you sure that wasn't there before?"

I glared at him.

"Just kidding. Of course, I'll pay for it and everything. No problem. I live right there." He pointed at the apartment building. He looked me straight in the face without even the slightest flicker of recognition.

"So do I," I said. "Obviously."

"OK," he said, "so you won't have any problem finding me." He smiled.

"Right."

"And I'll give you my"—he reached through the window of his car for a pen—"all my numbers." He pulled an old receipt out of his pocket, put it on the roof of my car, and started to write. When he was finished, he pointed to one of the numbers on the card. "This one is my cell phone. This is home, and this is my office."

"Are you a doctor?"

"No." He shook his head.

I knew he wasn't; I was just being rude about the self-importance of having so many phone numbers. I could tell by looking at him that he wasn't a doctor. His hair was long and messy. He was wearing jeans with holes in them, a T-shirt that should have been in a rag basket, and sandals. You never see doctors in sandals; you just don't. And I was certain that there were no doctors living in our complex; medical students, maybe, but no grown-up physicians. "And by the way, do you have insurance?" I asked him.

"It's illegal to drive without insurance in the state of California."

"*Do* you have insurance?" I asked again, in case he was just trying to evade the question.

"Yes, I do." He laughed. I hate when you're worried about something and someone is laughing about it. Then you're annoyed and insulted in addition to being worried.

"Good," I said. "How about writing down that information, too?"

"Sure," he said. He went around to the other side of the car, opened the door, and started rummaging in his glove compartment. I looked at the back of his car. There was nothing wrong with it. How was that possible?

"What's your name?" he said.

"Charlotte," I said. "Charlotte Dearborn." I expected him to get it now, to realize he used to know me a long time ago. I was cringing, waiting for the big reaction.

"Nice to meet you," he said. We shook hands. "I'm Dave. It's on the paper here. Have you lived here long? I don't think I've seen you here before."

"Several months," I said.

"Well. Give me a call if you have any problems."

"Sure," I said. "I'll do that." I got back into my car, and he got back into his. Mine wouldn't go, though. It started, but it wouldn't move. I got out. I went to his window. He was inserting a CD and didn't notice me. I tapped on the window. "You're going to have to help me push it." He looked surprised. "My car won't move."

Dave got out of his car. We tried to push mine, but that didn't work either. When we looked closer at the damage, we saw that the front fender was pressing on the tire so hard that the wheel wouldn't turn. Dave said, "What's this thing made of? Aluminum? I barely tapped it."

I said, "I've had this car for nine years, and it's never been a bit of trouble." My voice cracked.

"OK, OK," Dave said. "Sorry. It's a very nice, sturdy car. Again, I'm really sorry. I'll call a tow truck." He pulled out his cell phone.

Dave managed to get his car out, after all. He said he would stay and wait with me for the tow truck, but I encouraged him to leave. Finally he did. I went upstairs to put away my groceries, then came back down and sat on the curb for half an hour before the truck rumbled into the driveway. The driver pulled up in front of my car and got out.

"Hoo boy," he said. "That little mistake'll run ya."

"Someone ran into *me.* It wasn't *my* fault," I snapped.

He patted the air in front of him. "Did I say it was *your* mistake?" He shook his head and made a *shoo* sound, then shook his head again. He processed my Triple A card and hooked up my car. "Have a nice evening," he said and drove it away. I had this really sad feeling then, as I watched my car tipped up on its back tires, that I was never going to see it again. I was just being emotional, of course. Cars get in minor accidents all the time. Then they get fixed, and they're back on the road in a couple of days, a week tops.

Before any work was done on my car, I had to wait for an insurance adjuster to take a look at it. My sister gave me rides sometimes. Dave called a couple of times to see if I wanted him to take me anywhere. I didn't.

One morning as I arrived at school, Cindy Roland, the receptionist, said, "Charlotte, are you OK? You're all flushed and sweaty! And you're late!"

"Am I?" I said. "I walked. It took forty-five minutes."

"Great exercise," Cindy said.

"Well, see, my car got—"

"You better get in there. They already started."

"Who?" I said. "What already started?"

"The staff meeting?"

"Oh, yeah. Right. Do you think I really have to go to that? I was just going to go to my room and—"

"Yes," Cindy said, putting her hand to the middle of her chest and rolling her chair back in shock. "You do have to go. Staff meeting is very important!"

"Seriously?" I said. "Oh. Of course. What was I thinking?" I walked off as though I were on my way to the staff meeting, but when Cindy wasn't looking, I took a shortcut to my room. I'd found that the weekly staff meeting was one of the many time-wasters at school, a lot of people talking for long periods about things that didn't matter.

In the staff lounge at lunch, I sat at a table with the other first-grade teachers. Marilyn said to me, "Your class sure was noisy this morning. I almost sent someone over to see if you were all right! I thought they might have knocked you out and taken over." She and the other teachers laughed.

"We're working on that," I said. "The noise level."

Angela, another first-grade teacher, laughed. "I'll bet you are! Are you getting to any of the schoolwork? Or don't they have time for that?"

"We—we're working on a project," I said defensively. "We're writing to an author." I had just made this up to make it seem as though we were accomplishing something. But once I thought about it, it was a pretty good idea. "We're going to send e-mails."

"Well!" Brooke said. "If you're going to try to claim that's giving the kids computer experience, forget it."

I didn't reply.

Marilyn turned to the other teachers at the table. "You never know what's going on in Charlotte's room. Like the first day of school when that mother stayed all day!" The other teachers laughed.

This was an incident that I was trying to put out of my mind.

"Was this author you e-mailed a friend of yours, Charlotte? Someone you knew in your writing days?"

I shook my head. "Don't know him." I tried to keep my answers to questions about my former career as brief as possible.

"Oh, that's right," said Bernice, a fourth-grade teacher. "I heard you tried to be a writer. Did you ever publish anything?"

"Yes," I said.

"What?"

"Mostly novels, but also short stories, articles, essays, book reviews—"

"So, what are you doing *here?*" Bernice interrupted. Conversations at the other tables stopped as teachers turned to listen.

"I wasn't earning enough," I said quietly. "My books never took off the way I had hoped."

"So you got into teaching for the *money!*" Marilyn hooted. "You know, I don't think I've ever heard anyone say that!"

All the teachers laughed. When the hilarity subsided, a young kindergarten teacher commented, "You should have sold the movie rights to your books. *That* pays."

"I did," I said. "More than once. Unfortunately, not every movie option gets the kind of money you read about in *People* magazine."

"You should have sent your books to Oprah," said Mindy, the school librarian.

"I did," I said. "And my publicist did. My agent did. My sister and friends of mine did." I should just change the subject, I told myself, trying to think up another topic fast.

"And what happened? Oprah didn't like them?" Bernice wanted to know.

Against my better judgment, I began to explain. "See, they don't always tell you the—"

"You should have called to find out!" Bernice interrupted. "*I* would have. That way, you could learn from your mistakes. I'll tell you what would make a great story. You ought to write a book about this place! Of course, nobody would believe it. The crazy parents; the spoiled kids; the unyielding, uncompassionate—"

"Teachers," I filled in, nodding.

"*Administrators,* I was going to say." Bernice sniffed and took a sip of Diet Coke.

"Good idea," I said with a phony smile. "But you'll have to write that one. I'm not writing anymore. Ever. As long as I live."

"Listen to her! I bet she goes home after school and writes down everything we say in here," said Bernice. "Don't forget to cut us in on the profits!"

"No offense," I said, though I knew I should have let it go, "but it wouldn't make a very good story. In order to transform raw material into fiction, you have to develop—"

"So, your work is autobiographical, then," Bernice cut in.

"No, not really," I said. "I mean, *no.* It's not. Not at all."

"Boy, I'll tell you, I would not be sitting here in this room today if *I* could write a book," said Bernice to the other teachers. "If I had the ability to come up with an idea, write it down, and sell it, you better believe that I would be doing just that every single minute of every day."

"I did that for almost twenty years," I said. "Then I thought it would really be nice to have a paycheck, even a small one, that I could count on. And health insurance and retirement benefits—"

"Well, I've met some odd ducks in my time, but I think you win the prize!" said Bernice. Again, there was laughter.

I smiled, threw away my lunch trash, and went to check my mailbox. There were two messages for me. One was from the principal: "Please have someone fill you in on what you missed this morning at staff meeting. I would appreciate it if you would make every effort to attend *weekly* from now on. Thank you. Russ."

I shoved the paper in my pocket and looked at the other message. The garage that was repairing my car had called. I used the phone in the staff lounge. I was on hold a long time listening to an oldies radio station before the owner of the shop came on to talk to me. "Yeah, ma'am? This is Bill. Let me put it to you straight. The insurance guys are declaring the car a total loss."

I felt something dip in my stomach. I think I let out some kind of a moan.

"You'll probably get a message on your home machine from the guy. They'll give you a grand. My own opinion, I think that's generous. Repairs you need will run you about three. Thousand. That's for the front end and a lot of other things. See, it's not just the accident, but your engine's not what it used to be. There's not much under that hood that doesn't need to be replaced. You got oil leaks, a bad radiator, you need a new clutch—I could go on, but I know you're at work, so I'll make it brief. What I'm saying, I don't recommend going ahead with the work. Now, if you ask me, I'd say you need a new car. Repairs on this one would include a new engine, which, of course, would be a reconditioned engine from a similar model of similar age. I'd make sure you were getting a good one, but it's a used engine. You see what I'm saying? Then you got your body work, your paint, new bumper and headlight. It adds up. And let's say you decide to spend the three grand. You'd end up with your same old stained upholstery, worn carpeting, outdated safety features. Like I say, I don't recommend going ahead with this."

I just stood there for a couple of seconds. Then I said, "But my car! I *need* my car! It was running fine. It just got this little bump and then—*stained* upholstery? I've had that car for nine years and never once—"

"Hey, I understand," he said. "Big decision. Take some time, think about it. Let me know."

"OK," I said, "I'll let you know." I held tightly to the phone for a minute before I hung up.

Cindy, the receptionist, walked up to me. "Cupcake?"

"Yes?" I said. I thought, She sees how upset I am and she's using this endearment to make me feel better. She'll ask me what's wrong, and I'll have a chance to pour out the whole awful story. I might cry, but a little kindness and sensitivity will make me feel a lot better.

Cindy pushed a paper plate in my direction. "One of the kindergartners brought these in for her birthday. There were quite a few left over. Here you go."

"Oh!" I said. "You mean a *cupcake* cupcake. The kind you *eat!*" I took a cupcake from the tray and ate it in three bites before I noticed it had pink coconut all over the top and the cake part was imitation strawberry flavor. No wonder there were so many left over. I swallowed the sticky goo and licked my fingers. Then I just stood there for a minute, thinking about the conversation I'd just had with the mechanic. "My car, my poor car," I said to no one in particular.

There was no way I could afford a car right now, not after the move, the new couch, all the classroom supplies I'd had to buy. Buying a car was simply not an option.

* * *

At Car City, the salesman who was working with me, Jason, could not have been much more than a teenager. He had three holes in each ear lobe, but he wasn't wearing any earrings. Maybe Car City had an employee dress code that prohibited multiple earrings. When Jason pointed out the automatic transmission on the previously owned vehicle I was about to test-drive, I saw a tattoo just under his cuff, a rose the color of a bad bruise. "The front seats recline," he told me. "Nice radio there. Not too many miles."

He photocopied my driver's license, then came back to sit beside me. As I pulled out of the driveway of the dealership, he turned on the air conditioning full blast. "Good air," he said. "Can't be driving around southern California without air now, can you?" He looked out the window for a minute. "Take a right here. Beautiful handling. You feel that? You just went up a steep hill without any stress or strain whatsoever. Now left up here and you can take it on the freeway. That's it. Nice pep, don't you think? Peppy little car. Looks like the previous owners took real good care of it." He opened an ashtray, as if the lack of butts there proved his point. "You like the color? I think it's a real sporty color."

"White?" I said. "Yeah, it's OK." I drove it a few more miles. "I guess I'll try to buy this one," I said. It was a two-door, five-year-old Japanese import.

"I think you're making a great choice," said the salesman, probably already calculating his commission.

"Right. It will probably start falling apart about halfway through the payments."

"Oh, no," he said shaking his head vehemently. "You take care of a car, it'll take care of you. You do your regular maintenance, and you're going to be fine. And we have our famous Used Car Limited Warranty that's good for a full six months."

"Sure," I said. "Now give me your lowest price. I don't want to spend a lot of time on this. Really. Look at me. I'm forty-two. I know how this works. Just tell me the absolute least I can pay for this car. I really don't feel like negotiating anything."

"That's the beauty of Car City," Jason told me with a smile. "We don't do that here. We give you a good price and get you right on your way."

After five hours of haggling, I was leaving the Car City lot in my brand-new, previously owned vehicle. For the hundredth time, I recalculated the payments, what I owed my sister for the down payment, what I owed my credit cards. I added up my salary after taxes and my occasional tiny royalty checks that, of course, I shouldn't count on. If I didn't buy anything at all for the next six months, I might survive.

7

My second novel was called *Just My Luck.* It was about a young woman who wins a multi-million-dollar state lottery after buying a single ticket for the first time in her life. When ex-boyfriends, charity organizations, her family, friends, and neighbors keep harassing her for money, she changes her name and moves to another state. There a new friend, who knows nothing of her bad experience with lottery tickets, buys her one as a birthday surprise. She wins again. Anyway, it got a lot of good reviews but, like my first one, didn't sell very well. Between my second and third novels, March Blake called me. She was an editor from a huge, important publishing company, and she had become famous for taking unknown literary authors out of obscurity into startling celebrity. Remember that book of short stories about farm families whose unifying theme was canning recipes that was in the top five of the *New York Times* best-seller list for ninety-six weeks? She edited that. You might have read about the phenomenal success of the diary of a graduate student in anthropology, also a March Blake author. The film rights were optioned by Madonna, a close friend of March's. When I answered the phone, and the editor said her name, I nearly fainted. She said, "We *love* your novels, sweetheart. We want you over here with us. Collard & Stanton is not your real family. *We* are. We hope you know that."

I said, "I guess I—well, see, my sales aren't very—"

"Do you have anything for me, lovie?"

"Oh," I said. "You mean—well, right now, I've got a novel that's almost done. It will be finished in about two months."

"Excellent. Now take your time. Do everything you want with it. Because it's *yours,* your baby, and only you know how to nourish it and help it to thrive. But when it's finished, I want you to send it to me first. I want to be its godmother, its fairy godmother. You and I are going to work together. I feel that very strongly. Now, will you send it to me first? Will you promise me that, sweetheart?"

"Yes," I found myself saying without checking with Howard. "I will."

When I called Howard, he wasn't even mad at me for not letting him make the promises. "March Blake!" he gasped when I told him. "And she wants the new book? All right. Now. I want you to be calm. I want you to meditate half an hour every morning before you work and exercise for an hour every evening. At least an hour. You'll be like Rocky when you're writing this book. Focus, Charlotte. It's all about focus."

"Rocky? You're not going to make me drink raw eggs, are you?"

"If that's what it takes to sell your new book to March Blake, then raw eggs it is."

Howard and I developed a plan. "Every morning, before you start writing, I want you to visualize March Blake, holding the manuscript, telling you she loves it. March Blake embracing you, lifting your right arm high above your head, victorious. I want you to imagine hearing the phone ring, answering it, and it's March Blake, saying, 'Your new book is number one on the *New York Times* best-seller list.' I want you to picture—"

"Howard, since when do you—"

"I just signed a sports psychologist. My new client. This is how he gets his teams to win the Superbowl, the World Series, the World Cup, the—well, whatever their particular—"

"I see."

"And if it works on athletes, I don't see why it can't work for writers."

"Sure."

"So, go for the gold!"

I did what Howard told me. What could it hurt? I meditated. I visualized. I exercised. The rest of the time, I worked on my book. I hardly went out. I didn't read or watch TV or see my friends. In six weeks, I was ready to send my book to March Blake, but I sent it to Howard first. He read it quickly. After just five days, which included the time it took for the manuscript to get to him, he called me. "You've really done it this time. It's your best yet. She's going to love it. What's not to adore? Your readers will pull for the main character. In the end, they'll love it when she gets together with Jim. Frankly, I think I'm in love with her myself. I like the surprise with the lost ring and the walnut grove." Howard had a few small changes he wanted me to make, and then he sent it to March Blake.

I waited a week without even considering calling Howard. I waited two weeks before I even got a little bit antsy. With difficulty, I let a third week go by. After four, I called him. "What is going on over there? Has she read it? Have you heard from her? How long is this going to take?"

"Charlotte," he said. "It's been, what, like, two weeks? Oh, OK, four. Four weeks is a nanosecond in publishing. Four weeks is, well, it takes an editor longer than that to walk from the elevator to her desk."

"Couldn't you call her? Couldn't you just see if she's started to read it?"

"No, Charlotte. No, I could not. We like them to think we don't care what they think. Let them think that if it works out, great, if not, there's something better for us."

"But I do care. I *want* this. I care about this more than anything else in the world!"

"That's why you have me. If you could see my face right now, you would see the epitome of letting go. A Zen master, that's who I am. I am at one with destiny, at peace with the goodness of the universe."

"Howard? Since when do you subscribe to this kind of thinking?"

"Since this morning when I signed a self-help writer with a series of books and tapes."

"Congratulations. Now, could you please call March Blake?"

"You should not even be thinking about that book. You know what you should be doing? You should be writing another book. By now you should be so far into it you should have practically forgotten about the last book."

"You want to know what I'm doing? With two percent of my brain I'm writing chapter summaries for a psychology text. With the other ninety-eight percent, I'm wondering what March Blake thinks about my book. Couldn't you just call her?"

Howard sighed. I was messing up his beautiful strategy. "Against my better judgment, I'll make a lunch date, Charlotte. I'll ask her point blank how she likes the book, even though it is not the way I like to conduct business. And if it will make you happy, I promise to call you the minute she pushes her chair back from the table."

"Yes, that will make me happy. Thank you. Thank you very much."

But Howard didn't call. The bad news finally came in the form of a letter from March Blake herself.

Dear Charlotte:

Priority Mail has been read carefully by many of us here at Donner & Sons. It is with deep regret that I must tell you that we all wish you had done better. The characters are wonderful—engaging and easy to identify with; the plot is captivating, original, and surprising and clips along at a lively pace; the message is at once profound and uplifting. However, the book is lacking in what I call the "electric sparkle," that *extra* indescribable element that would distinguish it in a field crowded with entrancing, bewitching novels. In today's market, it is not enough for a book to have magic—it has to have magic *plus.* I am truly sorry to have to let this project go.

I wish you the best of luck in placing it elsewhere.

Sincerely,

March Blake

Enc.: *Priority Mail*

I didn't call Howard right away. I had to wait until I could speak without choking up, without falling apart. A few days after the letter came, when I was still sensitive and fragile, I was at Emily's house, watching her kids out in the yard. A dirty, mangy, half-starved stray kitten wandered in through the hedge. The kids took him inside, where he peed on a kitchen chair and clawed the couch. He hissed and arched every time we went near him. Naturally, the children fell instantly and deeply in love with him and insisted on keeping him forever. The next day, Emily and I took the kitten to the vet. The kitten had fleas, ringworm, tapeworm, and ear mites and rang up a two-hundred-dollar bill. The receptionist asked his name for their records. Emily looked down at the nasty little feline and said, "Magic Plus." We both laughed so hard that the receptionist had to hand us tissues to wipe our tears. Today, Magic Plus, or MP, is a healthy, fat, lethargic fixture in Emily's home.

When I finally got myself together and called Howard, I didn't have to read him March Blake's letter or even summarize it. He already knew. He just said, "I will never to speak her name again, and if you have any compassion for me at all, you won't either." I took another textbook job and sold *Priority Mail* to Collard & Stanton, who never even knew I was gone.

You just can't force a thing like the match between an editor and a writer. It has to be right.

A parent volunteer, Seth's mother, Mrs. Watson, typed each child's letters to author Tim Weeks, author of *Edie and Fred's First Day of School,* exactly as the children dictated them.

Dear Mr. Weeks,

I like the big bugs.

From Grace

Dear Mr. Weeks,

My dad got a new job. I like your book.

Jeffrey Dreyer

Dear Mr. Weeks,

Did you draw all the pictures yourself? They are good.

Amanda

Dear Mr. Weeks,

I like your story. Do you have one about dinosaurs? I like dinosaurs better than bugs.

Ryan H.

Mrs. Watson printed a copy of each letter to be added to the child's journal.

At recess, I copied the letters to Tim Weeks into the e-mail format. I added a note from me about the class, our school, and the fact that I was trying to start the year with integrated writing and reading projects that I thought had a high interest level. I said I liked the book and was happy to have found it for my class. I sent my note and the whole group of letters to Timothy Weeks's e-mail address, which was on the back of the book.

After school, I walked around the building looking for someone to talk to. Maybe if I had just one friend here, I thought to myself, I might feel more comfortable in my job. I would ask Angela and Brooke how their first years had gone. Maybe we could go to a movie together sometime. But both their rooms were locked and dark. I checked the media center and the work room, both empty. I went to Rick's room, which was also dark.

When I got home, I called my sister, but she was in the middle of cooking dinner and helping her kids with homework and couldn't talk.

I made myself some pasta and ate it watching a game show in which people tried to win money to pay off their debts.

* * *

One day, when I checked my mailbox at school, there was a note from Rick.

Charlotte,

I was wondering if you were paired up with anyone for a "buddy class." Last year I worked with a second-grade teacher, who isn't here anymore. I like to have my students get together with younger kids several times during the year for activities and projects. The older ones get a sense of leadership and responsibility. The younger ones get role models. For our first activity, I was thinking we could do some outdoor games later this week. If you're interested, Thursday at 10 works for us.

Let me know.

Rick Barnstable

I quickly scribbled an answer on a piece of scratch paper from the pile of old school lunch menus cut into quarters.

Rick,

Thursday at 10 is fine. My kids will love it! Thank you!

Charlotte

I left my note in his mailbox.

Rick's note was the first good thing I found in my mailbox that day. The second was a fat manila envelope postmarked San Francisco. It was from Timothy Weeks, the author my students had written to. Inside were twenty envelopes, each addressed to a member of my class. "Oh!" I said out loud. "Mail! He sent them each a *real* letter!"

Marilyn was checking her mailbox. She came over to look at the letters. "Look at that! One for each kid. *Somebody's* underemployed."

I let that go. "They're going to *love* this. I can put these in their journals with the letters they wrote!"

Marilyn nodded. "This will look good in their folders at parent-teacher conferences," she commented. "Good job, Charlotte!"

"It's like Valentine's Day," Rosie said at Carpet Time. "Everybody gets one."

I called each child up in turn to stand next to me, open his or her letter, and read it aloud. The letters were hand-printed. Some of the children could read their letters on their own; most needed help. For the nonreaders, I paused for words I knew they could get, such as their own names, and read the more challenging words myself.

Dear Jeffrey,

Congratulations on your dad's new job! I hope he gets a lot of vacations and days off.

I'm glad you liked my book. Thank you for telling me.

Your friend,
Tim Weeks

Dear Rosie,

I liked your letter. I will keep it in a special place: in a box in a drawer in my desk in my office in my house in San Francisco in the United States in the Western Hemisphere on the planet

Earth in the solar system in the Milky Way Galaxy in the Universe.

Your friend,
Tim Weeks

For a change, the children didn't have any problem sitting still and listening at Carpet Time.

I wrote to the author again, another e-mail.

Dear Mr. Weeks,

Thanks so much for responding to each child's letter. They were thrilled to get mail. I really appreciate your taking the time to do this for us. We thank you again for your excellent book.

Your fan,
Charlotte Dearborn

And to think that just a short while ago, I was worried that things might not work out for me here! It just showed how wrong you can be.

On Thursday, the day my class was getting together with Rick's class, I wore one of my favorite shirts, which I had bought at least fifteen years earlier at a Salvation Army Thrift Store in San Maria. The background was salmon-colored, and the pattern was twirling lassos. It was once the top of a pair of men's silk pajamas, but with the top button closed, as it was now, no one would ever guess. It just looked like an old-fashioned silk blouse. Today I wore this shirt with a pair of knee-length khaki shorts, which were loose enough that I could still fit into them, and brown cowboy boots. I wore my hair down, with a silver barrette decorated with a rope pattern on one side. I looked in the mirror assessing the effect: pulled together with a unifying theme that conveyed humor and spirit. I put on lipstick, a brownish-red, picked up all my folders of kids' papers, and left for school.

In my room, I checked my e-mail. The author, Tim Weeks, had written back.

Dear Miss Dearborn,

I appreciate your enthusiasm for my work. My new book will be available in October. It's around 5th-7th grade reading level so won't be of interest to your current students—yet. But I would be interested in hearing what you think.

Tim

It was almost October. Sometimes books are available before their official pub dates. I would ask my sister to order Tim Weeks's new book. The first bell rang.

When I went outside to bring in my class, Seth yelled, "Hey, Mrs. Dearborn! Is it Pajama Day?"

"Excuse me?" I said. "I don't know what you mean. I don't think so."

Ryan H. said, "Look at Mrs. Dearborn! She's in her p.j.s!"

"I am not! Boys!" I said. "Lower your voices! Please!" I didn't wait for them to quiet down. I just turned around and led them inside.

Moving into the classroom didn't get them to change the subject, though. "Mrs. D?" Seth was standing up beside his desk with his hand up. "In kindergarten, we had Pajama Day! Is it Pajama Day again? I didn't wear mine, Mrs. D. Can I call my mom? She could bring my p.j.s for me!"

Other kids got excited about this idea. Amanda said, "You shouldn't wear a long nightie on Pajama Day, because you might trip."

Grace looked panicky, as if she might burst into tears, "My mom didn't know it was Pajama Day, and I didn't—"

"Boys and girls," I said. I held up the peace sign. "I am wearing a shirt that *looks like* pajamas to *you,* but it is really a *shirt.* I am not wearing pajamas, because in first grade, we *do not* wear pajamas to school." I shook my head for emphasis. Do we? No. Pajama Day is only for kindergartners, and it's not today anyway. Do you understand? My shirt might *remind* you of pajamas, but it is not pajamas. Good. Now we're going to do reading first, because Mr. Barnstable is coming later this morning with his sixth-grade class. Each of you will get a sixth-grade buddy. We'll get together with them several times this year to—"

"Can I have Jason?" Seth blurted out. "He's my neighbor, and—"

"You can't choose your buddy," said Amanda. "The teacher has a list, and she tells you who—"

"Quiet!" I said. I knew better than to raise my voice at my kids this way, but it can be so frustrating when you can't finish a single sentence. Yelling didn't work anyway; they went right on talking, each one a little louder, to be heard over the one he or she was interrupting. I made a mental note that in the future I should not tell them about visitors beforehand because now it was impossible to get them to think about anything else. We hardly got any reading done. Some kids hadn't even started on their work sheets before Rick was at the door.

"Good morning, Miss Dearborn," he said, "are you ready to—"

"Hey, Mr. Barnstable!" Seth shouted. "Mrs. Dearborn's not wearing her p.j.s. It just *looks like* p.j.s, but she's wearing a *shirt!*"

Rick looked at me and said, "What?"

"Nothing," I said quickly. "Boys and girls, please line up."

Rick and I took both classes out to the grass. The first thing that went wrong was that my class kept interrupting Rick as he tried to give directions. "I'm going to pair you up—"

Seth shouted, "Jason! I want Jason!"

Amanda said, "Quit it, Seth. You can't choose your—"

Rick said, "I need everybody's attention."

When Seth was paired with a girl named Brittany, he shouted, "A girl! No way!" and stomped away from the group.

Rick signaled that I was to go after Seth, while he handled the two classes.

I started following Seth at a brisk walk across the field toward the houses next to the school. He looked over his shoulder, saw me, and started to run. I was afraid this was going to happen. With all my extra weight and in the cowboy boots on the lumpy field, I wasn't as fast as I would have liked. Once, accidentally stepping into a hole, I stumbled and almost went sprawling onto the grass. The thought of the two classes and Rick seeing me fall to the ground was what kept me from going down. Luckily, Seth slowed down when he got close to the edge of school property.

I said, "Seth, come back and join the class."

"OK, OK," he said. "But I'm not having a girl buddy!"

I tried to put my arm around him as we walked back, but he shrugged me off.

When we got back to the two classes, Rick squatted down so that he was at Seth's eye level. "Brittany has joined Chelsea, and they're both going to be Ryan J.'s buddies. For today, you're with me, Seth. Now, let me see you catch this bean bag." Seth didn't argue with this arrangement. For the first time, he went along with what the rest of the group was doing, participating agreeably. Whenever Rick spoke to the group, he kept one hand on Seth's shoulder. Several times while the two classes were together,

I saw Seth squint up at Rick with something like admiration. How does Rick do that? I wondered. Without even raising his voice, he's got everyone's attention. As the two classes separated, Seth said, "Bye, Mr. Barnstable. Thank you for being my partner."

Rick said, "Thank *you,* Seth," as politely and formally as if they were two adults who had just signed some kind of business agreement that would benefit them both for many years to come.

"Bye," Seth called again as Rick walked away. "I'll see you next time!" Rick turned around and waved at Seth.

8

A young, newly hired assistant in the publicity department at Collard & Stanton was extremely enthusiastic about my first book, *P.S. Will You Marry Me?* She made it her personal mission to get reviews of the novel. Her biggest successes were *Redbook* and *Glamour* magazines the same month the book was to arrive in the stores. I sent her flowers. These two reviews could be responsible for many sales, and her energy and support were refreshing and encouraging.

Due to some kind of glitch in distribution, however, the arrival of *P.S. Will You Marry Me?* in retail outlets was delayed. Cartons of my brand-new books seemed to have disappeared from the distributor's warehouse in Tennessee. The warehouse said the books had been shipped, but the trucking company had no record of the pickup. The books finally resurfaced in a warehouse that handled only academic texts, where they had been accepted accidentally. Then a series of snowstorms in the East and the Midwest slowed delivery further. My books were six weeks late getting to stores, so the novel wasn't available for sale until three weeks *after* the magazines that reviewed it were replaced by new issues. The publicist got discouraged and left C&S. I tried to talk her out of it. "You can't take these snafus personally," I said to Jennifer. The longer you keep working at something, the more likely it is that you'll succeed."

"Are you kidding?" she said. "Success in publishing is a random event, like having triplets without fertility drugs. Individuals have no control over the outcomes here. Listen, I majored in psychology, and I can recognize the situational factors that lead to hopelessness when I see them." Last I heard, Jennifer was selling cooking tools for one of those companies where you have parties in people's homes.

My sister called me when Timothy Weeks's new book came in. It was called *Snowbound,* and it was about a boy traveling from his mother's house in California to his father's house in Illinois in the middle of the school year. Against his wishes, he was going to have to stay in Illinois indefinitely, because his mother's new job involved a lot of travel. He had to change planes in Denver and got stranded at the airport overnight because of a snowstorm. While there, he met an elderly man who told him stories, and the two became friends. It was an older kids' book, so there were just a few illustrations, detailed pencil sketches of the main characters and people sleeping in airport chairs.

I e-mailed the author.

Dear Tim,

You write beautifully. SNOWBOUND is a moving story. The divorce theme and the boy's language gave it a contemporary feel, while the old man's stories had a timeless, almost fairy-tale quality. I liked the boy's electronic game and the rhyming story within the story. Is the game real? I want one. I hope you're planning a sequel. I had a hard time letting that boy go! I wish you tremendous success with this excellent new work.

Your fan,
Charlotte

Sometimes you feel you know a person by reading his books. Of course, you don't. You know nothing about the facts of his life, how he would behave in a group of strangers, what he would eat, the kinds of things he would like to get as presents for his birthday. But often you can feel familiar with him simply from reading what he has written. And I guess you might be right to a certain extent. You can get a sense, a feeling about what kind of heart an author has by reading the way he treats his characters. If he's sensitive to pain, loss, and alienation, it might be a good indicator that he possesses a good degree of empathy and compassion.

Tim Weeks wrote back.

Dear Charlotte,

Thanks (again!) for your positive words. They're keeping me going through a rough patch. Your class is blessed to have such a kind and generous teacher. They're too young to appreciate these qualities, but I do. My work is lonely sometimes. Thank you for keeping me company.

Tim

There was a picture of Timothy Weeks on one of his book jackets. It wasn't a studio photograph. I think my opinion of him would have been seriously damaged if he'd had one of those stiffly posed shots with a neutral background. (I never included an author photograph on one of my books. This is one of the few ways I refused to be flexible in my years as an author. I can't stand the idea of people trying to sum me up on the basis of my haircut or facial expression.) This photograph was much more relaxed than one of those professional shots, just a snapshot of him, looking a little self-conscious. He was kind of messy with a nice smile. His hair was a little on the long side, blowing straight up in one place in a breeze. He was wearing a rumpled, checked shirt. The photo only showed him from the waist up, but I pictured him wearing jeans. I read the tiny print of the photo credit along the side. If it had been taken by a woman with the same last name, Andrea or Jean or Betsy Weeks, say, I would have assumed that he was married and his wife took the photo. But as it happened, the credit read Mark Osgood, who might have been a photographer paid to take this picture. But I imagined he was a friend, doing a favor.

Oh! I suddenly thought. It was possible that Tim Weeks was gay, and Mark Osgood could be his "partner." How would I know? I read his bio again, carefully this time.

> *Timothy Weeks is the author and illustrator of several books for children, including the ALA Notable Book* And Make It Snappy, Sadie! *Mr. Weeks lives in San Francisco.*

I prefer reading author bios that give a lot of personal information, such as how old the author is and whether or not he has children. (When writing my own, I always kept my bio as skimpy as possible, not much more than a list of my books, specifically because I did not like busybody readers knowing about my personal life.)

I found myself returning to Tim Weeks's photo several times during the next few days, looking it over, scrutinizing it for details I might have missed. There wasn't much: part of a wooden fence in the background, a strand of hair that fell over one eyebrow, a left hand with no rings.

I wrote back. I started my reply on paper, then made some changes before I typed it on the computer. I didn't revise it too much, just made five or six word substitutions, deleted the first sentence, and changed the closing. I didn't tell him that I used to be a writer or that I knew how hard that could be. I didn't go into any of that. I just said

Dear Tim,

I know all about rough patches. This is my first year teaching, and it hasn't been an entirely smooth transition.

Discovering a writer I didn't know about always lifts my spirits. My sister owns a bookstore, and she has ordered all of your other books for me. Can't wait!

Your fan,
Charlotte

A message came back:

Charlotte,

It's hard to be new. But sometime soon you'll look up and be surprised to find yourself settled and comfortable. So, are you just out of school?

T

He wanted to know how old I was. I wanted to let him know that I wasn't twenty-three, but I didn't need to go into the details of how I got here. I would think this one over before I answered.

* * *

I could have stayed in my room during recess and lunch and corrected papers. Instead I went to the lounge with Marilyn and tried again to develop some kind of camaraderie with the teachers and staff. My plan was to try to offer them something they needed. I thought that this was the way I would find myself inside their group. But what could I offer them? Nothing. I had nothing they could possibly need. Being a new teacher wasn't so different from being a new kid. It was hard to figure out where to sit in the lounge when I didn't know anyone's regular spot. I waited for Marilyn to sit down, and I sat down next to her. Entering their conversations could be tricky, too, when I didn't know the teachers' personal histories, opinions, and backgrounds. But I had to be brave, I told myself, and force myself to jump in.

Coincidentally, a couple of teachers were talking about a new student, a fourth-grader.

"I can't even reach the parents," said Bernice Fitz, stabbing at a piece of lettuce in her plastic container. "By the time I get to school, they've already left the house. They don't get home until after I've gone home." Bernice reminded me of the teacher I had myself for second grade. Mine was called Mrs. Batson. If you lost your place in reading, she made you stand in the front of the class and face the chalkboard until recess. We lived in Pennsylvania then. I was so glad when we moved in the middle of the school year, even though it meant starting over from scratch. I tried to forget about Mrs. Batson and think about what these teachers were saying.

"You could call them from home," I said, trying to be helpful. Bernice didn't even look at me.

"What do they do?" Liz Muñoz wanted to know.

"I have no idea," Bernice said, shaking her head. "Business of some kind. I've never even seen them. The kid is at least a year below grade level in reading. Obviously, I'm going to need some cooperation from the parents. He needs extra reading time with an adult. And I refuse to have him pulled out of class for that. He's a slow worker anyway. I don't want him behind in *everything.* But apparently he's in daycare until six, which doesn't leave a lot of time for reading with the parents after school. I've got twenty-nine other children in my room. I cannot spoon-feed this one boy to get him caught up."

I was stirring sugar into my coffee. I was the only one on staff who used real sugar. I had to bring it from home.

"Of course not!" Liz echoed Bernice's indignation. "You cannot tailor the curriculum to suit each child. Parents are just going to have to accept that."

"You could send a note home, suggest that they call the district office and find a tutor," Marilyn suggested.

Bernice continued. "Cindy said the father just showed up and expected the kid to start school immediately. Some people believe the world revolves around them. Cindy said, 'We need the immunization record. We need to find a desk and books.' Well, the father did have the shot card with him, but then he said, 'How long will it take you to get those things organized? How hard can it be?' He and the kid parked themselves in the lobby. Robert had to drop everything to get a desk. Half an hour later, they stuck him in my class. The arrogance of some people!"

"Poor kid. It's really hard to be new in a big school like this. When I was growing up, my family moved a lot. Being the new kid was awful. Did you assign him a buddy to show him around and get him started with the work?" It was me butting in to their conversation again.

"By fourth grade, they should know enough to ask if they need something," Bernice said, letting me know she didn't welcome my comments.

"Sometimes," I went on, "we would feel so uncomfortable and out of place that we wouldn't use the school bathroom for the first couple of weeks. I have a twin sister, and we wouldn't drink anything and just hold it until we got home."

"Oh, great! All I need is a kid having an accident in my classroom!" Bernice said. "That'll win him a whole lot of friends! If I don't find someone to read with him—"

"I'll do it," I said. Here was my chance. "I could read with him in the afternoons. I'm usually here late anyway." Bernice and Liz turned to glare at me, as if I'd burped loudly without saying excuse me.

A couple of other teachers looked up from what they were eating or the papers they were grading.

Bernice snapped, "No, you couldn't. That would be overtime. You don't get paid for overtime here, you know." She folded a piece of wrinkled aluminum foil around an apple core and dropped it into the trash can.

They didn't seem to understand that I was offering to help. "I'd do it as a volunteer," I said. "I'd just do it for—to—just to help out. I could try to get him caught up. What's his name?"

"It's not your grade level," said a second-grade teacher, Laurie Clarke.

I laughed. "I think I can handle fourth-grade reading!" No one laughed with me. "He just needs someone to listen to him read, right? Some practice for fluency and some questions on comprehension, some vocab work, maybe? He'd need it every day for—what would it take?—half an hour or so—listening to him read? Sure. I'll do it. Be happy to. It's good practice for me." The other teachers looked at each other. "Good experience, you know?"

"She's still new," said a kindergarten teacher. Some of the teachers laughed knowingly.

I drank the rest of my coffee quickly. The bell was going to ring in two minutes. I washed out my cup and hung it on a hook.

Bernice said, "Well, isn't it nice that *you* have so much free time when the rest of us feel crazed and overloaded?"

I said, "Are you kidding? I'm used to doing rush textbook jobs during the day, while writing a novel at night. Before I did that, I waitressed eight to ten hours in addition to working on my books. Whenever I wasn't working at whatever job I had, I was trying to finish a book. This is the first time I've had real days off in, I don't know, since college! It's just a matter of what you're used to, you know? It's all relative. So I'll do it. I'll read with the boy." I smiled at Bernice to let her know that she could count on me.

"I'd take her up on it, if I were you." It was Rick. I didn't see him come in. He was feeding quarters into the soda machine. "She's offering you a hand. Why don't you just accept? What could it hurt?"

No one said anything for a few seconds. Rick's drink dropped out of the machine. He took it and left.

"Be my guest, then," Bernice said stiffly. "Knock yourself out. His name is Dylan Jones. I'll leave a message on their answering machine."

"Great. OK, then. Maybe you can give me a list of good fourth-grade books." I smiled to show her, again, that we were on the same side.

"Sure," Bernice said flatly. "Fine." I saw her give Liz Muñoz a put-upon look.

"OK, see you later," I said.

Marilyn got up to leave with me.

"Well, that went badly!" I whispered to her in the hall.

"No," she said, "it was very generous of you to offer to help the boy."

"So what are they so mad about?" I asked her.

"Mad?" Marilyn whispered back. "Who's mad?"

"The teachers. Just now."

"No, you misunderstood. I don't think they're *mad,* Charlotte. But they might be just a teeny bit hurt that you suggested your job here isn't as demanding as your old one. Some of the teachers feel kind of, well, overworked, underpaid, underappreciated, that kind of thing. A couple of years ago, we had a contract dispute. One of the issues was unpaid overtime. There's never enough prep time, for example, so we have to do a lot of it at home at night and on weekends. Bernice, who, after all, is this boy's own teacher, might think it makes her look bad when another teacher is willing to volunteer after-school time, and she's not."

"Oh. No." I ran a hand through my hair. "I just meant, the long vacations and the short days and well, gosh, I didn't mean to—should I say I won't do it, after all? Maybe Bernice might decide to read with him herself, and—"

Marilyn shook her head. "No. Bernice goes home right after school. She doesn't do anything extra here. Who *else* is going to help the boy? I'm sure his family will really appreciate it. And he *needs* it."

The bell rang, and Marilyn turned to go to her class. "See you later. Hope it works out."

"Yeah, thanks."

I was even worse off than when I'd started. Not only had I failed to make friends with the other teachers, I'd insulted them as well as taken on extra work.

My class was rambunctious and hard to control all afternoon. I was working on math with half of them, while two mothers divided the rest of them into two reading groups. The kids I was trying to talk to were listening to what the other kids were doing. Seth got up twice during math to see the pictures in the reading books. The kids in the moms' groups kept stopping what they were doing to listen and to answer the questions I asked my group. It wasn't any better when the groups switched places. When the bell rang, no one had finished either the reading or the math.

I had another headache, and I wanted to sit down in a quiet room and eat about fifty Oreos. But Ryan J.'s mother was late picking him up again, so I had him play a computer math game. He didn't understand how it worked, so I helped him for twenty minutes until his mother showed up.

Then I sat down at the computer.

Dear Tim,

I'm not just out of school. I was doing another job for a long time. It didn't work out. I used to work alone, and being with people all day is a bigger adjustment than I thought. The meetings and the staff lounge get to me.

Charlotte

Before I left, I straightened my room. Then I checked my e-mail again.

Charlotte,

I know just what you mean! I whine about being lonely, but I'd be lousy at working in an office or a store or a school. Can't stand to INTERACT all day long. What was your other job?

T.

I didn't answer that one, as I preferred to skip the question about what my other job had been. With e-mail, it's easy to control what information you give.

I got into the habit of checking my e-mail all the time—when the kids went out for recess, then again at lunchtime and a few times after school. I came to school on weekends and stayed a long time, even though I didn't really need to. I checked my e-mail several times on Saturday and Sunday. Whenever the blinking, darkened envelope indicated that I had a message, my heart fluttered. *I shouldn't be doing this,* I thought. *This will end badly.* But I didn't do anything to stop myself from writing new notes, and reading old ones over and over until they became as familiar as my social security number.

I knew the teachers weren't going to help me with book suggestions for Dylan Jones, so I had called my sister for recommendations. She said to try *Dear Mr. Henshaw,* by Beverly Cleary. She thought it might be a little easy for him, but that could be a good thing, in this case.

I went to the door of the daycare room. There was an art project—colored pipe cleaners, flower pots, and florist foam—set out on a table. Two girls, whom I recognized as first-graders in Marilyn's class, were putting on dress-up clothes. A younger boy was playing a computer game. I didn't see any other kids in the room.

To the daycare worker, a tall blonde woman in shorts, I said, "Is this it? Aren't there other kids?"

"Yeah, but they're playing capture the flag outside with Jimmy."

"I'm Charlotte Dearborn," I said. "I'm here to read with Dylan Jones."

"I'm Jen," said the woman. "Let me see." She checked a clipboard. "Wow, believe it or not, his teacher sent a note about that."

"So I guess I should go find him outside?"

"No, he's here," she said. "Just a sec."

She walked around the art table. Dylan was sitting on the floor, leaning against the wall. I hadn't noticed him before. He stood up and shuffled toward me. Dylan Jones was tall for a fourth-grader, almost as tall as I was. He was wearing tan shorts that stopped way above his knees, a short-sleeved, button-down shirt that just reached his hip bones, and white sneakers. The person who bought these clothes for him either did not know or did not care about what the other kids were wearing: long, baggy shorts below their knees; long baggy T-shirts; and black, navy, or dirt-colored sneakers. Looking at him was like watching a TV show about a teenager that gets all the slang and music wrong. It made me want to cringe and correct the mistakes.

"Hi, Dylan," I said. "I'm Ms. Dearborn. I'm going to be reading with you in the afternoons. Your parents wrote a note to Mrs. Fitz saying that would be OK. I hope it's OK with you, too."

"Not really."

"Oh," I said, startled. I didn't expect him to *want* to do this, but I hadn't expected him to be quite so truthful about it, either.

"But it's not like I have a choice," he added.

"Oh. Right. Yes, I see. We're going to use this desk. Here have a seat." The custodian had set up a desk and two chairs for me down the hall from Aftercare. I sat on one of the chairs, a child-sized one that made me feel like a giant. "OK. I brought this book I thought you might like. Have you read this?"

Dylan sat down. "No. I don't like reading."

"I see." I scrambled for common ground. "I hear you just moved here. My family moved a lot when I was growing up. I didn't like it. I remember that the first few weeks, before I had any friends, I would kind of watch everyone, trying to learn which kids were friends, the way they talked in the place. That way I got the feel for it before I actually joined in. Do you do that?"

"No."

"Of course, I guess I didn't *realize* I was doing it until after I grew up and thought about it. I had a twin sister, so that made it easier for me. But in those days, they never let twins be in the same class."

He looked at a pencil mark on the table, rubbed at it with his finger.

"So, OK, I thought we'd read for just a few minutes, since this is the first time. Let's give this book a try."

I slid the book over to his side of the table. He looked at the cover illustration without touching the book. I looked at my own copy.

"Start with the title, the name of the author, and the name of the illustrator."

"Dear Mr. Henshaw," he read. "By Beverly Cleary. Illustrations by Paul O. . . . Zinsky."

"Good. Very close. Ze*lin*sky. See the *l* there? Let's look at that picture. What do you think this book might be about?"

"I don't know."

"Guess."

"Um . . . a boy."

"OK . . . and?"

"A boy . . . and his pencil?" He smirked at his joke.

I laughed. "Pretty much. And the title? What clues does that give you?" He didn't answer. "Let's try it and see."

Dylan opened the book.

"You can skip the title page, since you've already read the title, author, and illustrator. Let's just go straight to the beginning of the story. Now what do you see? Does it look different from most first chapters? It doesn't say 'Chapter One' at the top of the page. What are we about to read?"

He shrugged.

"Can you guess?"

"I don't know." He was looking at the marks on the table.

"Dylan, look. It starts with the words 'Dear Mr. Henshaw' and ends with 'Sincerely, Leigh Botts.' What do you think?"

He glanced at the book. "Uh. I don't know. A letter?"

"Right. Good. It's a letter."

"Duh."

I needed a moment to think about this. If I confronted him, he might not cooperate; if I didn't confront him, he might get worse. "Right. Pretty obvious. OK, start reading," I said firmly.

He sighed wearily, paused, and began to read. The first letter was short and contained a joke. The character had written to an author that he "licked" his book. Dylan read the word "liked," instead, missing the joke.

"OK," I said, "let's go back a second. Look carefully at this word."

"Liked? Oh. Licked."

"Right. He's supposed to be a second-grader when he writes that one."

Dylan sat very still, hunched over the table, staring at the book.

"I did this with my class," I told him. "I had my first-graders write letters to an author. They were pretty funny."

He didn't reply.

"OK, read this," I said, pointing to the next letter.

When he got to the part that said the character had just moved and started a new school, he didn't show any sign that he identified.

He read slowly, but without a great number of errors. Bernice had told me that his problem was comprehension and to ask questions to make sure he was getting what he was reading.

"How do you think the boy is feeling in his new school and home?"

Dylan shrugged.

"Is he feeling happy or sad or what?"

"OK, sad. Whatever."

"Let's look at this sentence. Here."

He read the sentence to himself. "Sad. I *said* sad."

I pressed on. "Can you come up with some more words to describe how he feels? When he says he doesn't have a lot of friends in his new school, and down here when he says the kids in his school pay more attention to his lunch than they do to him, what feeling is he talking about?"

"Sad."

"He spends a lot of time by himself. He doesn't have any friends yet. What do you think?"

"I don't know."

"How about lonely?"

"Yeah, OK, lonely." He leaned his head on his hand.

I said, "Great. Let's go on. Read this."

After fifteen minutes, I said, "We're going to stop here."

He stood up to go back to daycare.

"I'll be back tomorrow," I said to the back of his shirt. "OK? See you then."

"That went badly, too," I would have said, if I'd had anyone to say it to. On the way back to my classroom, I checked my mailbox: nothing there. In my room, I called my answering machine at home: no messages. I read further in *Dear Mr. Henshaw,* but I didn't want to spoil the story for tomorrow, so I stopped, put it on a corner of my desk. I finished preparing an Ocober activity, haunted houses with window shutters that opened. Behind the shutters the children would glue pictures of things that started with the short *e* sound: egg, elephant, envelope. I cut open the shutters and glued backing sheets to each house. When I finished that, I really had nothing left to do, unless I wanted to start photocopying a bunch of stuff that I wasn't going to use until November.

I sat down at my computer table, typed in my password, clicked on the Internet server icon, clicked OK. A series of images zipped by: a flash of lightning, a bunch of planets out in space, the Earth from space, people circling a globe holding hands, then the "welcome" page of the Internet server. I clicked on the little mailbox icon in the corner of the screen. Then I just had to double-click on an envelope next to a message I had already read and click "Reply." On the blank screen that appeared, I typed:

Dear Tim,

A first-grade teacher gets lonely too.

Charlotte.

9

I was supposed to be on the *Shelley* talk show once. Shelley was that tiny, beautiful Olympic gymnast who went to college after winning her two gold medals and emerged with an ability to speak intelligently and look great at the same time. Now she owns both a TV network and a chain of sporting-goods stores. But this was years ago, when she was on the cover of every magazine and just starting to be huge.

Shelley wanted to talk to me about my third book because one of the characters was a former sixties radical who had settled down to a life of carpooling and gardening in the suburbs. Shelley's "people" called me. They said that Shelley was very interested in the ideas my book brought up about what had become of radicalism.

"Do you have any idea how many people watch that show?" Howard said.

"Don't tell me," I said. "I'm nervous enough."

"It's in the *tens of millions.*"

"Thanks. I needed that."

"This will change everything for us," he said. "Everything. I predicted this about you. Way back. Remember? I knew you had mass appeal the first time I read your work. I recognized the *largeness* there. And I'm always right. Hey, I hope you're not going to move to one of the monster agencies after all we've been through together."

"Howard," I said. "Come on."

"Stranger things have happened. Anyway, as I said, I just knew this was going to happen, sooner or later. Actually, I thought it was going to be sooner, but OK. You were ripening, maturing, deepening. And Shelley didn't have her show then. This is good; now you're ready. Now you can appreciate it."

Shelley's "team" gave me guidelines about what to wear. I bought a new dress, which was a little extravagant, but I knew I could wear it for other appearances. I went to Cincinnati, where the show was taped, and stayed in a fancy hotel for a night. Unfortunately, while I was sleeping in the nice bed, an international incident took place. Shelley and her staff quite reasonably thought, along with the rest of the world, that the United States was about to go to war. An assistant, a woman named Deb, phoned my room, just as I was assembling my clothes, to let me know that Shelley had changed the topic of her show to "Women at War," and they were going on live.

"So, you mean I'm not going to be interviewed?" I asked, slow to catch on.

"Right. Sorry. And don't take it personally. Happens all the time."

Instead of me, female representatives from each branch of the armed forces were flown to Cincinnati to speak about how they prepared their children for the fact that they were leaving indefinitely, that they might not come back. I'd be lying if I said that the show was not intense, gripping. I cried when they interviewed the kids. Shelley didn't mention my book, of course, because it didn't have anything to do with the topic.

I called Howard, "Aren't you going to make them reschedule?"

"*Make* them?" Howard said. "Charlotte, I can't do that."

"Why not? There isn't even a war. The whole thing blew over in three days!"

Howard said, "You just can't trust these fascist dictators, can you? Who knew the little bastard was capable of a retraction and an apology?"

"But my *book!*"

"Charlotte, Charlotte. It would have been great, I know, but I think, and I mean this in the most supportive way, I think Shelley made a little mistake. I think she realizes that now."

"Mistake?" I said. "Howard, what do you mean by that?"

"Just that, your, you know, your 'territory,' if you will, is a lot smaller than she thought."

"Territory? Smaller?"

"Smaller, yeah. I mean, she usually picks topics that take on more extreme examples of the human experience. Murder, addiction, kidnapping, corporate bullying, and, even better, combinations of the above. You know, big. Your stuff is small. One might say tiny. So I wonder if she even read the book initially."

"What are you saying, that she read the book after I was scheduled, hated it, and decided against having me on? That the 'Women at War' show was just an excuse to dump me?"

"Ah, who knows what goes on there? It's just—we'll never know, will we?"

"Howard, I resent your characterizing my work as *small.* And I think you're wrong. My work strikes a chord with a lot of people. It would be more, way more, if people just knew about it. I mean, minuscule details can have enormous resonance." I took a deep breath. I didn't like the high-pitched tone my voice had suddenly acquired. "I mean, small is—is, well—huge!"

"You're right. Don't listen to me. What do I know? I'm an *agent,* for God's sake, the lowest life form."

"Wait. I didn't say—"

"In any case, I can't get her to reschedule. Today she's doing that woman who writes the New Orleans police psychic novels. She won't be having another novelist on for two months at least. And as you know, if they don't get you as soon as the book comes out, it isn't going to happen. You're old news already. It's not right, but it's the way it works."

On a Monday morning the first week in October, there were identical orange notices in all the staff mailboxes. There was a jack-o'-lantern border around the message.

> Teachers, staff, and students are to wear costumes for the Halloween Parade ONLY. This activity should end by 9:00 A.M. Class parties should be no more than 30 minutes in duration. Teachers, please urge room parents to keep sweet snacks to an absolute MINIMUM with a reminder that the district is considering cancellation of future parades and parties. Thank you for your cooperation.
>
> Stephen Werner
> School Superintendent

"Wow!" I said. "We get a Halloween parade and a party? We get to wear costumes! That's so great. I love Halloween! I'm really going to enjoy this!"

Liz Muñoz, standing at the coffee machine nearby looked at me over her half glasses. "That makes one of you," she said.

"Oh. Really? I would think the kids would really enjoy it."

"Sure," she said. "The *kids* do. But try to teach them anything that day. Try to get them to focus after they come to school dressed as Dracula and the little string comes off their masks or they lose their fake fingernails or their hair is green and the rest of the kids want to feel it. We tried to ban celebrations altogether, but the superintendent, who is very cozy with some of the parents, wouldn't go for it."

"Oh. I see. I think I'm going to be a book character. I just have to decide which one. Alice, from *Alice in Wonderland,* maybe? But my kids wouldn't be familiar with those books. They only know the Disney movie. I could try to do Frog or Toad from the Arnold Lobel books, maybe. Or I could be Arthur from the Marc Brown books. But now that Arthur is on TV and there are all these tie-in products, it kind of eliminates that, too. Eloise wouldn't be too difficult: black skirt, white blouse, socks, Mary Janes, and a little red ribbon in my hair. But do the kids in my class know Eloise? No, of course not. Better to pick something more current. What are you going to be, Liz?"

"A witch," Liz said flatly and started back to her room.

At the first October meeting for the First Grade Team, I said, "What are you guys going to be for Halloween? I can't decide."

"I'm always a pumpkin," said Marilyn, without looking up from the master copies of the weekly homework she was handing to each of us. Already she was wearing a cardigan with ghosts, black cats, and jack-o'-lanterns knitted into it.

"Minnie Mouse for the last ten years," said Angela. "Before that, Dorothy from the *Wizard of Oz.* And I hate Halloween."

"I'm always a witch," said Brooke. "Not very original, but it works for me."

"Really?" I said. "You do the same costumes every year? Don't you get sick of it?"

"No," Brooke said. "I don't even think about it."

"Now, about the homework," Marilyn said. "I'm giving you all this packet that I—"

"Wait a second," I said. "Excuse me, Marilyn. Just one more thing about this. I was thinking of the character Eloise. Do you think—"

"Who?" said Brooke. She was a lot younger than I was, just a couple of years out of college. "Who's Louise?"

Angela said, "Is that from a TV show?"

"It's a series of *books,*" I said. "Eloise? We had them when I was a kid. She's this little girl who lives in the Plaza Hotel in New York and gets into all kinds of mischief? Don't you remember? The illustrations are classic. Hilary Knight."

"Hilary Knight?" Brooke shrugged. "Never heard of her."

"Him," I said. "The illustrator is a man."

"Are you sure about that? Hilary?" said Marilyn. "Like Bill's wife?"

"Yes, I am. Very sure. And the books are still in print. That's the thing about kids' books. They have this longevity that—"

"I'd go with something they know," Marilyn said. "Mama Berenstain, if you want to do a book, or maybe Clifford, the Big Red Dog."

"How about Marge Simpson?" said Angela.

"That's TV," I said.

"Oh, right."

"OK, could we get to the subject of homework?" said Marilyn.

"Sorry," I said. "By the way, do we have to give them homework? All the developmental literature I've read—"

Marilyn glared at me to let me know I shouldn't finish this sentence.

I said, "Sorry. I'll tell you later. When you're finished. Go on. What about homework?"

"Some of my parents are complaining that the homework is too much," said Angela.

I said, "That's exactly what I was trying—"

"And some of mine are complaining that it isn't enough," Marilyn interrupted quickly. "So I was thinking, how about some optional activities? The more practice they have at home, the easier our job is. Write five or more sentences about a particular topic, and then—"

"Your Halloween costume," I said. "How not to eat all your candy on the first night, and, oh! I know! The scariest—"

"Charlotte," Marilyn said under her breath, sighing in frustration.

"Oh. Sorry," I said scrunching lower in my seat. "I thought I'd just—you know, help you guys think up some writing topics with an October theme."

"But how would we add optional homework?" Angela wanted to know. "Give it to everybody, but tell them they don't have to do it? Choose who gets it? Give it to the parents who ask for it for their kids?"

We worked it out that we could each decide on our own system of giving extra homework. I didn't see a good opportunity to describe the study that I'd read in one of my classes last summer, which demonstrated convincingly that first-graders weren't ready to focus on school tasks for more than five hours a day, that their time at home was better spent playing with friends to develop social skills or with their families to strengthen bonds and feelings of well-being.

After school, I was coming upstairs with groceries. I had two heavy bags. I was planning to make a vegetable casserole and freeze it in small portions so I could take something healthy and nonfattening to school for lunches. As I was going up, Dave

Conklin was coming down with a huge bag of dirty laundry. The bag looked about my size and probably weighed as much. All the clothes I owned, including things I didn't like enough to wear, would not fill up a bag that size. I was wondering how long he must have gone without washing anything, when he started coming toward me, walking diagonally down the steps. He couldn't see me, of course, because the bag was in front of his face. Before I had a chance to say anything, he ran right into me, and I lost my grip on my own bags. My egg carton, which had been on top, squished and popped open, a glob of cold egg running down my front.

"Oh!" I said, the coldness of the egg making me cry out.

"Sorry," Dave said. "I didn't think anyone was—"

"Going to use the stairs but you!" I finished for him.

"Sorry. Really," he said. "I was in a hurry, and I just—Sorry. What a mess! Look at that!"

He had dropped his giant laundry bag without spilling anything, but he bent to help me pick up my groceries. He handed me a box of tampons, an egg-covered *TV Guide,* and a box of powdered Slim Fast. Dave seemed to be reading the back of the box as he handed it to me.

"Thank you," I said snatching it from him.

"Sorry," he said again. He bent down to pick up a bottle of shampoo.

"Really," I said. "It's OK. It was just a little accident." I sounded more irritated than I meant to.

Quickly, I gathered up what I could and started to my unit. Behind me, I could hear Dave picking up more of my stuff. I left the bag at my door and went back to pick up the rest of it, passing Dave on his way up.

"Every time I see you," he said, "there's some kind of crash!"

"It's only been twice," I said. I gathered up the few remaining items and passed Dave again on his way down.

"Well, it was great bumping into you!" he said, smiling.

"Yeah," I said.

"I was kidding," he said.

"I know."

"OK, I guess I'll go to the laundry room, if you have everything."

"I do."

"So long, then."

"Good-bye."

He bent down to pick up his bag but straightened up again. "Hey, how's your car?"

"My car was a total loss, according to the insurance company."

"What!" he said, putting his hand over his heart.

"I had to buy another one."

"Oh, no," he said. "That is the worst thing I've ever heard!" He slapped his hand against his forehead.

"Well," I said. "No, I mean, I wasn't hurt or anything, and—"

"But it was all my fault!"

I said, "No, the car was—I would have had to buy a new one anyway. I mean, eventually."

"That car? It was a good car with no problems, you said! Didn't you say you just got this new job and moved in here? Then your car gets totaled, and here you are turning over a huge chunk of your salary to the loan people!"

"Well, yeah. But you know, I got a *used* car. It's not that nice, so it didn't cost that much."

"You don't even *like* the car I forced you to buy!" He sat on the top step and dropped his head into his hands.

He looked miserable. Now I felt guilty. "You know, sometimes it's a good thing—a blessing in disguise—to start over from zero and, you know, have everything, well, fresh, and . . . and new!"

"Zero," he said, shaking his head. "*I* did this to someone. You're going to have to let me help you."

"Help me? Help me what? Don't be silly. I'm fine."

"No, you're not. You're in debt, and you're unhappy."

"I am not unhappy," I snapped. "And everyone's in debt. Don't you listen to the news? Five thousand dollars in credit-card debt for the average American household. That's not even counting car and house payments. And what makes you think I'm unhappy? I'm happy."

He shook his head. "No, you're not."

"How would you know that?"

"Your groceries," he said. He shrugged.

I laughed. "You can't tell anything about me from my groceries! How do you know—I mean, what makes you think—I might have been buying them for someone else!"

"Listen. I'm going to make it up to you, OK?"

"No! Really, you don't have to do that." Why did I tell him about the car? Now I was never going to get rid of him. This was going to be just like high school. "I wanted a new car! I did. I was planning—"

"Whatever. But listen. From now on, whenever you need anything, think of me. OK? I want to help. I really do. It would make me feel better. You'll be doing me a favor every time you ask me for help."

"Please, I—"

He held up his hand. "It's settled." With a slight grunt, he picked up his laundry bag and took off down the steps.

"I don't think there's anything weird about an e-mail romance," my sister was telling me on the phone later. "Relationships start in all kinds of ways. And look at all the epistolary romances of earlier generations."

"Those are in books," I said. I sat down on the couch.

"Some of them really happened!" she countered. "That's how

the novelists got the idea! Anyway, he looks nice. You know, on his book jacket. His books sound nice. I think you can know something about a person from his books, not everything, but you can get a general feel for a person."

"Oh, come on," I said, "he writes children's *fiction.* It doesn't say anything about *him.*"

"Well, take you, for instance. You don't write—"

"*Didn't* write. I'm not a writer anymore."

"OK, *didn't* write about your own life. Still, your readers have some idea about your sense of humor, what moves you, what you—"

"I sure hope not. That would make me feel so exposed."

"Well, they *do*—"

"Did."

"Whether you're willing to recognize it or not. If you feel weird about the e-mail, why don't you go up there? Meet him."

"I couldn't just—"

"Isn't there a teacher's conference or something you could attend? My kids' teachers are always going to these meetings—"

"Next month, there's a meeting on journal writing in the primary grades that I was thinking of going to. I guess if I really—"

"Perfect!"

"Well."

"Just casually mention that you *might* be in the area," my sister said. "Then he'll suggest getting together."

"I don't know."

"Do it! You're not going to meet anyone at school. Sounds like it's just a bunch of cranky women."

"And a few cranky men. I guess I could try mentioning to Tim Weeks that I might be going to San Francisco. See if he—"

"He will. He's interested. I can tell!"

"OK. I'll e-mail him."

Sometimes, even though I know what I want to do, I like to have my sister tell me to first.

I was pushing my cart around Vons. I was looking for some red lentils to make soup. They're so much prettier than the regular ones, but I couldn't find them. I picked up one of those bags of fifteen different varieties of beans and looked at the recipe on the back, when something crashed into my shopping cart. I had been leaning on it, so I momentarily lost my balance and had to grab onto a shelf. I bumped into a can of ready-cut tomatoes, which slammed to the floor, narrowly missing my big toe. I was wearing sandals.

When I recovered, I looked up, expecting to see an addled old lady or a toddler too small to see where his cart was going. Dave Conklin was standing there grinning at me. "Surprise!" he said. "Just kidding."

I glared at him.

"Oops," he said. "Bad day? It was just a little joke. I'm sorry. Didn't mean to upset you. I saw your car. I checked it out in your space last night. It's nice!"

"Thanks." I bent to pick up the can. It was dented. I put it back on the shelf.

He looked away for a second. I looked back at my recipe. "Making soup?" he said. "You're going to have a lot on your hands there. That bag is going to make enough for a family of twelve!"

I didn't answer. He thought I didn't have any friends or family. He probably thought I was lonely and disconnected and wanted me to invite him over. I said, "It's for a party, a big one, at the school where I teach. And actually I'll need two bags." I picked up another bag.

"You know what would be good with that?" he said. I didn't

ask what, but he told me anyway. "A loaf of cheddar bread from the Village Mill Bread on El Camino Real. Ever go there?"

"No, and see, it's potluck, so everyone just has to bring one thing."

"Kind of a get-to-know-each-other gathering? That will be good for you."

"No," I said. "They all know each other. It's a fiftieth birthday party for one of the teachers, a surprise."

"That must be hard, being new in an established group."

I said, "Hard? Not at all. I'm enjoying getting to know everybody. They're all really, you know, nice." I nodded *yes* for emphasis.

"You're lucky, then. Sometimes being new can be hard. Well, anyway, it was great bumping into you again!" He grinned at me. "And think about that bread. Want me to tell you how to get to the bakery? When you come out of this parking lot, you go right, then at the light—"

"Thanks, but I'm just bringing the one thing."

"Just thought I'd, you know, tell you about it. In case you hadn't been there."

"Well, thanks." I pushed my cart in the opposite direction from the way Dave was going.

At home, I had just finished putting away my groceries, and I was eating some Mystic Mints that I shouldn't have bought, when there was a knock on the door. Of course it would be Dave, and of course I couldn't try to pretend not to be home because he knew my car.

I opened the door and found him holding a Crock Pot and a white paper bag. "What's this?"

"The bread," he said, handing me the bag. "You can serve it warm or not. Whatever. Everyone will love it. Guaranteed. And you can borrow my Crock Pot. Just cook the soup in this, then bring it to the party, and plug it in to keep the soup warm."

"That's OK," I said. "I'm just going to—"

"I wasn't going to use it today." He brushed past me to set it down on my table. "I hardly ever use it. Let me know how they like the bread," he said on his way out.

"OK," I said. "Well, thanks."

The principal was going to call the second-grade teacher, Arlene, at home and say there was an emergency meeting at school, which normally only happened when someone died.

I arrived with my soup and Dave's bread. What else was I going to do with it? The party was in the school library, which was just off the front entrance to the school. Other people brought chips and dip or vegetables on a plate surrounding some kind of dressing. There were coolers of drinks, napkins with balloons on them, as well as real balloons, black ones, and black streamers hanging from the ceiling. The birthday teacher hadn't arrived.

I don't like parties. Does anyone? You get there and you just want to run. All these people are standing around laughing and talking, and you're just this extra piece that doesn't go anywhere. When you first arrive, before you've spoken to anybody, there's a tiny window during which you could turn around, get back in your car, and go home. I've done it. Of course, at home, I always felt like a jerk in my lipstick and my semi-special, but not-too-dressy outfit in front of my own TV. Then I torture myself about what fun I might have had, the incredible people or person I might have met. But at least at home by myself I don't have to try to think of things to say.

I was wearing my newest jeans (less than six months old) and a vest I made out of silk neckties that I'd collected over the years from thrift shops. Under it, I had on a white tuxedo shirt. I thought the vest added color and interest to the outfit while, at the same time, covering the way the waist of my jeans dug hard into my middle and diverted attention from the way my butt stress-tested their seams.

I stood there for a few seconds, holding my offerings, and scanned the room. I put the soup down on the table next to a pan of brownies. One of the second-grade teachers came up to me. "Hey, whatcha got there, Charlotte?"

"Soup," I said. "I made soup."

"Great!" she said. "Most everybody else brought a dessert or an hors d'oeuvre."

"Oh, good," I said. "I wasn't sure if—"

"Gifts go on that table over there? 'K?"

"OK," I said. I set Dave's Crock Pot down on a table full of biographies and plugged it in. My present, which I carried under my left arm, was a book, naturally. My sister and I had spent a long time picking it out. It's hard to get a book for someone you don't know very well. But Emily happens to be very good at this. She asked the teacher's interests.

"She collects bird houses and makes quilts," I told her.

My sister said, "What about the Eudora Welty collection that just came out?"

I shook my head. "Too, too—no, not that. What about something along the lines of approachable wisdom? Something inspirational. You know, because she's fifty."

She looked at me. "You hate that kind of stuff."

"Yeah, but it's not for me! Don't you have one of those books with the positive quotes that recognize how hard everything is?"

"Like this?" My sister held up a best-seller on the subject of life.

"Yeah!" I said. "And isn't there a companion journal to go with it?" She found it for me. "I'll take those two." Emily wrapped the books in nice paper and chose a card for me. I signed it, and she taped it to the present.

I set my gift on the table with the others. I went back to one of the food tables and dipped a carrot into some kind of creamy dressing. I looked around the room again. I took some potato chips. Bernice came over to get a napkin. "What did you bring, Charlotte?"

"Bean soup," I said.

"That's not party food!" she said, scowling.

"It's not?" I said. "Oh, and this bread."

"Ooo!" she said, taking a slice of the bread. "Is that from the bakery down on—"

"El Camino Real. Yeah. Village Mill."

"Mm. Good," Bernice said with her mouth full and moved on to talk to a group of other teachers.

One of the sixth-grade teachers—I couldn't remember her name—came over to the food table, lifted the lid of the Crock Pot, and put it down again.

"Hi," I said. "Wow, pretty good attendance here tonight."

"Yeah," she said. "Oo, is that tiramisu? Yum."

The lights went out, and everybody got quiet. Arlene's car had been spotted in the parking lot. We all hid behind the stacks. I squatted down next to Phyllis, who taught kindergarten, and Beth, one of the fourth-grade aides. My knees gave a loud crack. We all heard the front door open. Arlene walked in. The principal met her at the entrance to the media center. "I guess you're wondering why I called you here tonight."

"Well, yeah, what's the big—"

"SURPRISE!" we all yelled, jumping out from behind the books.

Arlene looked very surprised. In fact, as she put her hand to her chest, I worried for a second that it was too much of a surprise. But then she said, "You guys! Oh, my gosh, you guys! How did you—of all the—" Then I knew she was faking. I checked out her clothes: coordinating pants, top, and jacket. Her hair was brushed and her makeup looked recent. She knew.

Everyone gathered around to hug Arlene. One of the second-grade teachers led her over to the presents and put a can of Diet Pepsi—her favorite beverage—in her hand. Someone had brought in a rocking chair for her to sit in and an afghan to put over her knees. She sat down and opened her gifts. There were a lot of joke presents: a cane, anti-flatulence tablets, a big magnifying glass. Not very funny, but par for the course for these parties, I guess. I watched the whole ritual with a stiff smile plastered across my face. When she opened mine, she looked it over quickly and said, "Nice." She put it on the pile.

After the presents, everyone milled around eating and talking. There was no music. There should be music, I thought. I ate some of the vegetables and some of the chips. Then I ate a couple of desserts. I was just going to have a brownie, but then I added a chocolate chip cookie, because they looked so good. People go to a lot of trouble to make this stuff for a party, and it's a shame when it doesn't get eaten. The cookies weren't warm or anything but very fresh anyway, the chips still gooey and the cookie soft. As soon as I could, I was going to leave. I ate another cookie, white chocolate chips this time, and walnuts. The walnuts were a mistake, I thought, chewing, just one step too far. I took another of the regular chocolate chip cookies to erase the last one. Much better.

If I moved slowly without drawing attention to myself, I could get out of the room without anyone noticing.

"Hi, Charlotte." It was the music teacher, Connie. My class shared our session with all the other first-grade classes, and our school shared her with two other schools. I had only seen her twice, so far. She was small and wiry, about my age. "I heard you used to write," Connie said.

I nodded.

"I have a great idea for a novel," she said, taking hold of my arm. Her fingernails were sharp. "Bernice said I should talk to you."

"Oh, well, I no longer—"

"Oh, I know. Bernice told me your book was a complete catastrophe." I didn't correct her on her facts—that I'd had five catastrophes, not just one. "But I was thinking that you could give me your agent's number. And I was wondering if you'd proofread my book."

"I don't proofread," I said, smiling. She couldn't help it if she didn't know how this worked. "I've done a lot of things, but never that. Sorry. I thought you said it was only an idea. You don't need an agent or a proofreader for an idea."

"I'm about to start."

"Good luck!" I said, and I meant it. I tried to break away before she could describe her idea, but she had my arm.

"It's about a music teacher who's extremely talented but never got to—"

I gasped and held up my free hand. "Stop!" I said urgently. "Don't you know? You should *never* say your idea out loud!" I shook my head.

"But what if I've already—"

"Protect it. Nurture it. Keep it safe inside you until you're ready to let it out." I cupped my hands in front of me as if holding a small, tender bud.

"Oh," she said. "You mean I shouldn't—"

"Never! No. Uh-uh." I continued to shake my head.

She put her hand to her mouth. "I almost—"

"Good thing you didn't!" I said quickly.

"Thank you!" she said.

I took another cookie. Rick walked in then. My mouth was full, so I waved. "Hi, Charlotte," he said. "Anything good to eat?"

I hurried to chew and swallow so I could answer, but he moved quickly to Arlene. "Happy birthday!" he said, handing her a present.

She opened it. I stood on tiptoe to see. Eudora Welty's short stories! I should have given her that. Of course, if I had, she would have gotten two.

"Oh!" Arlene said. "My favorite! How did you know I—"

"I've worked here a long time!" he said. "Her photos are in there, too. It's new, so I was pretty sure you didn't have it."

"I don't. It's wonderful!" She hugged the book to her chest and looked so touched that I thought for a second she was going to cry. "Thank you, *all!* You guys! This is so nice! I'm overwhelmed."

Rick walked over to the food table, where I was still standing. "These cookies are really good." I held out the plate.

"Thanks," he said, "but I'm going to sneak out. My daughters are waiting in the car for me to take them to a movie."

"Oh!" I said. "They should come in!"

Rick shook his head. "No, but maybe I'll take some cookies for them."

He loaded a napkin with cookies. "See you, Charlotte. Have fun!"

"Wait!"

He turned around.

"How did you know she would like that book?" I asked.

"Oh," he said. "It was hard! I never know what to get people. Last night, I stood in a bookstore for two hours, reading first chapters until I found something good."

I nodded.

"See you Monday, Charlotte."

"See you."

I went to the gift table, where Marilyn was now folding up the discarded wrapping paper. She said, "I think these will make excellent—oh, I don't know, but something. Did you get any food, Charlotte?"

"Too much." I picked up a piece of yellow paper with balloons on it. "Hey, here's a nice piece. It's hardly ripped at all." I smoothed it and handed it to her.

"Great. I think I'll use these for journal covers."

"Cute," I said. When I looked up from pressing the wrinkles out of wrapping paper, I noticed that a few of the teachers were leaving. Good, I can go, I thought. "I'm going," I said to Marilyn. "See you Monday."

I said happy birthday to Arlene. She said, "Thanks so much for your gift!"

"Oh, you're welcome," I said. "I'm so glad you liked it." She probably didn't remember which one it was, but when she did, later, she would appreciate that I had given her a real present, not a joke.

I unplugged Dave's Crock Pot. It was still full. The bread was gone, though. Good, I wouldn't have to take it home. Instead of going straight to my car, I stopped off first in my classroom.

I turned the light on, put the Crock Pot on a desk, and went to the computer. I typed in my password, which I could now type faster than my own name, and clicked OK. I watched the universe, the galaxy, the solar system, the earth light up my screen, then the little mailman holding a letter. I clicked on the letter.

Dear Charlotte,

So nice to hear back from you so quickly. As I've said, your students are very lucky. Do you have children of your own?

I am working on a book that is giving me a hard time right now. I'm sure that you, as a teacher, never have to experience this particular form of misery. But a book can be very uncooperative. I've tried everything I can think of, short of throwing it out the window. Nothing works. So it's really a relief for me to have this pleasant and unexpected conversation start up.

Tim

Dear Tim,

I do know what you mean about the book giving you a hard time. Don't throw it away. Keep working on it; it's probably about to start behaving itself any minute.

By the way, I might be in your area in a couple of weeks. There's a teachers' conference I'm considering attending.

Charlotte

I clicked Send Now, waited for it to go, and quit. I went home.

10

The sub-rights woman at Collard & Stanton, Veronica, had some success with my book *Priority Mail.* First, it was an alternate selection for one of the minor book clubs. Then she sold the German rights. But she called me personally with the best news. "Charlotte, this is so cool. Listen. I sold audio rights to *Priority,* and Joan Cusack is going to be the reader!" I screamed when she told me. My sister and I loved Joan Cusack. This was before she was as famous as she is now. Her voice was just right for the main character of that novel, a superstitious letter carrier with obsessive-compulsive tendencies, who walks from San Diego to New York to deliver a letter to her idol, Susan Lucci. From then on, whenever I opened that book, I heard Joan's voice, which had easily replaced my own as the narrator.

Unfortunately, Joan had "a conflict" and couldn't do the audio for my book, after all. For a while, it seemed as though someone else might do it, but eventually the project got dropped. It hadn't gotten as far as a contract or anything.

Still, whenever I saw Joan in a movie or on TV, I felt we were personally connected, as if we were cousins or ex-next-door neighbors or something. She seemed to belong to me somehow.

Sunday morning, I got up early to work on my Halloween costume. It was still dark when I began pinning the pattern to the fabric. I was going to be Mrs. Beetleman from the Tim Weeks book. I was using a pattern for a bee costume as a starting point, but I had to make a lot of modifications to have it match the book (and to satisfy Seth, who would expect a lot). Miraculously, I had found a shimmering lime-green and orange synthetic fabric for the beetle's body. As it moved in the light, the fabric had all the iridescent colors you would see on top of an oily puddle. I had some translucent black stuff for the wings. I would need to wire them somehow to make them stand up. When it was all done, I would have someone take a picture of me in it. If I weren't so fat, I would send a copy of it to Tim Weeks.

The next day, I would have been happy to stay home all day again and sew. Instead I got up before it was light and chose an outfit for school: a loose-fitting rayon shirt with pictures of surfboards on it, a pair of black pedal pushers, platform sandals. The sandals made me taller, giving me a longer, slimmer shape. I hoped.

At school, the first thing I did was check my e-mail.

Charlotte,

If you come up to SF, be sure to let me know. Maybe we could get together.

Tim

The Grasshopper Group was working on a story. They were taking turns reading two sentences in Book 2 of our phonics reader series.

It was Amanda's turn. "Pup is up in the hut." She read quickly and easily when it was her turn and waited impatiently when it wasn't. There was a line drawing of a dog in a shack on a hill. We all turned to the next page. "Pup has a bug." The dog was looking cross-eyed at a black blob on its nose. We turned the page.

"Pup . . ." Seth started his sentences. Then there was a long pause. With considerable difficulty, the other readers in the group were restraining themselves from finishing the page for him.

When she couldn't stand it anymore, Amanda urged, "Try the first sound."

I caught her eye and shook my head. We had talked about this, and Amanda had promised to try to let me be the teacher.

"J—" Seth began.

"Right," I said. "Now the second sound,"

"P?" He looked up at me.

"That's coming. But it's not next. This one right here. It's a vowel. What vowel are we working on? Remember? Look at pup again. It's the same sound as in pup. Listen: *p-u-u-u-p.*" I drew out the short *u* sound to make it impossible for him to miss. "It's the sound we're working on in this book. It's been on every page so far. And look at the picture for another clue. What's the pup doing?"

"Hopping? The pup hopped?"

"Yes, but does *hopped* start with the *j* sound?"

Seth looked up at me. Tentatively, he shook his head.

"OK, so say the first sound."

"J?"

"And now the second sound?"

"I?" He tried a short *i.* The only time during the day that Seth spoke quietly was during reading.

I shook my head.

He blurted out a short *a* sound. *"A?"*

"That would be the letter *a,* wouldn't it, Seth? Listen. It's *j-u-*. Now this sound?"

"M?"

"Right. Good, Seth. Now try this last one. You had it before."

"P?"

"Good. Now, say them all together and you'll have the word."

"Um . . ."

"J-u-u-u-m-p," I prompted.

Seth looked at the ceiling.

"OK, it's jump. Good work. Let's go on to the next page."

Seth shouted, "I'm going to be a taco for Halloween. We buyed it last night at Party Plus."

"You bought your costume at Party Plus? I love that store. I can't wait to see you as a taco. Now, why don't we—"

"What are you going to be, Mrs. Dearborn?" Seth demanded.

"That's a surprise."

"Tell us, come on," Seth whined.

"I'm not telling. Let's go on to—"

"A witch?"

"No."

Amanda said, "A pumpkin."

I shook my head.

"An alien?" Patience said.

"*Tell* me. I can't stand it!" Seth yelled.

"Inside voice, Seth. Wait and see. Grasshoppers, we'll work on this book some more tomorrow. Now it's time for you to take your seats and work in your spelling books. Ants! You're next for reading."

One of the kids in the Ant Group stood up. Two were playing with math manipulatives that they had gotten out without permission. One child was missing. Had I said anyone could go to the bathroom? The remaining member of the group was sitting on the carpet eating his lunch. "Ants!" I barked. "Now!"

Before I left school, I got ready for the next morning. I put a phonics work sheet on each child's desk. I got out the number lines we were going to use for math. I checked my schedule. When I looked over the list of activities for tomorrow—math, spelling, library—a wave of weariness washed over me. As usual, I would be spending the day failing at my attempts to get twenty kids to listen to me and do what I asked. But it was only October, I said to myself, and it was only my first year; I might improve.

When I got home, I saw Dave's car in the parking lot. What was he doing home at 4:30? That was a pretty short work day. I found I was almost tiptoeing past his door.

I worked on my Halloween costume until it was time to go to my sister's house for dinner. I was bringing dessert, which I had already made, an ice-cream pie that was in the freezer.

The costume was coming along pretty well. The fabric was difficult to work with, but the pattern was a fairly simple one. I found myself thinking about Tim Weeks as I worked. Would he get a kick out of seeing this costume I made? I would, if I were the author of a children's book. But in it, I would be a lot fatter than his Mrs. Beetleman, and that was just too embarrassing. Emily would look great in the costume. I wondered what our weight difference was right now. Fifteen pounds? Twenty? OK, maybe twenty-five. This hadn't happened to us before. But I couldn't ask her to—I couldn't believe I'd even had such a thought. The fact was she did look almost exactly like me, except for the weight, and some people didn't even notice that. It had been like this only for the past two years.

At first, I thought it was because I worked at home. Emily

worked in the store, where she could keep herself away from food. I thought that when I started teaching, I would lose weight. But even though I was away from food all day long, I made up for it at night—bad habits.

When we were little girls, Emily and I switched classrooms a couple of times. Kids we thought would catch on immediately, our closest friends, didn't even notice. This hurt our feelings, so we didn't find it as much fun to trick people as we expected. The teachers were never more than mildly annoyed at the inconvenience it caused. I'd see Emily's teacher mentally going over the time I'd been in her classroom, thinking, Why didn't I catch on? And I'd want to tell her, "You couldn't know. How would you know?"

Our mother didn't dress us alike. She didn't believe in it. She wanted us in separate classrooms in every school, and she encouraged us to make our own friends, have our own interests. The trouble was, we wanted to dress alike. We envied twins we knew whose mothers bought them the same dresses, underwear, socks, and shoes, who decided together which outfit to put on in the morning, came to an agreement, and arrived at school looking like, well, twins. We wished our names started with the same letter. (As children, we didn't appreciate the fact that our mother named us after two novelists who were sisters. As an adult, I found it intimidating to have such a famous namesake.) We improvised matching outfits for ourselves, finding clothes in our wardrobes that were similar and putting together outfits of them. Seeing us in the morning, our mother would say, "Oh, girls," and shake her head. "Now I suppose if I had insisted on dressing you alike, you probably would have defied me and made sure to wear the matching outfits on different days. Wouldn't you?" We said, "No, we wouldn't."

We wanted to be together all the time. When we invited a

friend over, we usually just invited one girl and shared her. We would have loved to be in the same class, sitting right next to each other. But that was not allowed in those days.

If you saw us standing together, you'd notice the similarities right away. We both wear glasses for reading. Without even discussing it, we made appointments for the eye doctor, got identical prescriptions, ordered the glasses, and ended up with the very same frames, not just the same shape or color, but the same brand, too. And sometimes, when I buy a CD and tell my sister about it, she'll say, "I just bought that this morning." We almost always have the same haircut. We have bought the same bathrobe twice, bathing suit three times, many pairs of the same shoes, the same Christmas sweatshirt, sheet sets (four times), toaster ovens, and vacuum cleaners. For a while, we had the same kind of car. We don't mean to do this. It just happens that we think alike.

But there were differences, big ones that might not have been apparent at first glance. There was our weight, as I've said, but that was recent. And there was the very important fact that she had a family and I did not. We're not exactly sure why this is. We attended the same college and both had boyfriends. She and Brad got married right after graduation and had their first child five years later.

My college boyfriend's name was Joe. Although I expected to marry him, he had no such plan in mind. In fact, after two years of practically living in our apartment, he cheated on me with one of our roommates then took off suddenly, dropping out of school and moving back home to Indiana. I never heard from him again.

I was Emily's maid of honor. I had a yellow dress. Brad's brother was best man. Our mother wore a long, flowery dress and a hat. When you look at the pictures now, it all looks so dated. Brad had long hair. Emily and I had long hair, too. At the time, we worried a lot about split ends and tried a lot of different methods of treating and preventing them. Truth be told, long hair didn't suit us, and neither did our dresses. I avoid looking at those pictures now. Anyway, that was ages ago.

For many years, I expected to fall in love any minute and have a family like Emily's. I'd had three serious boyfriends, including Andrew, but never even gotten close to marrying one of them. I'm the maiden aunt of Emily's children, Janie, Ted, and Will. And now I'm a spinster schoolteacher. Imagine that. It's just like some old novel, except that those spinster teachers were about twenty-six, and I am forty-two.

I have come in handy for Emily. All of her children were poor sleepers and fussy eaters with a tendency to fly into tantrums for more years than any of us likes to admit. I have taken one or more of the children overnight without notice, and have driven to their house in my nightgown when Brad was out of town and more than one child was throwing up. I've hidden birthday and Christmas presents bought on sale at my place for months, and I've stepped in to drag all three to the beach or the movies when Emily was ready to lose her patience or her mind. I knew she would have done the same for me.

Instead she tirelessly promoted my books in her store, went over each one of them with me through countless drafts. She was my audience. I always wrote with Emily in mind. She was the one who would get the jokes, appreciate the overarching themes, predict that there would be tremendous success for me the minute people discovered my work. She would hound and pester me until I finished each book. My sister was the secret to my productivity. Every writer should have an impatient twin, nagging and complaining about how long it took to write each novel. I considered her a collaborator, though she never thought of herself this way. "I'm just a fan," she always said. "I'm your biggest fan."

And every time I finished a book, she would say, "This is your best one yet, Charlotte. Really. I think so. I cried. I had to put it down and sob." She always put a Post-it on the pages that made her cry or laugh out loud. "People are going to gobble this one up," she always told me, believing it every time. I always put Emily in my acknowledgments, and I had dedicated two novels to her. I dedicated the other three to her kids, one at a time, oldest to youngest. Fortunately, each child had a book before I quit writing.

At six o'clock, I brushed my hair and put on a sweater. I made whipped cream in a stainless-steel bowl that I had chilled. Then I got the ice-cream pie I'd made before school out of the freezer and picked up my keys. Before I stepped out the door, I looked both ways for Dave. He wasn't around. I went out and locked my door.

Emily's house was the third one she'd had in San Diego. Brad liked to buy new, and the best schools tended to be near the most recent construction.

I turned slowly into their cul-de-sac. There were usually a few kids out playing in the street, even after dark. Emily's oldest, Janie, was Rollerblading around some cones she had set up, and Will was batting at a hockey puck with a stick that was too long for him. He was wearing regular shoes, though, so they must be about ready to go in. I parked in the driveway in front of the smaller garage door. They had a three-car garage. The basketball hoop was there, too, but no one was using it now.

"Aunt Charlotte, watch this!" Janie called. She did a trick, skating on one leg while bending at the waist, the other leg extended horizontally behind her.

"Beautiful!" I said. "You've been practicing."

"No, I haven't," she said. "I just came out here."

"It looks like you have. That's the nicest spiral I've ever seen you do."

"Thank you," she said. "What did you bring for dessert?"

"Ice-cream pie."

"Yes!" said Will.

"Let's go in and help your mom," I said.

"Oh, she doesn't need any help," said Janie.

"Is the table set?" I said. "Are the plates and glasses out? Come on. Why do *I* always have to do everything?" I imitated their whining.

"OK, OK," said Janie, "but wait. Watch this." She did a twirl with both legs together and her arms up straight above her head. It was a little slow, but she was getting there.

"Fabulous!" I said. "Now take those things off your feet. This is starting to melt."

Will said, "Aunt Charlotte, did you bring whipped cream?"

"I thought you were getting it!" I said.

His face fell.

"Kidding," I said. "I was kidding." I held up the bowl of whipped cream.

Will took it from me and headed into the house.

"Where's Ted?" I said.

Janie was now sitting on the curb removing her Rollerblades. "Getting stitches in his chin. Dad took him."

"*What?* Why didn't anybody tell me? What happened?"

"He fell on his face."

"I'm going to find your mom."

"OK."

"Emily!" I called inside the front door. "Em, what happened to Ted?"

Emily was putting place mats on the table. "He fell off his skateboard and hit his chin. It wasn't too bad, but there was a lot of blood, so Brad thought he should get it sewn up. Wouldn't you know, Brad came home early for a change, and now he's spent the whole afternoon in the doctor's office."

"Why didn't you call me?"

"It wasn't that bad. And I thought you'd still be at school anyway."

"I was for a while, but then I was home sewing."

"How's that coming?"

"Great. I think it's going to be nice."

"Did you tell him you were doing it?"

"Who?" I said, though I knew who she meant.

"Tim, the e-mail guy. I bet he'd be so flattered. You know, that someone liked his book enough to make a costume from one of the illustrations. You should send him a picture."

"Oh, I wouldn't—"

"You *should.*"

"I'm too fat," I said. "I'd be embarrassed."

"You're not. You look fine."

"Not as fine as you do."

"You look great. No one ever notices that we are the slightest bit—"

"What am I doing, standing here holding this ice cream?" I went to the refrigerator. She had one of those big ones with two sides, one for the freezer and one for the refrigerator. You could get cold water or ice cubes from dispensers in the front. "What are you going to be?"

"I don't know," Emily said. "Janie wants you to go out with her, you know. I'm going with the boys, and Brad's going to open the door here."

"Who's Janie going with? Michelle and Taylor?"

"Yeah."

"I won't be using Mrs. Beetleman's outfit with them, though."

"Why not?"

"They'd be too embarrassed."

"I guess you're right."

"You want to wear it when you take the boys out?"

"Sure. So, what are you guys talking about lately?"

"Hm? Who?"

"Tim Weeks," she said. "The author."

"Oh, right," I said.

"Does he still e-mail?"

"Yes," I said.

"And?"

"What if he's married? Or living with someone? Or gay?"

"Well, he's not *gay.* I can tell you that much."

"How do you know?"

"Because he keeps writing to you."

"He's a writer; he's lonely. It's the constant struggle to connect. That whole thing." I looked at my watch. "How long have they been gone? Shouldn't they be home by now?"

"I'm going to call and see what's happening," Emily said. "I should have gone with them. I hate waiting. Waiting is way harder than holding him while they stick the needle in."

Emily dialed. But before anyone answered, the garage door rumbled open. Janie clomped in through the front door on her Rollerblades. Will was right behind her with a ball.

Emily and I went to the dining room door and simultaneously scowled at the children, hands on our hips. I thought she was busy on the phone or I wouldn't have done this. She thought I was going to check on Brad and Ted.

Will laughed. "You guys look like a cartoon."

"Put that ball away and wash your hands," Emily said. "It's time for dinner. And Janie—"

"I know, I know. I'm going." She rolled to the garage door,

slowing herself by touching the arm of the couch, an end table, a door knob, and clomped down one step into the garage.

Emily and I followed her to the garage door, where Brad was turning off the car and Ted was getting out. He had a big gauze pad over his chin.

"How many stitches did you get?" Will wanted to know.

"Honey?" Emily called. "How did it go?"

Brad said, "We had to wait a long time. But we got one of the good doctors. The one with the beard. Resnick. Stitches come out on Thursday." He went back out to the garage.

"Oh, sweetheart," said Emily as Ted walked to the door.

"It's OK, Mom," he said. There was dried blood all over his shirt, and the part of his chin that we could see was swollen and shiny. "Did you guys already eat? I'm hungry."

"No, of course not," I said. "We waited for you."

"Take that shirt off and throw it in the washer," Emily said.

Ted handed the shirt to me. In the garage, I met Brad, who was dropping a bloody towel into the washing machine.

"Is that going to come out?" Ted said, shirtless, at the garage door. "I love that shirt."

I said, "I don't know. We'll see. Blood is hard to get out. Let's squirt some of this goop on it." I dribbled a clear liquid stain remover onto the stain and rubbed.

"Good," Ted said, nodding.

From the kitchen, Emily called, "I'm putting the spaghetti in! It only takes eight minutes. Wash your hands, Ted."

We went inside. "I'm glad you're OK," I said to Ted. "Let's go find you another shirt."

I followed Ted upstairs to his messy room. When they moved here a year ago, the house seemed huge. Now, with all their stuff all over the place, it didn't seem so big, after all. Ted pulled a clean T-shirt out of his drawer. I took it from him and stretched the neck opening so he could put it on over his head without touching his face.

"Did it hurt a lot?" I said. "I've never gotten stitches."

"They gave me a shot so it wouldn't. *That* hurt. But the worst part was that they actually *sewed me up!* With a *needle.* It was disgusting. I could see him pull it through. I could *hear* it. *Ew.* It made me sick."

"You're very brave," I said.

Ted shook his head. "I cried the whole time. Dad had to hold me. He was squeezing my arms down so I wouldn't grab the needle out of the doctor's hand."

"See, brave doesn't mean that you don't *mind* having your chin sewn up, that it's OK with you. It means that you *do* mind, that you really hate it a lot, but you manage to get through it anyway."

"What are we having?" Ted said, heading out into the hall.

"Spaghetti," I said.

"Oh, yeah. I forgot. Did you make that ice-cream pie?"

"I did, sir. Just as you ordered."

"Good. I'm starving." Instead of bounding down the steps, he walked slowly, tenderly, holding on to the banister. Emily gave him three chewable grape Tylenol tablets, hoping that they would start to work before the Novocain wore off.

At home, I finished marking my class's spelling papers. Then I cut out some jack-o'-lanterns for the children to put on the fronts of their folders. I was sitting on the floor, my back against the couch, watching an old *St. Elsewhere,* thinking how difficult it was not to talk to Emily about my class. I had not mentioned to her that they never listened to me, how some of them hardly stayed in their seats for more than a few minutes at a time. She didn't know that several had been in trouble with the principal for fighting and saying bad words to the teachers on duty at lunch. While I didn't want Emily to solve this for me, it would have been nice to have her say, "Oh, my God! I can't believe it!" And I would have liked to ask her, "Is this what you thought my first-grade class would be like? Because it isn't what I expected. It's way, way harder." But I was trying not to do that. I wanted to make this work. Emily had spent enough of her time worrying about me and trying to help me out of problems.

I finished the pumpkins and got back to work on my Halloween costume. Once I got started, it was hard to stop. I kept telling myself, "One more thing, and then I'm going to bed." I knew I was getting carried away—the other teachers weren't doing much at all—but I was enjoying myself.

At 1:30 in the morning, I finished the costume. I felt a little flutter in my heart when I realized I had just sewn the last stitch. I wasn't even tired. Immediately, I took off my jeans and T-shirt and put the beetle outfit on right there in the living room. I mean, why not? One of the advantages of living alone is that you can take your clothes off anywhere. The costume fit, though the elastic around the thighs was a little snug. I checked the seat. Not too bad. I would be able to sit down in this. And anyway, I was only allowed to wear it for a little while in the morning. I went to look in the mirror. I looked just like the character in the book, only a little rounder. I had done a good job. All I needed was a tiara and a pair of tights. I looked back at the picture to see the shoes: black jogging shoes. That was kind of Tim to put the teacher in comfortable shoes. Not many writer/illustrators would have thought of that. And I even had some.

I took off the costume and hung it on a hanger. Then I hung it over my bedroom door so that I could admire it whenever I wanted to.

11

Publishers often ask established writers for endorsements of novelists who are just starting out. "The finest novel I've read in several decades!" a blurb by a best-selling novelist might declare on the book jacket of an unknown writer. The veteran shines some of the light of his or her success on the newcomer. As a beginning novelist you're supposed to come up with a list of writers you have connections to. If you don't have any connections, you make a list of writers you believe might like your work. These tend to be your heroes, of course, the writers you've always loved, the writers whose blessings you yearn for. The blurb-gathering process is not pleasant, as there is tremendous potential for rejection. It can feel something like asking older relatives for money or like asking the most popular boy in school for a date, embarrassing at best and sometimes downright humiliating.

My publisher's requests for blurbs on my books had been turned down by some of the world's finest living writers. I can't say who they are, because, as I've mentioned, their answer was no.

Most of them simply didn't respond to requests for support. Those who did had a variety of reasons not to give it. "Of course I know Charlotte Dearborn's work. She is a fine writer. Unfortunately, I just got a puppy and will be unable to read the new novel. I wish her the best of luck with it, however," a prize-winning female novelist wrote. A famous male author wrote, "A long time ago, I vowed never to endorse anybody. I can't remember why now. No matter. I simply don't do it. But have fun!"

My favorite writer in the world, now an old lady, was someone I'd started to read when I was in my teens. Without mentioning her name, I'll just say that she wrote a series of books about a Welsh family. If you start at the beginning and read all nineteen books, you move from the eighteenth century right into the twenty-first. The characters become your best friends and, between books, you live in suspense, waiting to hear from them again. I can't tell you her name, but maybe you love her as much as I did. I think I became a writer in the hope that she would read my books. But I never put her on my blurb list. For my first book, the publicist suggested that she get in touch with my Welsh idol. "No way!" I said. "Are you kidding? She never does that! Have you ever seen her name on someone else's book jacket? Please don't!" The publicist said, "Since you feel so strongly about it, we'll respect your wishes. But you know, you're only hurting yourself."

For my second book, a new publicist, Julie, insisted on contacting the Welsh author. "I want to go for it," she told me.

"No," I said. "*Please.* She doesn't do this. And what if she does read it? She might hate it, and then I'll feel bad."

Julie said, "She'll love it! I know she will. Charlotte, if you don't take a risk now and then, you're never going to get anywhere. And sometimes the really famous people are the most helpful. You'd be surprised. Anyway, I'm not asking you. I'm telling you: This is what I'm doing."

This author was hard to reach. She lives on an island off the coast of Wales with no fax or e-mail.

After I knew she'd sent off the manuscript, I kept calling Julie, to ask if she'd heard from the Welsh writer. She said, "She only has a P.O. box, so we couldn't FedEx. She's probably still reading it." Then, "No, Charlotte. You have to be patient." A few weeks later, Julie said, "I wish she'd hurry! We only have about a week left to stick on a quote!"

Somehow Julie tracked down the author's phone number. "No!" I said, horrified. "You didn't *call* her! I can't believe you're—That's *such* an invasion! What did she say?"

"I told her you were a big fan, had been since you were a kid, and that it would really mean a lot to you to have her support."

"What did she say?" I bit my lower lip hard.

"Are you sure you want to know?"

"No. But tell me anyway."

"She said, 'You tell your author that if her book were any good, she wouldn't need to beg for compliments!' "

"Did you tell her that it wasn't my idea? Did you say I was completely against it and I—"

"I didn't get a chance," Julie said. "She hung up on me."

"Oh," I said.

"It's OK, Charlotte. My feelings weren't hurt. I'm used to it. Are you disappointed?"

"No," I said. "I'm used to it, too."

I didn't even cry when I told Emily. But she cried, hearing about it. Then I cried because she was crying. I think it's that way with a lot of twins.

* * *

When I checked my e-mail, there was a message from Dylan Jones's father.

> Would you be interested in some additional hours with Dylan after school at my home? His teacher is not enthusiastic about his progress, and I think it would help. How about M, W, F 3 P.M.–5 P.M. or whatever would suit you? We'd pay you, of course. Let me know if you're interested.
>
> Matthew Jones

When I mentioned this proposal in the teacher's lounge, there was a lot of disapproval. "I wouldn't do it," said Bernice. She put up her hands in front of her.

"Why not?"

"They're using you for daycare!" she said.

"Maybe they're concerned about him being behind the rest of the class," I said. "Maybe they just want him to catch up."

"Are they going to be there when you're working with him?" said Bernice. "The kid is not easy, you know. And it's not just my opinion. He's been in detention a couple of times already for bad behavior on the playground."

"All I'd be doing is sitting with him while he does his homework. How bad could that be?" I said.

"Wait and see," said Bernice.

"I just wouldn't want to get so personally involved with these people," said Liz.

"I wouldn't be *personally* involved. I'd be tutoring."

"See what happens, then," Bernice said. "But these seem like uninvolved parents who are looking for someone to do what they should be doing themselves."

"At least they recognize that the boy needs more help than they can offer."

"I suppose it's something." Bernice finished her Diet Coke and left the room.

How could I say no? I could use some extra money for the car payments. And I would probably make more progress with Dylan if I spent more time with him. Besides, now that I had worked with him a few times, it would be mean to make him start over with someone new.

I made an appointment to meet Dylan's parents at their house on Saturday morning. It was a big, new house, a couple of miles from my place. The yard was dirt, still unlandscaped. A big dog with dirty paws jumped on me at the door. Unfortunately, along with a turquoise bowling shirt embroidered with the word *Highrollers,* I had on my white pants.

"Get away from her, mutt," said a tall man, who met me at the door. He had gray hair and a neatly trimmed beard that looked businesslike, rather than bohemian. "He's new, not trained yet. Hi, I'm Dylan's father," he said. "We're not completely settled here. We just moved in. Maybe Dylan told you."

"Yes. And how's that going? I know it's a big adjustment."

"For Dylan?" he said. "Sure. Friends and school. Big change. Have a seat," the father said. "He's been through it before, though. So it shouldn't be a surprise. Oh, I'm Matt, by the way." He shook my hand.

"Nice to meet you."

"My wife's here somewhere." He looked out the door to a long hallway. "Colleen!" he called. "You coming? The tutor's here!" We were both silent for a second. There was no answer. Dylan's father went on. "So what I was thinking was that maybe you and Dylan could sit down with the homework in the afternoons and go over the assignments. He's way behind most of the class. He had a bad year last year, and he wasn't in the best school to begin with. Let me show you what we've got set up for him." He led me to a family room, where there was a desk with a lamp on it and a small electronic dictionary. There was a pencil jar full of pens and pencils, and a calculator. He picked up the calculator. "Do they use these? We weren't sure."

"No," I said, shaking my head. "Not allowed until middle school."

"Oh," he said and put the calculator into his pocket. "That's the end of that, then. So this is the setup. Does this look about right to you?"

"It looks fine."

"Good. Now, I don't really know the going rate for tutoring. So let me be blunt. How much money would you want?"

"I, um, I hadn't quite—"

"Name your price. You've definitely got the upper hand here. We've got no idea where else to look for a tutor."

"Oh," I said. "If you need some additional choices, you could call the school district office. They keep a list of teachers who do tutoring." I guess I was hoping that he would tell me Dylan wanted me and only me to help him with his homework.

But he didn't say that. He said, "Frankly we're both swamped right now. We just don't have the time."

"Well, I wouldn't want to take advantage of your situation."

"Sorry to rush this, but I've got to get back to the office. Forty an hour sound all right? We could shake on that and be done with it right now."

"Forty dollars? An hour, you mean? Well—" I hesitated. It sounded like a lot to me, too much.

"OK, fifty, then," he said. "You twisted my arm."

"I didn't mean—"

"Sorry to be in such a hurry," he said. "But I've got this meeting that I really can't—"

"Sure," I said. "No, I understand."

"So you'll be meeting Dylan here after school to go over the assignments with him. Make sure that he understands what he's supposed to do and that he does the work. Sometimes he's very spacey, and I'm not sure he's taking school as seriously as he should. He needs someone to keep him on track."

"But he's a good boy. He's very . . . honest." I felt it was important to always say something positive about the student, no matter what the problems were.

Mr. Jones laughed. "I guess that's true," he said. "Do you need some time to think about this, or can we shake on it right here and now?"

"I think I'm ready to shake on it," I said. I stuck out my hand.

He flashed a business smile. "Excellent. Dylan will be expecting you Monday then, if you can make it that soon."

"Monday is fine."

"Keep track of your hours and just leave us a note at the end of each week. Thank you for coming. Have a nice day, Miss Dearborn."

"Charlotte. Same to you."

I went out, and he shut the door behind me.

This would be good. I certainly could use the money. I didn't see the mother, I was thinking as I got in the car. Wouldn't the mother want to have something to say about this?

When I got back to my apartment, the answering machine was recording a message. "So I wouldn't take it," Emily was saying. "Tell them no. Three days a week is a huge commitment. Sounds like he's a problem kid. And what are they paying anyway? Probably not nearly enough. It never is. Say *no* as soon as possible so they won't—"

I lifted the receiver. "Too late. I already said yes. The dad offered me fifty bucks an hour."

"On the other hand," my sister said. "Things can work out in surprising and wonderful ways! When do you start? You'll need a couple of weeks to gear up and get ready."

"Monday."

"Oh, perfect."

My first session at Dylan's house didn't go very well. Dylan opened the door with a soda can in one hand, a Pop-Tart in the other.

"Hi, Dylan," I said. "Ready to start on your homework?"

"No. I just got here. And I'm eating."

"Time to get to work. Finish up, and I'll meet you at your desk."

I went to the desk and looked around for Dylan's books, which I couldn't find. I waited several minutes, then went back to the kitchen. "Dylan, let's get started."

He was sitting at a table watching television. He sighed and stood up. Slowly, he picked up his backpack from the floor beside him and walked to his desk in the other room. I turned off the TV.

Dylan sat down in a leather chair across the room from his desk. "Let's sit at the desk," I said. "I want to be able to see what you're reading."

"I like it here," he said, opening a book and not looking up.

I got a chair from the desk and dragged it over. "Social studies? Good. Fourth-grade social studies is the best! California history is really fun. There's the gold rush and—"

"I have to make a mission," he said, as if challenging me.

"I made a mission in fourth grade," I said. I tried not to dwell on my memory of a lopsided cardboard mess that had earned me a low grade. "We'll work on it together!"

He didn't say anything. "I mean, maybe I can help you gather supplies and plan how you're going to do it. Unless you were going to do that with your dad. Or mom."

Dylan turned the page in his book. "They don't do that kind of stuff."

"Before you get started on that, why don't we go over what the assignments are for today."

Slowly, he pulled his binder out of his backpack. He handed it to me. There was an assignment sheet in the front. "OK, we've got some spelling, social studies, math, and reading. Well, Mrs. Fitz is not going to let you have too much time on your hands, is she? What's the hardest thing you have to do here?"

Reluctantly, he looked it over. He shrugged. "I don't want to do any of it."

"Which one is the hardest?" I asked more firmly.

He shrugged again. "The math?"

"And what's the easiest?"

"The spelling?"

"OK," I said. "And reading and social studies are somewhere in between. We'll do it like this, then. First math, then reading, then social studies, and spelling is last."

"Why do I have to start with the thing I hate the most?"

"So you'll have it behind you first. Where's your math book?"

"It's not a book, it's a packet. They love packets at this school."

"Please take out your math packet and go to the desk." I sounded like Mrs. Fitz. "Come on," I said, touching his shoulder, trying to sound less like a battle-ax and more like a teenage big sister on a TV sitcom. "Let's try out that beautiful new desk of yours."

He grunted and walked over to the desk. I dragged the extra chair across the carpet again.

This was only the first day. It takes time to build a relationship with a kid. I pictured the way it would be after I'd earned Dylan's trust. He'd tell me things no one knew about him, his whole face would light up as soon as he saw me, I'd bring him treats that I'd made at home for him. I might feel a little guilty about leaving him when his schoolwork got so good that he didn't need me anymore. But we'd keep in touch. Sometimes doing good work means putting yourself out of a job, and there would be other kids who would need my help as badly as Dylan did now. He'd move on, and I'd—

"Are you just going to sit there and stare at me?" Dylan said. "Because I don't know how to do this."

"OK," I said. "What have we got here? Ah, double-digit multiplication. These problems are just like two small multiplication problems. First you do five times three. Put the five here, carry the one, then do five times four, add the one you just carried. Then multiply these two by this one. Two times three, then two times four, but these are tens. So leave a space here. Now add these, and there's your answer. Now you do this one. What's four times four?"

"Uh . . . That's . . . I don't know." He didn't look at me but kept his head down, staring closely at the paper.

"All right, then. Let's do it as an addition problem. Four plus four plus four plus four." I wrote this on a piece of scratch paper, then pushed it over to him.

He worked on it for what seemed like a long time, then he said, "Fifteen? Is it fifteen? Fourteen? Fourteen! I'm sure."

Math took over an hour. Then we did reading, which was another forty-five minutes. I let him take a break—he watched a cartoon and didn't speak to me. Social studies, a reading about some of the California Indian tribes who were here before European explorers arrived, and two pages of questions, took another hour and a half. I had gone way over the time I was supposed to be here, but Dylan's parents weren't home yet. It was six-thirty when I heard a car in the driveway and the garage door going up.

Mrs. Jones entered through the laundry room. "Shit!" was the first thing I heard her say. “Dylan! Why is the dog’s water next to the back door?” She obviously didn’t know that I was here.

Dylan didn’t answer.

“Uh, hello? Mrs. Jones?”

She came into the kitchen with a puzzled look on her face.

“I’m Charlotte Dearborn, Dylan’s tutor?” I said, reaching out to shake her hand.

She was wearing a straight red dress with pearls. One of her spiky black shoes was in her hand, dripping. She switched the shoe to the other hand. “I’m Colleen. Dog water,” she said, meaning the shoe. “So, are you finished?”

“A little while ago. I didn’t want to leave Dylan alone. He wasn’t sure what time you—”

“Oh, he’s fine! I’ve got my cell phone, if there’s anything. So homework’s all done then?”

I nodded.

“Excellent. Because I’m beat. I certainly do not feel like listening to a million questions about Indians and multiplication at the end of the day.” She looked at me, as if to say, “So why aren’t you leaving?” Instead, she said, “Do we owe you—did my husband—”

“He said he’d pay me Fridays. So I guess I’ll go, then,” I said, picking up my purse from the floor. “Dylan, you worked really hard. Good job. See you Wednesday. I’ll let myself out.”

I was exhausted myself and not at all excited about the spelling, reading, and math papers from my own class that I still had to mark and the lessons that I had to prepare for the next day.

12

When I was ready to sell my fifth novel, *My Self-Portrait of Someone Else,* Howard said, "We've got to get C&S to do more for this book than they did for the others."

"How are we going to do that?"

"Kip Prentiss loves you," Howard said. "I think that's got to be your starting point." Kip Prentiss was a vice-president in charge of sales and marketing. "If he weren't married, you might think he was—hey, I know! Why don't you go and talk to him when they have that sales conference out there. It might make you feel better to find out exactly how they plan to sell more of this book. Seeing him face to face might cause him to make some promises that I couldn't get out of him."

"That's unlikely, Howard, but I'll give it a try."

I met Prentiss at six in the morning in the restaurant of his hotel. He had to catch a plane back to New York. His cell phone was next to his coffee cup resting on the pale pink tablecloth. "Charlotte, one of my favorite authors!"

"Good morning," I said.

"How are you?" He gave me a business hug, a kind of distant embrace, if such a thing is possible. He offered me breakfast, which I declined. I ordered a cup of coffee just to have something on the table in front of me.

"So, now," he said. "I want you to know that at C&S there are a lot of people who just adore you. Love you. Absolutely unconditionally. Frieda in publicity is a devoted fan. Our chain-store rep—you know Donna Palladino, right?—is nuts about you. Especially about the new book. You should have heard her at the meeting yesterday! Then there's Adam Finch, our sales rep for the Northeast except New York, head over heels. Big fan. And Elaine—well, Elaine's leaving, but what I'm saying is that you've got a tremendous base of support here. A whole fan club! We are all thrilled to have this new book."

"Thank you," I said. "I really appreciate that. But my sales have been—"

He held up one finger to silence me. "And going over your sales figures, I think we ought to be able to do better. A lot better."

"That would be good."

"I can imagine that you've been very disappointed in us."

"I'm very fond of everyone I've worked with at C&S, of course. They're all great people. I hope everyone knows that I appreciate their commitment and all they've done. It's just been a little hard to survive. I have to get all these other jobs, and that makes it really difficult to—"

"You're going to see an improvement. And I don't mean a little rise." He made his hand do a small hop in the air. "I'm talking about an *exponential* increase." His hand imitated an airplane taking off, a steep ascent into the wild blue yonder. "Because the readers are *there.* We just have to go out and *get* them!" With both hands, he grabbed imaginary readers by their throats, pulling them forcefully toward him.

"That sounds good," I said, nodding.

"Great," he said. With one hand he reached for his check; with the other, he reached for his cell phone.

"Uh, Kip?" I said. "I'd like to know more about how you plan to get those readers."

He put the phone down and looked at me blankly.

"Promotion? Marketing?" I said. "What do you plan to do, exactly? Before I commit another book to C&S, I'd like to know exactly how you're going to improve my sales. Specifics of your plan. Because with each successive book it gets harder to—"

"Oh, it's way too early for details. The book isn't even scheduled yet. But listen to me." He looked me in the eye. "You have my personal word on this. I promise you here and now that I will do everything in my power to sell *Self-Portrait* in huge numbers. I believe in it, Charlotte."

"Thank you," I said.

He reached for his phone again. "I hope you don't mind, but I—"

"I want a marketing plan."

"A—"

"I think the key to making this work is to have a strategy ahead of time and follow it through, step by step."

A little smile curled his lips upward, as if I were a toddler who had inadvertently used a bad word. "We don't work that way, Charlotte," he said. "Hasn't Howard explained *anything* to you?"

I said, "This is my fifth book. I know exactly how you work."

He looked into my eyes. "You have my solemn oath, my *pledge* to you. I will see to it *myself* that this book not only succeeds but *flourishes.* It means as much to me as it does to you."

"Thank you. I appreciate that. I do."

This time when he reached for his phone, I stood up.

"I'm so glad we got a chance to really talk," he said.

We shook hands.

The phrase that stuck with me was *exponential increase.* It's hard to remember now whether I believed him at the time. I do remember that I started praying every morning and every night. "Please, God," I repeated many times a day, "can you cast your radiant light on my new book?"

The book might have sold a couple hundred more copies than its predecessors, but it was not because of any change in my publisher's approach, because there wasn't any.

On Halloween, I drove to school in my costume. It was a warm bright day, so I had my sunglasses on in addition to the antennae, which were brushing against the ceiling of my car, and my tiara. I parked in my spot, number 27, and got out a stack of folders, papers I had graded the night before.

"Happy Halloween," I said to Cindy as I passed the receptionist's desk.

"Holy smokes!" she said, staring at me.

I went to my room and unlocked it, put the folders on my desk, and wrote "Happy Halloween" on the board in orange chalk. I had a journal activity ready for after the parade.

The door opened, and Marilyn walked in.

"Cindy buzzed me from the desk and said that you went completely overboard. I had to see. Oh, my gosh!" Marilyn yelled. "Look at you!" I stood up, and Marilyn compared me to the dust jacket of the book that was propped in my chalk tray. "How many hours did you put into that? Does the phrase 'Get a life' mean anything to you?" She laughed.

Marilyn was wearing a giant orange sweatshirt stuffed with something. There were black felt jack-o'-lantern features glued to the front of the sweatshirt. She had on green leggings and a green beanie.

I said, "Is that, could that possibly be an actual Girl Scout beanie?"

"Yeah." Marilyn touched her hat. "Everything comes in handy sooner or later." She stepped back and looked me over again. "Well, well, well."

"I'm going to get coffee," I said.

In the staff room, there was a line in front of the coffee machine. "Where'd you get your costume?" Cindy the receptionist asked me. She was a movie star or something with a lot of makeup and big sunglasses. Otherwise, she was dressed the way she always dressed.

"I made it," I said. "It's a character from a book I read to my class."

"Nice," she said as her turn for the coffee came. "Kind of a lot of work for forty-five minutes, isn't it?" She left the machine and found a seat.

"I had fun making it." I poured my coffee. "I'll use it again."

"Here we go," said Bernice Fitz in a sneering voice. "The *creative* one. The *author* has arrived in her perfect little outfit to make us all look bad."

I looked up. Bernice was wearing a black jumper with a black turtleneck under it. She had on black cat earrings; she probably had a pointed witch hat back in her room.

"You look great, Bernice!" I said. "I love your earrings."

Rick came in, heading for the coffee machine. He was a vampire, a black cape around his shoulders, and blood dripping from one corner of his mouth. By sixth grade, kids enjoyed fake blood. Down in first grade this might produce tears, nightmares, and other unpredictable problems.

Rick said, "Hi, Charlotte. Nice costume."

Marilyn said, "Do you know she *made* it? It's based on a character in a book she read to her class. How long did it take you, Charlotte? How many hours?"

"I don't know," I said. "I didn't keep track."

"Your kids will go nuts over that," Rick said.

"I hope not. We have enough trouble with focus and behavior, as it is."

The principal, Mr. Dean, walked in then with a clipboard and a travel coffee cup. He was dressed as a scarecrow. He scratched at his wrist where straw was hanging out of his cuffs. "Good morning, all. Happy Halloween. Our parade route will be the same as last year. For those of you who weren't here, we walk in a clockwise circle around the perimeter of the playground. Blacktop only, as there is bound to be dog crap out on the field. Please try to assemble your classes very quickly outside. As soon as the bell rings, attendance, Pledge, and go. We'd like to have everyone back inside by nine. Some of the parents have already called to complain about wasting school time on a Halloween parade. Our position, in case you're asked, is that this is a school tradition. No one is *required* to dress up. No one *has* to participate in the parade. If we do it fast, get on with our normal day almost immediately, we'll have fewer complaints. Have the kids change as quickly as possible after the parade. I expect you to have your classes in school clothes, celebrations over, by nine-fifteen, nine-thirty at the outside. Please have your own clothes changed by the end of recess. I'll need your full cooperation on this."

Suddenly, my face burned and my heart pounded. I hadn't brought any other clothes! I could just see the bag of clothes I'd left by my front door, all set to come with me today. I had walked right by it this morning without a thought. Was there time for me to go home and change during the fifteen minutes of recess?

No. Did I have anything in my car or classroom that I could put on? No. Out of sheer anxiety, I coughed and cleared my throat.

"Are you all right, Charlotte?" Mr. Dean asked.

"Fine," I said and smiled weakly.

I had sent the notes home to the parents about the Halloween parade. I had told the children that they should be able to change easily and quickly into their regular school clothes. *Shoot.* Why did I have to be such an incompetent idiot?

Mr. Dean was finishing up. For a split second, I had hope that I could race home immediately and get my clothes. I looked at my watch: seven minutes until the first bell. I'd never make it. If Emily had been home or in her store today, I could have asked her to pick up my clothes and drop them off here. Unfortunately, she would be at her kids' school all day, running Halloween activities for their classes. This was going to be embarrassing. Marilyn and I walked to the so-called portables together. Marilyn was yakking away about spelling tests, one of her pet peeves. "So they were saying it enhances word recognition. Ha! There are plenty of other ways to get there."

"Mm-hm," I said.

"Are you OK?" she said.

"Yeah, sorry," I said. "Just a little distracted. Which way were we supposed to walk again? For the parade?"

"Clockwise. Don't worry. They'll have cones all over the place. And sorry to disappoint you, but they don't give out prizes for best costumes or anything."

"Right," I said. "I knew that."

"I was kidding. See you out there."

The kids in my class were lined up by the door in their costumes, waiting for me. Looking around with exaggerated confusion, I said, "I usually find my class here every morning, but they aren't here today! I see a princess; a firefighter; a butcher—no, a surgeon, *excuse* me—a Dracula; one, two, three witches; Superman. Well, all of you will just have to come in and sit down in my boys' and girls' seats, since they aren't here. Oh! Ryan H., stop that, please. Give Amanda her wig back this minute. I said now! Amanda, wait! Don't—if you scratch him or kick him, I'm going to have to send you both to Mr. Dean! You'll miss the parade!"

Inside, I said, "Good morning, boys and girls. You all have wonderful costumes!"

"Hey! Mrs. D! You're the beetle lady from the book!" Seth shouted full volume.

"You're right, Seth. I'm Ms. Beetleman. You got it. Inside voice, please."

"I like your crown," said Patience, who was dressed as some kind of princess or queen.

"And I like yours very much," I told her.

"Thank you," she said. She was wearing lipstick and green eye shadow with sparkles. "I'm Princess Diana."

"You're very beautiful. Now. Let's all stand to say the Pledge."

"She's dead," Patience went on.

"I know," I said. "Very sad."

"My mom has this book, and she—"

"Patience, I mean, Princess Diana, you're our Pledge leader this week."

The class stood up. Patience said, "Place your right hand over your heart. Ready, begin."

As soon as we were finished with the Pledge, I got my attendance book. "Now, we're due out on the playground for our parade, so we need to be very quiet and *cooperative* while I see who's here. No one is absent! And how many hot lunchers today? Eight? No, seven. Is your hand up or down, Rosie? OK, seven." I looked at my Helping Hands chart. "Seth, please take the attendance sheet to the office and come right back, but *don't run!*"

When Seth came back, the children lined up at the door of my portable. "Now, I want you to remember that the whole school will be participating in this parade. That's a lot of children. Find a partner, hold hands, and stay with that person for the *entire* parade. And I expect your very *best* behavior." There was some scuffling around while they paired off. Inevitably, there was one child left over. It was Ryan H. "Mrs. Dearborn, I don't have anybody."

"Ryan H., you go with Seth and Ryan J." There was a short moan from Seth and Ryan J. I glared at them. "Thank you, boys. Patience, who is your partner?"

"William."

"OK. Hold hands, please."

I opened the door and led them down the portable ramp. Everywhere kids in costumes all moving in the same direction, converging on the blacktop playground. I had to keep looking behind me to make sure that mine were all still there and not getting distracted and wandering off with the wrong class. Rosie and Michelle, last in our line, were looking panicky. They stopped every few feet and looked around, in awe of the spectacle. I stopped and held up my hand in a stop sign. Several kids ran into each other, and a couple fell down. "Rosie and Michelle, I want you to come up here, please." The girls came forward.

"No fair," said Patience and William in unison. "We were first!"

"Soon you will be in a circle," I said, "and no one will be first."

We joined the rest of the school in a circular parade around the playground. There were a lot of parents there; many were wearing costumes. A couple of fathers were dressed as doctors in green scrubs. Of course, they probably *were* doctors. Many of the mothers were dressed as witches but with their hair nicely blow-dried and a lot of lipstick. We marched around the playground twice and then started back to the classroom. Everything took a long time. Every once in a while, there would be a little slowdown in front of us, which would create minor chaos behind me. The children in front of me would stop, I would stop, and then Rosie and Michelle, who were right behind me, would step on the backs of my shoes and crash into me.

After the parade, there was a Halloween party back in our room with the room parents, Amanda's mother and William's mother, in charge of five or six other mothers. A cauldron of punch emitting dry-ice vapor was on my desk. Each child's desk had a plastic pumpkin full of candy and a cupcake with a plastic black-cat toothpick on top. Seth's mother was holding a pumpkin piñata. "Where do you guys want me to hang this?" she called to the other mothers.

"Out by the lunch tables!" Amanda's mother yelled.

I had a math packet ready, a story, and a writing activity that I wanted to get done before lunch. "Uh . . . Ann?" I said to Amanda's mother. "How long do you think this will take?"

She shrugged "An hour, hour and a half, or so."

I said, "Well, see, we're really supposed to finish up in the next fifteen minutes. Mr. Dean was pretty firm about this."

"Fifteen *minutes?* No way. Uh-uh. No can do." She shook her head hard. "We've got games and crafts and a song and dance we're going to teach them! We had two planning meetings about this. I took the whole morning off work! We can't disappoint the kids!"

I said, "The kids know that it's to be a low-key event. We went over this a couple of times. Remember when I gave you that schedule?"

Amanda's mother looked around the room at all the Halloween stuff. Was she about to cry, or was that anger I saw flashing across her face?

I said, "OK, so maybe we can take a little longer than fifteen minutes." I looked at my watch. "Do you think we could skip the piñata, though? If there's candy in that, it looks like we have a lot of sugar here already. And I do want to get them to focus at some point today."

"The piñata? Seth's mother made it!"

"I understand," I said. "Fine. We'll do the piñata, too, then."

"You go change. We'll take care of everything."

"I didn't bring my regular clothes," I whispered to her behind my hand.

"You better hide from Principal Dean for the rest of the day."

The party was like one of those nightmares where you're trying to get somewhere and everything you do seems to take you farther away. I sat at my desk watching the kids rotate from station to station. Every new phase of the party seemed to have a different kind of treat to go with it. Finally, at 10:25, just before the recess bell, I clapped my hands three times. A few of the kids put their hands on the tops of their heads, the way I had taught them to. "Boys and girls, it's time to clean up."

"But what about the song and the—" one mother tried to interrupt.

Loudly, I said, "And what do we *say* to our room parents, boys and girls?"

"Thank you, room parents!" all the children chanted together.

"Don't you think we have time for just one more—"

"No!" I snapped. "It's time to clean up." I was just turning around to get my wastebasket to collect trash. I forgot about the cauldron on the edge of my desk. I knocked it with my hip, and it toppled to the floor. Green punch and small chunks of dry ice spread across the linoleum. There was a collective gasp from the mothers at the same time that the whole class ran over to see the dry ice.

"Don't touch it!" yelled Seth. "It can burn a hole right through your hand!"

The bell rang for recess. Chaos was in full operation when the door opened, and Mr. Dean walked in. The way things happen, good and bad, all comes down to timing.

"Boys and girls," I said, trying to keep the frantic edge out of my voice. "Please line up quickly and quietly for recess."

"I'll find the custodian," Mr. Dean said, backing out the door.

After the kids left, Seth's mother shook her head, "Oh, boy. You've got a job ahead of you."

"It's going to take a mop and bucket, I think," I said.

"I meant Dean. Once you're on his bad side, it's really hard to win him back."

I poured two cups of leftover green punch down the sink.

After school, I went home to change and then straight over to my sister's house. I brought the Mrs. Beetleman costume with me for Emily to wear when she went out with the boys. As soon as she put it on, I said, "Oh, that looks fantastic!" Then I added, "If I do say so myself. Hold on now. I have to take a picture of you. Stand over here. Good. Like that, yeah. OK, now smile." I pushed the button.

"Did anyone take a picture of you at school with the kids?"

"No," I said, pressing the button again.

"Oh, that's a shame. You should have gotten one of the room parents to do it. You could collect pictures of Halloween every year."

"Smile just one more time. This is much better. You're thin. Good. Great. Just like that. OK, done. Thanks."

"I want one of those. Don't forget. OK, let's get the kids fed. It will be dark before you know it. I wonder how long Brad is going to be."

"What time did you tell him?"

"Five-twenty," Emily said.

I looked at my watch. "Then he'll be here in twenty-five minutes. What are we making for the kids?"

"Just macaroni and cheese and fruit. I didn't give them after-school snacks, but they had plenty of junk at school."

"If their classes were like mine, they did. Our party was in the morning. It was supposed to be short and low-key. It blew the whole day! The principal walked in at the end when the room was a mess, and the kids were all hyped up on sugar, which we were supposed to keep to a minimum. But I couldn't help it! The room parents took over! They're so bossy and controlling! You must know."

"Of course I do," Emily said. "I'm one of them. Was the principal mad?"

"Yes. And supposedly once you're on his bad list, it's hard to move back to his good list."

"Charlotte, I know you're not on his bad list. If he's a principal, he's worked in elementary schools all his adult life. Therefore, he knows that Halloween is a wasted day."

"Well," I said. I didn't fill her in about the deadline for parties ending, the spilled punch, or my forgotten clothes. I cleared a bunch of papers off the kitchen table. "The kids didn't settle down for five minutes all day." I got out the place mats.

"It's always like that, Charlotte. You just have to figure on losing several days a year to celebrations. The day before Christmas vacation will be like that, too."

I also didn't tell her that my class was noisy and out of control every day, even when there wasn't a party. Instead, I put the forks on the table.

After dinner, I walked with Janie two streets away to her friend Taylor's house. Janie was a witch with a long purple wig and a green face. She was carrying a pillowcase for her candy. "You look great," I said. "Where did you get the green makeup?"

"The party shop. It itches."

"Can you stand it for a couple of hours?"

"I think so."

"I hope we don't have to stay out until you fill up that whole pillowcase!"

"Last year I got it up to here. Remember?" She pointed to the two-thirds mark, an exaggeration.

"I remember. And you still had some at Easter."

"I'm a saver," she said with satisfaction.

"It's a good thing to be," I told her.

Taylor was a black cat. We picked up their friend Michelle, who was also a witch with a green face, but her hair was blue, instead of purple. Janie and her friends were not the type who liked to stand out. I took pictures of them in Michelle's living room. They all made horrible faces.

We set off down the street. The girls had a certain route they wanted to cover. I had on a black sweatshirt with a glow-in-the-dark jack-o'-lantern on the front, black leggings, and black high-top sneakers. It was really too warm for a sweatshirt. I would have been more comfortable in a T-shirt. As we walked, I was alternately pulling my sweatshirt down—it didn't quite cover my rear the way it had last year—and wiping perspiration off my face. I was hoping that it was dark enough that no one would notice me. I tried not to talk too much to the girls but just to follow unobtrusively behind them. There were hordes of kids out with adults following. I had to walk fast to keep up and watch the girls carefully so that I didn't end up following the wrong group. We did a lot of walking. I was thinking, This is good exercise. I hadn't eaten any of the macaroni and cheese, or any of the treats at school, so I was doing very well for Halloween.

We were supposed to drop off Taylor and Michelle at their houses no later than nine. But by eight-thirty, all three of them were starting to drag. They complained that their pillowcases, about a third full, were too heavy to carry anymore. Taylor's feet hurt. "I'm dying to wash this crud off my face," Janie said. We walked the girls home early.

I stayed at Emily's for a few more minutes. The boys were sorting their candy into piles. "How many Butterfingers did you get?" Ted asked Will.

"Hold on." Will counted. "Twelve."

"I got fourteen, and I don't even like them."

Emily said, "Give them to Aunt Charlotte. She loves them."

"No, don't!" I said. I held up my hands. "*Please.* Don't give me any Butterfingers."

"OK," said Emily. "Put everything you don't want into this bowl. I'll take it to work. The customers can eat it."

"Thank you. I've done very well all day, and I don't want to wreck it now." I stood up, yanked my sweatshirt down. "I better get going. Happy Halloween, everybody!" Emily gave me my Mrs. Beetleman costume in a shopping bag from Vons. I kissed everyone and went to my car. It was only ten to nine, but most of the kids were in now. I only saw a couple of groups of high-school boys as I left Emily's development.

On the way home, I stopped at Rite Aid to drop off my film.

My apartment complex was quiet. I didn't see anyone, let alone children in costumes ringing doorbells. I let myself in and changed into my nightgown. It felt so good to get into something loose. For a minute, I had to scratch at my side where the waistband of my leggings had dug into me. I sat down on the couch and turned on the TV. Then without the slightest hesitation, I went to the closet, where I had stashed five bags of Halloween candy. I had meant to give these to Emily tonight, but I forgot. I tore open a bag of treat-sized Butterfingers, took one out, bit a rip in the paper, and popped the candy into my mouth whole. I had another and then a few more.

There was a knock on the door. So I was going to have trick-or-treaters, after all. When you move somewhere new, you really don't know how Halloween is going to go. I dumped the remains of the bag of Butterfingers into a bowl that was on my coffee table. (They really don't give you very many in a bag, I thought.) Quickly, I reached for the Vons bag and grabbed my tiara and wings, which I could put on easily over my nightgown. I'm the Tooth Fairy, I'll say, if the kids ask, I planned. I held the bowl of candy in front of my stomach and opened the door.

Dave was standing there. He said, "Hi. The dome light was on in your car."

"Pardon?" I took a step backward to look out the window at my car, and just that much open space was enough for Dave to feel invited inside.

He stepped around the door. "You know the little ceiling light? You left the door open just a little, and—Oh, thanks." Noticing the bowl I was holding, he took a candy bar.

"Oh, shoot," I said. "OK, I'll get my keys. All I need is a dead battery in the—"

"No need," he said. "I did it."

"Oh."

"Yeah, I just bumped my hip into it, and—"

"So, you just came to tell me that? There's no problem, you just wanted me to know."

"Yeah." He took another Butterfinger.

"Oh. OK. Well. Thanks."

"You're welcome."

Now he was staring at me, tipping his head to the side, squinting.

"I'm the Tooth Fairy," I said, annoyed.

"You are?" The concept seemed to confuse him.

"It's October thirty-first?" I said. *"Halloween."*

"Halloween. Oh, right. Sure, sure, sure. I guess I forgot about that."

"How could you possibly? Even the bank tellers and the checkers in Rite Aid are dressed up!"

"Didn't go out much today. Well. Hm." He kept looking at me. "You look great, though. Really."

"Oh, this isn't my real costume. See, for school, I had this—oh, never mind. Anyway, thank you for telling me. About the light."

"You bet," he said. "Also, I was going to get some dinner. Would you like to come with me?"

"Dinner? Oh, no thanks," I said. "I already ate."

"Butterfingers?" He pointed to a pile of empty wrappers—seven of them, all mine—in a crumpled pile on the couch. "Come on, that's not dinner. It looks like you need to talk. I'll bet you're trying to figure out some big problem. I can help. Really. I'm very sympathetic."

If you see something private like candy wrappers on someone's couch when you stop by uninvited, you should just keep quiet about it. You'd think anyone would know that.

I said, "As a matter of fact, I had a lovely dinner earlier. With my sister and her family. But thanks so much for thinking of me." I gave him a fake smile.

He backed out my front door, saying, "Maybe some other time, maybe over the weekend?"

"Maybe," I said. "Happy Halloween."

The next day I picked up my pictures. I took one of the ones of Emily and slid it into a note I had written to Tim Weeks. I said I thought he'd like to see the costume I made. I wasn't trying to deceive him by giving him a picture of Emily, instead of myself. I told him it was a picture of my identical twin.

13

A women's magazine was going to run an excerpt of my third novel. The timing would be perfect, just before publication. The magazine's books editor called Howard, Howard called me.

"Good news, for a change," he said. "Sabrina Siebel from *A Woman's Outlook* called. She loves the work. She wants to run an excerpt in the June book."

"Oh, my gosh," I said. "That's great. Their circulation is—"

"Eight million," he filled in. "She said she hasn't seen anything this good in the thirteen years that she's been working at the magazine. She's really got herself in a lather over this. She wants to meet you, wants you to come to New York. She's going to call you about what you think your work is most like, you know, who and what she can compare you to."

"OK, you mean, a nineties Francesca Bailey or a modern, um—"

"That's it! Say, Jane Austen."

"But I'm nothing like Jane Austen. I don't even like—"

"That doesn't matter. The point is that there are all those movies out now that are based on Jane Austen novels. Major stars. Big dough. It doesn't really matter *who* you say you're like, as long as it's something that sells."

"I don't like to mislead people. If a whole lot of people buy my book expecting Jane Austen—"

"Then you'll have some money. See how that works?"

"Anyway, it's going to run in June?"

Howard said, "There are a few hoops still. Little ones that I'm sure you'll fly through without even getting winded. There's an editorial meeting Friday. She presents it to the rest of the editors. Then they read it."

"So they *all* have to like it or it won't run?"

"No, not all. Of course not. Sabrina's voice, of course, carries all the weight here. She's the books editor. And she's already on our side. The others pretty much go with what she chooses. They probably don't even pay attention to the fiction. They couldn't possibly have the time to—"

"So why the meeting? Why do they all have to read it?"

"Charlotte, come *on.* You're not a beginner. You know how these things go. They have to go through the motions of having everyone involved, makes all the players feel important. But I've never heard Sabrina so whipped into a froth in all the years I've been sitting here. Never."

"That's a good sign."

"It's more than a good sign, Charlotte. Just write a memo that compares your work to all the jumbo-sales popular fiction you can think of. Throw in a movie and a couple of TV shows for good measure. Fax me that as soon as you can, so she can take it to her meeting on Friday. You know what this means, don't you? You know what kind of sales this will lead to? You're about to break out, and it's long overdue, if you ask me. We've been waiting for this."

"This is great, Howard," I said. "I'm so excited."

"It was just a matter of time. I always told you that."

"When are we going to know for sure?"

"You know what I have to say on that."

"'It's never for sure until the check clears?'" I said.

"You got it, kid. I'm waiting for your fax."

"I'm going to write it right now."

I compared myself to three authors, one classic and two current; a classic film, a current film; and two TV shows, one cutting-edge and one that had run for over a decade. Howard said the fax was exactly what he needed. He couldn't have done it better himself, he said. He even signed his name to it, as if he *had* done it himself, and faxed it to Sabrina. He heard right back from her that this was perfect, just the right touch.

I waited a week. I waited another week. I called Howard. "What about *A Woman's Outlook?*"

"Oh, that, yeah. Well, that's going a little slower than we expected. You see, Sabrina met with a little resistance."

"Resistance?"

"Yeah, there are a couple of factions there, turns out. And one of these factions was trying to push for something else for June."

"Oh, my gosh! You made it sound like—"

"I was pretty sure that it was going to go through. I told you I've never heard Sabrina sound so excited about an author."

"Yeah . . . ," I said, "and? So how did this happen?"

"Geez, Charlotte. Wish I could tell you what goes on in these meetings. If I'd been there, I can promise you it wouldn't have turned out this way. Anyhow, your book is going to Ms. Big Cheese at the magazine. I forget her name, Terry, or something. She's new. Came from some other industry. I forget what. Cars or soap or something. Anyway, she's The Great Almighty over there, and she decides. She's taking the book home over the weekend. Monday, she casts the deciding vote."

I had a stomachache. I wanted to get off the phone now. "OK, well, thanks for letting me know."

"We'll talk, 'K?"

"Yeah."

As soon as I hung up, I burst into tears. But wait, I told myself mid-sob, it's not over yet. The Almighty Cheese might absolutely love my novel. It was possible. Of course it was. I called my sister. The two of us performed our good-luck rituals. We lit candles and silently chanted. My chant was, "Everyone loves my book. My book is irresistible." I found a picture of Ms. Almighty in the most recent issue of the magazine. I cut it out and glued it to an index card with a bubble coming out of her mouth that said, "Charlotte Dearborn is my favorite author."

Howard didn't call the following week, and I didn't call him. I waited through another week without calling. Finally, he called to say, "You got a good review in *Library Journal,* a 'highly recommended.' Congratulations!"

"Oh," I said flatly. "Oh, goody, goody."

"This will help. It's quotable too. I'll get C&S to put it on the jacket. There's still time. I'm going to fax it to you. I'm dialing your machine right now." I heard the buttons of his fax machine beeping. "I'm feeding in the review."

My fax machine started working. I said, "The Sabrina Siebel thing fell through, didn't it?"

"That—oh, you mean the *Outlook* deal? Yeah, actually, it did." He took a deep breath to put a positive spin on the bad news. "That magazine goes for the real broad-appeal kind of stuff. You know, these female characters that absolutely everybody can identify with."

"*My* work has a broad appeal. It does."

"You're really too good for them. Too literary, too well-written. You're so much more sophisticated than the drivel they usually publish."

"But eight million readers, Howard. There must be at least a few hundred thousand among them who would have enjoyed my work."

"Maybe," Howard said. "Now we'll never know. I'm working on something else for you now. Something way bigger. Don't you worry."

"OK, great," I said without enthusiasm.

"Charlotte," Howard said, "I'm sorry. I really tried. I promise you I did. Sabrina was as crushed as you are, maybe more. She's been in women's magazines for thirteen years, that's twelve years and eight months longer than what's-her-name, who had the deciding vote. It isn't fair, it isn't right, but we're just going to have to accept it and move on."

"Howard," I said. "Thank you. I appreciate everything you've done for me. Do. All the time, every day, for all these years. Now, if you don't mind, I'd like to hang up and cry."

"Sure," he said. "I understand. I might just do the same."

If there really was a big thing he was working on for me, I never heard about it again. Maybe it was just one of those things that agents say to make it seem as though the bad news isn't really bad.

For our November journals, my class was writing stories. I wrote the words "Thanksgiving," "vacation," "turkey," "leaves," and "grandmother" on the board.

"Miss Dearborn," said Ryan H. "How do you spell 'trouble'?"

"Mrs. Dearborn," said Seth, "how do you spell 'weird'?"

"Miss Dearborn—"

"Boys and girls, please," I said. "I'm going to have to remind you about something. Does anyone know what it is?"

Grace yelled, "Not to call out!"

"Right," I said. "And also, use your inventive spelling. If you can't spell a word, put down the sounds you think it has. Keep writing, even if you can't spell a word. This will help your writing *and* your reading. We'll type the stories on the computer later, and then we can correct all the spelling errors."

"Mrs. Dearborn," whined Seth. "I can't think of anything."

"Then use one of the words on the board as a starting point."

"I don't want to write about Thanksgiving."

"What would you like to write about?"

"Monday Night Football."

"Fine."

"But I don't know what to write!"

"Seth, write one sentence about *Monday Night Football.* 'I like to watch *Monday Night Football,'* or 'There are too many commercials on *Monday Night Football.'* Then add to that. Write another sentence. Then—"

"I don't want to write about commercials."

"OK, you could tell about a game you watched."

"No, I—"

Be very firm with him, I told myself. He needs to know that journal writing is expected, and he can't get out of it by whining. "Seth, stop!" I said. I put up a hand, palm out, like a traffic cop. He was really getting under my skin lately. I tried to get a hold of myself. "Other children are working, and you're disturbing them." Actually, no one was. Everybody was waiting to see how this was going to turn out. "One sentence," I said. "Now!" Seth moaned softly, then pressed his lips together and picked up his pencil.

He sat there for a long time, not writing anything. He even cried a little. Then it was time to move on to something else.

Being firm hadn't worked. I had bullied him, and the result was we both felt bad, and the assignment didn't get done.

"I don't have very much homework today," Dylan told me at the door.

"Great," I said. "Lucky you!"

"So you can go."

"I'll stay, thanks." I had to squeeze by him to get into the house. I went into the kitchen and turned off the TV. There was another one in the family room, tuned to a different channel. Dylan was still standing by the front door. He was wearing a velour sweatsuit in kelly green with navy blue trim. What were his parents thinking?

"Come on, Dylan," I called to him from the family room, where I was dragging the extra chair over to the desk. I picked up his backpack, pulled his binder out, and placed it on the desk. "Let's get started. Dylan?" There was no answer. I waited. "The sooner we get started, the sooner we'll be finished."

"Duh," he said softly as he came into the room. He had six Oreos in his hand and put a whole one into his mouth.

"Did you get any of your homework back, the stuff we did the other day?"

Dylan shook his head.

"May I see the assignments for today?"

Dylan didn't answer, as he was busy chewing, his cheeks bulging with cookie.

I opened the binder as he slumped in his seat. There were a lot of assignments written in the little boxes under Wednesday, including, "studdy for test!!!!!!!" in the social studies box. "You have a test tomorrow in social studies?" I said. "OK, we'll study for that. And what else here? Some math problems, spelling. We'll get the spelling and math out of the way first. Then we're going to spend the rest of our time on the social studies. Any reading? Just a little. OK, then. Let's start with the math problems."

I put the math book on the table and turned to the right page. I handed him a pencil. He copied the first problem, then sat there a minute.

"What's four times six, Dylan?"

He shrugged.

"We're going to need to review the times tables. But for now, let's use this chart. It sticks right on your desk, see?" I peeled the backing off a times table sticker.

Dylan looked at it. "You're giving me the answers? That's cheating. You're telling me to cheat, you know." It was the first time I had ever seen him smile.

"I'm giving you a tool for practicing, like flash cards. If you use this over and over, say each answer to yourself as you use the chart, you will memorize the times tables. Finish the problem, please."

Slowly, he worked the problem. He got it right. "Good, Dylan. That's excellent. It helps to say the problems to yourself, to repeat them and the answer so that you hear it, and stamp it in your memory. Now let's go on to this one."

It took a long time, but we made it through all the problems. The spelling was a little easier. The reading assignment was another struggle. Over and over, I showed him where to look for answers to questions. He had read the whole chapter but didn't seem to remember it.

"Good!" I said when he got a question right after three tries.

"It's not *good,*" he said with a sneer. "I was purposely giving you the wrong answers. You say good about everything."

"I say good when I think you're trying. If you can do better, show me. I promise to be impressed."

"That's just it. *Everything* impresses you. You get paid to tell me I'm doing a good job."

I could think of other ways to spend my time than sitting here with this nasty kid. I wanted to make some patchwork seat cushions for my kitchen chairs, and I had just the scraps I wanted to use—

"I'm right, aren't I?" Dylan said. "How much does my dad pay you?"

"I prefer not to answer that."

"Yeah, well, he'll tell me if I ask him."

"That's between the two of you. Read the next question, please."

Dylan read the question very quietly so that I could barely hear him.

I said, "Any ideas?"

"No."

"Read this." I pointed to a short paragraph containing the answer. I wanted to go. I looked down at my watch without moving my head.

"You can go, you know," Dylan said. "You don't have to stay here all night or anything."

"I was just checking how much time we're going to have left for social studies. I want to make sure we cover everything thoroughly."

"Yeah, right." He wrote his answer. It was incomplete, but I didn't make him redo it.

We moved on to the next question. "How about this one?" I said. "Remember where you read about that?"

"Let me see," he said.

He squeezed his eyes tightly closed, as if he was straining to remember.

"You can always—"

Dylan farted. "Oops! I guess I was thinking too hard."

Not every kid is likable. Maybe it's not his fault. Whatever. I really didn't have to do this. To be effective as a teacher, you should *like* the student, have some positive feelings about him. "Say excuse me," I ordered.

He made an exaggerated look of innocence. "What? What? I had a little gas. I can't help it."

"Say excuse me, and answer this question." I was growling through clenched teeth. "If you'd like me to ask Mrs. Fitz to work with you after school, instead, I think she would be happy to take over for me here. Maybe it would be better for you to work with the same teacher on your homework that you have all day in class. No need to make a transition from one person to another." Bernice would never do it, of course. She left the school building exactly fifteen minutes after classes ended every day. But Dylan didn't know that. Nevertheless, my threat was effective.

"Excuse me," he said out of the side of his mouth.

"You're excused. Continue with the next question, please."

As we worked through the rest of the questions and reviewed the social studies chapters, I was thinking about what I would say to Dylan's father. *I'm afraid I'm finding that I have more work than I can handle, just with my first-graders . . . Dylan needs help daily, and unfortunately I won't be able to commit that much time to . . . My first year, and I'm still adjusting . . . Wonderful boy, and I'm sure any number of teachers would be happy to have the additional income . . .*

It was not necessary for me to be miserable. I went into teaching to improve the quality of my life, not to swap one form of misery for another.

An hour and a half later, Dylan was watching television, and Matt Jones was handing me a check. "Thank you," he said, looking me in the eye. "You're really helping him."

"Oh," I said, startled by the compliment. "Do you think so? That's great. I wasn't sure. Sometimes it's hard to know if I'm getting through. In fact, I was—"

Matt Jones's cell phone rang.

" 'Night," he said, detaching the phone from his belt. He turned away, pressing a button on his phone. "This is Matt Jones."

Dylan walked in, as his father was looking out the dark sliding glass door to the unfinished pool in the backyard. "Hi, Dad! Dad? Oh, you're on the phone." He seemed to drop his head as he scuffled off down the hall without saying good-bye to me.

I let myself out and drove home.

"If he's rude and doesn't try, what's the point? You're just making yourself miserable," Emily was saying to me later over the phone.

I had decided that it was OK to let her know how badly tutoring was going because it wasn't my main job.

"But they don't pay attention to him," I said. "It's so sad."

Emily said, "Charlotte, I hate to tell you how many kids have parents like that."

"So you just want me to abandon him, too? That's not right. Everybody needs someone who is going to stick with them, no matter what."

"You just said yourself that you're not doing him any favors going there every other day and wishing you were somewhere else. He must know that you don't like him."

"He doesn't like me either."

"Then the responsible thing to do would be to find someone else for him. Maybe there's someone at school who would click with him."

Rick would be perfect, I was thinking. Dylan would never act up like this with Rick. I said, "I can click! I can. I just need some more time. It's not that bad. Really. I exaggerated. I can handle it. And maybe it will get better. I think he's growing on me. A little bit."

"Charlotte," she said. And although I couldn't see her, I knew she was shaking her head at the way I deluded myself.

14

Years ago I had tried to do as many appearances as possible, readings and signings in bookstores, to help publicize my early books. My first Collard & Stanton publicist, Joelle, told me when my first book was about to come out, "Readings are the way you build a following. If you reach just one person, it will be worth it," Joelle emphasized. Sometimes the appearances didn't even work out that well. I'd traveled to a distant state to a bookstore to find that even its own employees were unaware I was coming. The best readings—the ones where ten or so people showed up and two or three bought books—were exceptions. Since my early novels, C&S had revised its policy regarding author tours. If I reached just one person, then my publisher had wasted a lot of money on airfare and a hotel.

So when Nina, the C&S publicist for my fourth novel *Hello, You're on the Air,* called me about a reading at Jasper's Books in Los Angeles, she was almost apologetic. She had to talk me into it.

"Jasper James *himself* called to ask you to read in his store," Nina told me.

"He did?"

"As you know, Jasper's Books is the most important independent bookstore in California, maybe even in the West. It's really an honor to read there. You know Jasper is a big Jane Austen enthusiast, and—"

"I never liked—"

"Please don't tell him that! Anyway, the point is he likes *you, too.*"

"That's very flattering, but—"

"Now wait. I told him you didn't know anyone in L.A. I told him about how many times you've gone to read somewhere and no one showed up. He said, 'You tell Charlotte that I personally will see to it that there are people in my store to listen to her read. Good people. People who have taste and will buy her book!' "

"Do you believe that?" I said. "I mean, it's nice of him, and I really appreciate his enthusiasm, but I don't even get reviews in California. Who does he plan to—"

"If anyone can do it, he can."

I had to go, of course. I wore a black skirt—I always wore a black skirt—and a long black top.

When I got there, one of Jasper's salespeople, Elizabeth, greeted me. Elizabeth is almost famous herself for doing all the book groups and for the gentle but persuasive way she pushes emerging writers on the store's clientele.

"Charlotte," she said, as if I were a long-lost relative, "Jasper is so excited about having you!"

"I'm flattered," I told her, "and I appreciate all the support—"

Elizabeth lowered her voice. "I mean this is unusual. He's *staying* for your reading tonight. He just doesn't do that. He has a family, you know. He *goes home* in the evenings." She squeezed my hand for emphasis. "Listen to this—I don't think he meant for it to be a surprise or anything." Still, she looked over her shoulder before she said it. *"He bought a cake."*

"How nice!" I said.

"It's more than nice, Charlotte, I assure you. You don't know him, but I've worked here for seventeen years. He didn't buy a cake for Amy Tan or Carol Shields. He didn't buy one for Elizabeth Berg or Jan Karon. Not even Jamaica Kincaid got cake! He *adores* you. He's head over heels. I mean it."

"Wow," I said. "A cake."

OK, I was flattered. My heart lifted a little. I felt, maybe not happy or relieved, but let's say I allowed for the possibility that a positive turn of events was remotely conceivable. And I was grateful as anything for even that much lightening of my increasingly leaden spirit.

Jasper came down from his office above the store. Elizabeth introduced us, and he both shook my hand and kissed me on the cheek. He said I smelled good. He showed me an introduction he had written that he was going to read himself. It was a full page, handwritten, about *my work,* on a sheet from a yellow legal pad. Here's what he said about the book I was promoting:

> *The new novel by Charlotte Dearborn is a quietly breathtaking exploration of life and love. Ginny Randolf, widowed at age twenty-three, is faced with two daunting tasks: to support her toddler twins alone and to reinfuse her heart with hope. A series of funny misadventures lands her a job as the unlikely host of a San Diego radio call-in program. When an elderly caller complains of loneliness, Ginny offers, "Come over to my house, and we'll make dinner for us and my kids." When a nineteen-year-old caller bursts into tears because it's her first birthday away*

from home, Ginny says, "I'm going to get you a present. Now, don't ask me what it is. It's a surprise." Ginny's radio persona offers not only entertainment to her listeners and solace to her callers, but ultimately her own salvation. By turns hilarious and heartwrenching, this one is a winner.

I can quote all this because he gave me the piece of paper, and I saved it. There was more, but I'll cut to the chase: No one came. Not a single soul. For an hour and a half, I sat at a table in the café with Jasper. We ate cake. If we had eaten the cardboard box it came in, I wouldn't have enjoyed it any less. We talked about—never mind what we talked about. All I was thinking the whole time was *Can I go yet? May I please just go somewhere else, cry for a while, and start to move on?*

I was in a Starbucks in San Francisco, waiting for Tim Weeks. I was wearing my denim dress, which I still fit into. I didn't think he would recognize me from the picture of Emily in the Ms. Beetleman costume. So it was up to me. I figured he was the type who wore those button-down plaid shirts pretty much all the time, but there were a lot of men like that here. I would concentrate on the hair, which was curly. I did a survey. There was just one man with curly hair in the store at the moment, and he was wearing a three-piece suit and hurrying out the door with his cell phone and his personal travel mug. Definitely not a writer.

I watched the door and sipped my coffee. I would have liked to have a chocolate chip scone with butter, but I restrained myself. Someone came in the door who I thought might be a possibility. I straightened up and looked at his face carefully. He was about thirty-five, I guessed. I didn't think Tim Weeks was that young, but it was possible. No, this man had a completely different nose. I kept watching the door. Two women came in. Someone sat down beside me. I looked. He was in his late fifties, overweight, and bald. I considered telling him that the seat was taken, but there was another one open on the other side of me.

A pregnant woman pushing a two-year-old in a stroller came in. Then there was a pause and no one came in for a few minutes. I drank some more coffee. Two more men came in. One was on the phone; the other was listening and waiting expectantly, as if to find out some important news. The pregnant woman had her cup and, with difficulty, maneuvered her stroller between the chairs with one hand. Her little boy was shoving a big cookie into his mouth. They were coming closer. *Don't stop here,* I mentally urged them. The woman parked the stroller next to my feet and sat down beside me. "Hi," she said.

"Hi," I returned.

I was going to get up and move. I looked for another table. Maybe outside, I was thinking.

"Charlotte," someone said.

The bald man next to me knew my name. Geez, now what? I was thinking. I looked at him. He didn't look the slightest bit familiar. Maybe he was someone I had met briefly at a bookstore appearance or something. Not now, I was thinking, Tim Weeks will be here *any minute,* and I don't want to be talking to *you.*

"Are you Charlotte?" the man asked me.

"Yes," I said.

He thrust out his hand. "I'm Tim," he said. "Tim Weeks."

"Oh!" I said, as if I'd just seen a mouse run under the table. "How nice to meet you!"

I stretched my lips across my face in a polite smile. Where was his curly hair! And he was older than *I* was! He grinned at me, and little pleats appeared around his eyes. Parentheses enclosed his mouth. Now I could see the shadow of the face on the book jacket. But a lot had happened since that picture was taken.

"Here we were sitting right next to each other and didn't even—"

"Know it!" I squeaked too loudly.

"Well," he said, staring at me. "So, what time do you have to be at the conference? Maybe we could—"

"I have an hour," I said quickly. He really looked different, not like his jacket photo at all, a whole different person. But it might not have been a big mistake coming here. I knew the writer of those books had a generous heart. That was what had drawn me here, really, not his hair, not his face, or his age. "But my schedule is flexible," I added.

"Right," he said. "But I have to—I have a deadline I'm trying to—"

"Sure, I understand," I said. He was going to make an excuse, come up with a reason that he couldn't be with me. "So, tell me, how's the book coming along? The one you were having trouble with?"

"Trouble?" he bristled. I guess I wasn't supposed to mention that. "Maybe every once in a while, I hit a little snag. But generally things are going well. I've got a number of projects I'm working on, various irons in the fire."

"Great," I said, nodding.

"Yeah, there's a television series in development and a possible feature film that I'm—"

"Wonderful!" I said enthusiastically.

"Yeah, it will be if I ever see any of the money."

"The contracts can be very—"

"No, it's not that. It's just that my soon-to-be ex-wife is trying to claim most of the proceeds, and everything's tied up in court."

"Oh," I said. "So, you're married?"

"No, not really. Separated six months now."

"Oh," I said. "So how long were you together?"

"Twenty-seven years," he said, nodding. "She has somehow convinced herself that she's entitled to my income. It's ugly. You ever been married?"

"No, I haven't."

"Lucky." He clutched his coffee and slugged back a major gulp.

"Was your wife working during the marriage?"

"She's a writer."

"Oh, you're both writers. Wow. That must be very—"

"Actually, she was the writer and I'm the illustrator. Of those books you saw."

"You didn't write them? I thought you wrote them. I don't understand. Your name was on them as the author/illustrator."

"Well, yeah. It was, but see, way back—we were just out of school—we agreed to just use one name and publish everything as a single entity."

"Why? She got no credit."

"This was, oh, years ago, and I wanted, I mean we decided—together—to just use my name—"

"And you're actually going to try to prevent her from getting the money from her own stories?"

"I offered her a very reasonable deal."

"Don't tell me," I said. My hands went up, and my voice got loud. "You want to give her a cash settlement and no royalties. Is that it?"

"You make it sound as though I want to rip her off. Believe me, it was a very generous offer. I just don't want the partnership to continue. And neither does she. She's the one who asked for the divorce!"

I don't blame her, I was thinking. "Do you really think it would be fair for her not to continue to share in profits from *her* stories? I'd fight that, too, if it were me."

He grunted. "You probably would."

"What's that supposed to mean?"

"You know, you're not what I expected."

"Oh?" I said.

"You didn't look so heavy in your picture."

"Ha! You didn't look so mean in yours." I got up. I felt tears coming into my eyes and my throat closing. I had lost a good friend, a dear friend that I never really had; my imaginary friend had died. "I have to go," I squeaked. I thought about the time I'd wasted driving, the anxiety I'd spent on my clothes, the daydreaming I'd done about what might happen here. "I have to get to a meeting."

There wasn't any meeting. I had just made that up so it would sound like I had a reason to be in San Francisco. I drove to a gas station, filled up my tank, and then headed south with the radio on loud. I didn't stop until San Luis Obispo, when I was almost out of gas again. I used the bathroom, got a Coke and some potato chips, and got back in the car. I drove all the way to my sister's house without stopping.

It was almost eleven when I got there. Emily came to the door in her nightgown. "He was a jerk," she said when she saw me.

I nodded and burst into tears.

"Did you drive straight back? You must have. Oh, Charlotte. I'm sorry."

"He didn't even write the books! His wife wrote them. He's divorcing her and trying to deal her out of her royalties!"

She gasped, then shook her head in sympathy. "The scum!"

"And he didn't look anything like his picture. I think it was taken about twenty years ago."

"I'll make you a hot chocolate," Emily said. "Come on."

"Mom?" came a voice from the top of the stairs.

"It's OK, Janie," said Emily. "Aunt Charlotte just stopped by."

"Aunt Charlotte?"

"Yes?" I said.

"Did you like him?"

"No!" I said.

"Oh. Can I hear the story, Mom?"

"It's late, Janie."

I said, "Honey, I promise I'll tell you next time I come. Or you can call me. OK?"

"All right," she said grudgingly. "I never get to hear anything the first time through, you know. It's not as good after you've practiced it a couple of times."

"Sleep well, Janie," Emily said. "I love you."

"And so do I!" I said. I sniffed.

"Oh, Aunt Charlotte!" Janie ran down the stairs in a big T-shirt and bare feet. "I love you, too!" She hugged me, and a tear dripped off my nose into her hair. Then she went to bed.

Emily and I had hot chocolate and chocolate-covered graham crackers in the kitchen. Brad was asleep.

"I didn't expect him to be like *that,*" she said when I told her the story.

"That's because you were reading the wife's work. You were hearing the wife's voice," I said. "I probably would have gotten along great with the wife!"

"You should have called her," Emily said, biting into her cookie. "I bet she's really nice. You can feel that from the books."

"But you have to remember that the notes we sent each other were short. They didn't reveal much. I never even told him that I used to be a writer. This is so embarrassing."

"I would have done the same thing."

"You would?" I took a cookie. "I better go, so we can both get some sleep."

At the door, my sister hugged me, and I went alone to my car.

15

I got a bad review in the *New York Times Book Review* that took up half a page. The reviewer must have read my book very fast, because her plot summary was way off, getting some of the most important events completely wrong. It was hard to agree with the way she was chosen to review my book. She had recently published a historical cookbook; my book had some recipes in it. It was one of those cutesy pairings that might seem clever on the surface, but for me it was damaging. The reviewer's criticisms focused on the cooking in the book and nearly disregarded the story. "Far better recipes for black bean soup are available in . . ." and she named a cookbook. "It's a novel!" I yelled at the newspaper. "My character is supposed to be a *bad* cook!"

One misconception about harsh, public criticism is that someone not liking your work is what causes your pain. Though certainly reading a negative review of your own work is no fun, what hurts even more is the experience of being publicly misunderstood.

The most severe humiliation is brought about by the reviewer who gets the plot wrong, who says your work is an imitation of an author you've never read, or who doesn't get your jokes. And what's really unfair about it is that there's nowhere to publicly state that the reviewer did a lousy job without looking like a bad sport.

Some people think that writers develop thick skins and that, after a while, bad reviews and rejections stop hurting or no longer penetrate to their soft, unprotected centers. Unfortunately, this is not the case. What happens, instead, is that the experience, while no less painful after many repetitions, begins to follow a predictable pattern. I called it post-rejection syndrome, or PRS. The first stage of PRS was crying for a full day, which was followed by extreme emotional tenderness and not wanting to leave the house. Then came plans for a completely different career. Finally, a time came when you could sit at the computer and write something. You could not rush any of this or skip any of the stages. You simply had to let PRS play itself out completely before you could expect to feel hopeful and ready to try again.

"We . . . came?" Seth said, looking up at me hesitantly.

It was Seth's turn to read. The other Grasshoppers were waiting for their turns. Seth took a long time to puzzle out each word. "Look at the word again," I said. "What—"

"What's that vowel, Seth?" Amanda said with exasperation. "It's an *o,* not an *a!* Come, not came!"

"Amanda," I warned.

"Come?" Seth said.

"Good," I said.

He looked at the picture: a house. "Home?"

"Right, but the word is *i-n.* What sound are we working on? Short *i.* So look at the word. *I-n* What does that spell?"

"We come home? Inside? In! It's in!"

"Good," I said.

He turned the page and looked at the picture: a table with food on it and a family sitting together, eating. "We had food?"

"Look at the words, Seth," I urged.

"We? I *said* we!"

"Great. Now what's the *next* word. It starts with a long *e.*"

"Eat? We eat?"

"Good. We eat what?"

"Food?"

Amanda sighed loudly and flopped backward in her seat. I glared at her.

I said, "The word has a short *i* sound. But instead of guessing, let's look at *each* of the letters, one at a time. The second letter is a short *i.* What does a short *i* say?"

Seth made a long *i* sound.

"She said, *'short i,'* " Amanda muttered in annoyance.

"Amanda," I said firmly. "Please wait quietly for your turn." I said to Seth, "*Short i,* as in i-i-i-t."

"Fish! . . . it's fish! Is it fish?"

"Yes, it is. Good"

Seth suddenly looked up at me, and for a second I thought he had it. He said, "Mrs. Dearborn, do you know what? I'm getting a frog."

"You told me, Seth. It's very exciting. Now, let's just get the rest of this sentence, and then it will be someone else's turn."

"We eat fish for dinner!" Amanda exploded. " 'We eat fish for dinner!' He can't read! He's just guessing!"

"Amanda," I said. "Go to your seat and finish your clock work sheet!"

"Hey!" she said. "I didn't get a turn!"

"I'm going, too," Seth said. "I don't want to read anymore. This is not a good story. It's boring."

He stood up and started back toward his desk. "Seth," I said, "you're not—"

But the bell rang. It was time for lunch. All the kids started rummaging for their food and lining up by the door.

I didn't blame Amanda for feeling frustrated. I felt the same way sometimes. On the other hand, I could understand Seth's frustration, too. Due to a slower rate of maturity, environmental factors, maybe even some neurological glitch, he wasn't reading as well as most of the other kids. I was supposed to let them develop at their own rates, mix up the reading groups so the kids wouldn't feel labeled and pigeonholed. Meanwhile, Seth was painfully conscious of his struggle for each word, and Amanda got in trouble for butting in.

"Mrs. Dearborn?" Rosie stood up in front of me, as we were working on the date and the weather. "My head itches."

"Scratch it," I said. "And sit down, please, so everyone can see."

We decided it was partly cloudy. William attached a felt cloud partially covering the sun onto the weather square of the calendar. Rosie said, "Mrs. Dearborn? My sister had lice. Do you think I have lice?"

"You may sit down, William," I said. "Thank you. When did your sister have lice, Rosie? A long time ago, or—"

"Yesterday," Rosie said.

I stood up. "Rosie, just to be on the safe side, I'd like you to go down to the nurse's office to have her check your hair. OK? Thank you. I'll call and say you're coming."

As Rosie walked out the door, I called the front office. "This is Ms. Dearborn," I said to Cindy at the front desk. "Is the nurse here today?"

"She's been cut down to once every two weeks. Someone sick?"

"I just sent Rosie down to be checked for head lice." I was trying to keep my voice even. Bugs and rodents were a problem for me.

"All right, I guess I'll be doing the checking, then," Cindy said. "I'll get someone to cover the phones. Now, if she's got lice, I'm going to need your whole class down here to get checked."

"All right," I said.

The phone rang a couple of minutes later. I asked my class, "Who is Phone Person this week? Grace?"

"Miss Dearborn's room, Grace speaking. . . . OK. . . . OK. . . . OK, bye." Grace hung up the phone. "Rosie has to go home. And we're all supposed to go to the nurse's office *right now!*"

"Thank you, Grace." I went to Rosie's chair and got her backpack and sweatshirt. "Boys and girls, please line up quietly by the door."

I stood at the front of the line. There was a little itch on my scalp just above my right ear. It took a lot of effort not to scratch it. "Does everybody know what lice are? They're very small bugs that like to live in hair. Mrs. Roland in the office is going to look very closely at your hair and scalp. I'll be first so you can see what's going to happen. Now, if you have lice, it just means that you have to go home, get some special shampoo, and wash your hair with it. Is that a big deal? No, it is not. And if some boys and girls have to go home, we are not going to talk about that outside of our classroom. Not at all. That's private information. We're just going to save all their work until they can join us again. These bugs can get in anybody's hair, even Ms. Dearborn's. I just washed my hair this morning, and maybe you washed yours last night or—"

"I didn't take a shower 'cause I was watching this show, and I fell asleep, so my mom—"

"Seth." I put my finger to my lips. "If I had lice, it would just mean that I sat close to someone else who had lice. They like living in *anyone's* hair. Do you all understand that? Good. Now hands at your sides. Seth, I mean you, too, please. Thank you. No talking, and let's go, girls and boys."

Cindy was waiting for us in the nurse's office with a jar full of what looked like tongue depressors. Behind her, Rosie was sitting on the examining table, crying loudly. I walked to her quickly. She jumped off the table and flung herself against me. "I have to go *home!* They called my mom at *work!* She's coming to *get* me!"

"Oh, but, Rosie, you're going to be back with us very soon. And we're going to keep a folder of all your work. Look! Here's your mom now!"

Rosie ran from me and hurled herself against her mother. "Oh, Rosie," her mother said, rolling her eyes. She looked at me. "Isn't this a disgusting little development! I just washed all the sheets and comforters yesterday when her sister had lice. I knew I should have shampooed them both!"

"Oh, boy," I said sympathetically. I walked over with her things and handed them to her mother. I knelt beside my sobbing student. I took her hand in both of mine. "Rosie, this will all be cleared up in no time. Don't you worry about a thing."

Rosie gulped back a sob. "OK."

I stood up. Rosie took her mother's hand and walked out the front door.

"Bye, Rosie," some of the kids murmured.

"Hope all your lice get dead!" Seth shouted.

"Now, boys and girls, Mrs. Roland is going to check my hair and scalp for lice. I'm going to sit in this chair and hold very still. There she goes. It's not hurting me at all. I just have to be patient for a minute." I was getting sweaty. I really didn't want to have lice. If I did, I might just start crying like Rosie.

"You're clear," said Cindy.

I bounced out of the chair. "See that? It was as easy as pie! OK, Ryan H., honey, you're next. There we go."

Three more kids—Ryan J., Katie, and William—had to be sent home. "We're the survivors!" Seth announced loudly.

"Quiet now, boys and girls, and we'll walk back to our classroom."

Back in the classroom, I debriefed them. "It's important to remember that lice are looking for heads to live on. They could choose your head or my head or—"

"They don't care whose it is!" Seth asserted.

"You got it, Seth," I said. "They would love to be on all of our heads, but we won't give them the chance."

Seth began to rub his head. Patience was scratching the back of her neck. Before I could stop myself, I shuddered.

"What?" Seth wanted to know. "Why were you shaking your shoulders?"

"Chilly in here," I said. I zipped my sweatshirt for realism.

"I thought you were getting the creepy-crawlies from talking about lice so much!" Seth said with a grin.

"Seth, I don't want to say it again—"

"Don't call out and don't interrupt!" Seth bellowed.

"Right. Oh, look at the time. It's ten-thirty. Now, when we go out for recess, we don't discuss lice with anyone outside of our classroom. Does everybody understand that? That might be embarrassing for our friends who had to go home. We wouldn't want to do anything to hurt their feelings. Thank you very much." The bell rang. "Line up please, boys and girls."

They lined up. I opened the door, and they charged out. "A whole bunch of kids had lice!" Seth was yelling to the world in general as he ran.

If I'd had a plastic shower cap, I would have put it on and worn it for the rest of the day. My head kept itching, and I kept feeling as though something tiny and almost weightless was making its way across my scalp.

I went to the staff room to get some coffee. "Lice?" Bernice Fitz was saying. "Ew. Yuck. Whose class?"

"Charlotte Dearborn's," Cindy Roland said. "Four kids went home. You should have seen her face. One of the kids was crying, but Charlotte wouldn't go near her!" The two of them laughed loudly.

"I did so," I said in my own defense. "And her mother was there!"

"Oh, hi, Charlotte. You didn't look too happy a little while ago."

"Sorry, that gave me the creeps," I admitted.

Marilyn walked in then. "What's that?"

"Lice. Four of my kids went home."

"Oh, dear," she said. "Were they very upset? I have a book you can read to them."

"I was going to try to forget about the whole thing, move on as quickly as possible to another topic, something nice," I said.

Marilyn shook her head. "That's not going to happen. This is your theme for the next couple of days. The kids won't let this go. They'll be talking about it, asking about it. They've got to process. Make up a rhyme. Draw pictures. Have the kids make up math problems. 'Four children had lice yesterday. Today three more had lice. In all, how many children have had lice?' "

"Do you think there will be more?" I asked in horror.

"Oh, yeah," Cindy said, nodding with certainty.

"Yup," said Bernice, smiling.

"Of *course,*" said Marilyn. She took my shoulders in both of her hands, looking into my eyes, imploring. "I'm telling you, think of it as a *theme,* like Saint Patrick's Day. You can *use* this. It's like a little *gift!*"

"I see," I said and shuddered again.

* * *

Seth was working on short *e.* "What's this one?" I asked him.

"Egg?" he said.

"Good," I said. "You're getting it!"

"No," he said gloomily. "I just looked at the picture."

"The picture is part of it," I said. "You're supposed to look at the picture for clues."

"That's not reading," said Amanda, shaking her head.

I shot her a warning look. "What's this one? It rhymes with egg and starts with an *l.*"

"Um," Seth looked frantically at the picture.

"OK," I said. "Now, listen to me. *E-e-e-egg.*" I pointed to the *l* in the word. "*L* then *eg.* What's that?" He looked at me. "Look down here at the picture. *L—eg. L—eg.* What's that?"

Seth shrugged. "Foot?"

Amanda sighed, got up from the circle, and went to her desk. I saw her take out her math book. I thought about what to do. Should I insist that she come back when I knew she would make Seth feel bad? No, let her do math.

Seth sighed and rubbed his eyes.

I knew he was tired and wanted me to go on to someone else. But if I kept doing that, he wouldn't learn to read. "It's leg," I said, pronouncing each letter clearly. I turned the page. "How about this one? What sound does it start with?"

Seth looked at the ceiling.

"Look at the book, sweetie," I said. "What sound does this letter make?"

Seth glanced at the book and then up at the ceiling again.

"B-b-b," he said.

"Good," I said. "Now what's the word?"

"Beg?" he said without looking at the book.

"Good," I said. "That's *very* good!" I looked up at the ceiling. "Seth, what are you looking at? The book's down here."

Seth looked down and then rubbed his eyes. "Can I be done?"

I sighed. I didn't mean to. I just did it without thinking. "Sure. Are you tired?"

"I'm not tired! I just don't like reading!" Seth said emphatically.

"It will get easier."

When the bell rang at the end of the day, I felt like curling into a fetal position on the blue carpet and closing my eyes. Luckily, I didn't have Dylan today. I made up some reading questions, typed them on my computer, and printed them. I checked a huge stack of papers and filed them for my kids to take home the next day.

At six-thirty, I was getting my keys out of my purse when someone knocked and the door opened. "Hi, Miss Dearborn." It was Jen from Aftercare. Dylan shuffled in behind her. "Dylan's mom and dad must be running a little late tonight. And both their cell phones are turned off. After six, it's a dollar a minute, with a thirty-minute limit. They've passed that, and I have to go to my other job now. Dylan says he doesn't know any of his neighbors. There's no one down on his emergency card, and I just didn't know—"

"OK," I said, forcing the corners of my tired mouth to turn up. "Thanks, Jen. You go ahead. Dylan, you can stay with me until your mom and dad come. Any homework left to do?"

"I really appreciate it, Charlotte," Jennifer said. "Bye, Dylan. See you Tuesday, OK, bud?"

Dylan mumbled, "Bye."

Jennifer took off across the dark playground at a run. Dylan was busy studying my Helping Hands chart and trying not to let himself cry.

I said, "I bet you're hungry. Let's go up to the front office, where your parents will come in. We'll order a pizza."

We ordered half pepperoni, for Dylan, and half mushroom, for me. With my luck, I thought, the parents will get here before the pizza, and I'll be stuck with it. But I was wrong. We worked on reading and spelling, ate the pizza, threw away the box, and were playing hangman when Dylan's mother showed up at 7:30. "Oh, hi," she said. "You do daycare, too! Good to know! Hey, Dyl," she said. "We forgot about you! I came in with dinner, and Dad said, 'Where's Dylan?' I said, 'I thought *you* were getting him! I had that late meeting.' He said, 'I had a late meeting, too! I told you this morning.' Of course, he didn't!" She laughed. Dylan packed up the homework we had done together, and I got my purse.

"This must happen all the time, right?" Dylan's mother said.

"Not that I know of," I said.

"Once again! Mother of the Year!" she said, laughing.

"We had pizza," I said.

"Oh," she said. "Great! So he's all fed and everything. What do I owe you?"

"The pizza was thirteen dollars."

She put her hand against her cheek. She'd had her nails done recently, and I found myself wondering if I'd been with Dylan when she was with the manicurist. "I don't have any cash right now. We'll just add it on at the end of the week, if that's OK. Come on, Dyl. Hurry up! *You've* eaten, but *I'm* starving, and my food is getting cold at home."

Dylan put his backpack on, stumbled slightly under its weight, and followed his mother out the door. Halfway out, he did a quarter-turn and waved at me.

"Next time, you say, 'I am not on call for you twenty-four hours a day!' " My sister was giving me advice about the Dylan problem. "I mean, what is this, like the fourth or fifth time they've been more than an hour late?"

"Who would I say that to? Dylan? Because he's the only one there when I have to decide what to do. And usually I'm already at their house. I can't leave him alone."

"And they know that, so they're taking advantage of you."

"Right, but if there's no one else—"

"Just tell the parents."

"See, you don't get it. The parents are selfish and irresponsible. I can't make them grow up. And I can't leave a fourth-grader by himself at night. So I have to wait until the parents come home."

Emily thought a minute. "I guess I would, too."

"See? If I don't stay with him, it's just one more adult who has better things to do than be with him."

"I see what you mean."

"The worst part is that he doesn't even like me."

"He does," Emily said, patting my arm. "He's just a fourth-grader trying to be a tough guy."

"Sure," I said. "Oh, sure."

16

I was in the teacher's lounge, eating a rice cake with melted jack cheese and salsa. This was going to be my main meal of the day, because I was really trying to cut way back on food. Portion control was key, just cutting down on the amount you eat can make a huge difference. I was letting my teeth descend through the gooey hot cheese, the cold but spicy salsa, and down into the crunchy rice cake. A medley of contrasts, I was thinking, when a fifth-grade teacher, Ron Clarke, sat down beside me.

"I have an idea for a novel," Ron said as an opener. "A *great* idea." He lowered his voice to match the weighty significance of this, then looked at me, waiting for a reaction. He had never spoken to me until now.

I licked a drop of salsa from the tip of my finger. "Good for you," I said. "Congratulations." I was still thinking about the contrasts: crunchy/gooey, cold/hot, bland/spicy. I took another bite.

"Listen," the teacher whispered, in case the kindergarten teacher standing in front of the microwave, stirring her instant soup, might have a tape recorder to scoop up his great idea and claim it as her own. "It opens with a murder right after a site council meeting," he said.

"What's a site council?" I said.

"Oh, that's a group of parents, teachers, and school board members who decide—"

"OK," I said. "I get it. Are you on the site council, by any chance? Never mind. Doesn't matter. Go on."

"Well, yeah, I am. So anyway, a board member is dead, stabbed to death with his own ballpoint pen. It's a brutal, bloody murder." He closed his eyes and shook his head, as if the horror of it were almost too much to bear. He opened his eyes and took a breath. "OK. Now. Everyone on that council has a motivation for killing him." I didn't interrupt him to question the murder weapon. If I did, he would explain his justification to me, and this whole thing would take longer. He leaned forward, talking fast, bubbly saliva collecting in the corners of his mouth.

Now he was telling me each character's motivation. Meanwhile, I planned my afternoon. I would have a longer session of reading aloud to my kids than usual, because yesterday it had been cut short by an assembly. For PE, I would have my class run around the field once without stopping. Then we would play dodge ball.

"And then for the love interest," the would-be first novelist was saying, "because you've got to have love interest. It's a requirement, practically, right?" He didn't wait for me to reply.

I slid my eyes ever so slightly sideways to look at the wall clock. If I got out of here within the next two minutes and the photocopy machine was free, I'd have time to copy a math packet for tomorrow.

"So," the teacher said. "As they're leaving the funeral, he brushes against her, and she says, 'Was that an accident or intentional?' "

Then there was a huge pause. I said, "Is that the end?"

"Yeah," he said. "As you can see, I have it all worked out." He touched his temple. "It's all there. The whole book. Every single detail. I think it's going to really be a hot seller. And for the film, I think Rene Russo and Nicholas Cage. Ed Harris for the detective."

"Excellent," I said. I stood up and threw my paper plate away. Now I could go. I looked at the clock again. I was running out of time to do my copying.

"So, all I need is a publisher. I was wondering if you could just give me your editor's phone number." He looked at me eagerly, followed me to the trash can, waiting for me to say something.

"Actually," I said, "you need a little more than a publisher."

He snorted at my ignorance. "Like what?" He put a hand to his hip and tipped his head back.

"Well, a couple of things. Have you written it yet?"

"Not exactly, but it wouldn't take—"

"Of course. Writing the book is just a little thing, but I just thought I'd mention it. That means, oh, say, conservatively, from fifteen hundred to three thousand hours of hard work, during which time you'll have to discard your first idea because, chances are, it won't work, or it takes only thirteen pages to tell, or the characters are unlikable, or—I don't know—any combination of other possible problems. You'll have to be willing to throw out a few hundred pages, once, if you're lucky, several times if you're not, and start over from scratch. Then, assuming you can stick out this kind of torture for a couple years, you'll need a huge lucky break if you want to sell it to a publisher. After that, you'll need a *series* of miracles—the odds are about equivalent to lightning striking in exactly the same spot every day for a month—a publisher who wants to spend money on promotion and who has even the remotest inkling about what sells books, a publicist who cares about your book and has connections, good reviews in huge publications with enormous circulations, excellent public-speaking skills, lucky coincidences that get you on TV and radio, and so on and on. And then, yeah, sure, you'll probably make a million bucks. More maybe. But remember, what you have now is an idea. And an *idea* is nothing. Zip. Squat. *Everybody* has an *idea.* An idea is not a *book,* not even close. But good luck with it." I looked at my watch. "Excuse me, I might still have time to make some photocopies."

Sometimes it seems that everybody in the world believes that they have fully formed books inside them just waiting to pop out whole, ready, and most incredibly, marketable.

I had this in the back of my mind until I went home: the large number of people who believe that they already have a book, even though they haven't written anything yet. That's why writers are always writing books about how to write, I thought. Books about how to write books is a whole market in itself. As a matter of fact, I could write one myself. Of course I could. As soon as I got home, I put down my book bag and sat down at my computer. It wasn't returning to writing, really. This was another form of teaching.

I wrote:

1. Start.

For some people, this is the hardest part. They put it off and make excuses. Years go by during which they repeat again and again that they have this idea—and it's really a great one. It's all there, they say, pointing to a temple: every detail worked out, sharpened, honed, finely tuned until it practically crackles with readiness. Now all they have to do is write it. And they will, for sure, as soon as the kids go back to school or when this project is completed at the office or when the landscaping is done or the house painted or the dog spayed. Let me tell you something right here and now. If that dog had an idea for a book, it would be every bit as valuable as yours, because until the idea is on paper, it doesn't count. Worthless. What distinguishes an idea from a book is this: A book is something; an idea is nothing, a mere thought, as marketable as *I really should vacuum the living room.*

So pick a moment in time, an incident, an event, an occasion, and write it down. Choose a voice—a first-person narrator, an omniscient third-person observer—and let that voice speak. Write a scene.

2. Keep going.

Now write what happens next. This is the second most important step to producing a book. You'll need a lot of pages. What you write is not nearly as important, at this stage, as that you write. That perfect and special idea that got you going in the first place may fall apart by page three. Or you may not have had an idea in the first place. Do not concern yourself with these small details. Just keep going. You might find out what your book is about for the first time by reading what your hands are busy writing.

Warning: When you make a discovery concerning what the book is about, do not go back to correct earlier portions to align them with your new vision. Keep moving forward to the end.

3. Stop.

Reach an ending and declare the first draft finished. Do not show this to anyone. If you are working on a computer, you do not even need to print out this draft. Simply proceed to Step 4.

4. Start over.

Knowing what you now know about your story, go back to the beginning and expand upon what you have. For example, perhaps you decided on page 147 that your character has an estranged brother hiding out in Missoula, Montana, that the book was going to be about your character's search for him. You kept going after you discovered this plotline and reached the end of the first draft. Now is your chance to put the family pictures of the two brothers on the piano in Chapter 1, insert a passage in which your main character receives an undated postcard with a smeared postmark from him in Chapter 5, and so on.

Warning: Do not read the manuscript beginning at page 1 and try to determine whether or not it is good. Let me save you the trouble: It's not good. It's not supposed to be. This is a first draft, not a book.

When you've rewritten everything to the last page and perhaps added a new ending, this is the end of draft 2.

5. Start over.

Go back, beginning at page 1, and rewrite, adding layers if necessary.

Again, I caution you not to look at the book in terms of whether or not it is good. You are working toward an overall unity, making all the parts of the book—characters, plot, themes—work together consistently. When you hit upon an idea that resonates, allow it to echo throughout the book.

Later on, others will let you know their thoughts on whether or not your book is good. Some of them will have received advanced degrees in analyzing literature or in creative writing. They will have done this many times before. They might even get paid for it. However, no two of them will agree. So you can see that your own review is not only outside of the task of novel writing, it's also completely subjective and therefore beside the point.

6. Keep rewriting until you can't stand it anymore.

Chances are there will be no single moment when you say to yourself, "Now I am finished. I have fully expressed what I wanted to say. Now everything about my book is as good as it can be, and it is ready to go to a publisher." If you do have such a moment, it is probably a sign that you should go back to your old job and forget about writing altogether.

On the other hand, you might reach a stage where every time you open up your book to work on it, the words you see make you nauseated. You retch and gag every time you look at or even think about your own words. Your head throbs and aches, and you feel an overwhelming urge to close your eyes and never look at this mess of a manuscript again. You just want to get the disgusting thing out of your sight, as far away as possible. You hope you never see it again.

Congratulations! It's time to send your book to a publisher in New York.

(Do not spend too much time trying to decide which one will be right for your book. If you are going to wait to find a company that will nurture you as an author and promote your book as if its success really mattered, you might as well skip steps 1–6, not write your book, and just keep telling everybody that you could write a great book if only you had the time.)

7. Start another book.

You will have to wait a long time before you hear word one from anybody. If you decide to call them up and ask what the hell happened to that book you sent them months ago, you will probably get an automated phone system that, unfortunately, will not include manuscript tracking as one of its numbered options. If you do manage to reach an actual person who has something to do with the editorial process, he or she will sigh, as if all the books in the world were at that very moment being supported by his or her capable but overburdened shoulders. He or she will tell you that he or she can't possibly get to your book until after the holiday (whichever one is coming next). In truth, he or she may have already lost your book. At some point, you'll find this out and have to send another copy. Don't trouble yourself with trying to get in touch with the publisher.

I know what you're thinking. You're thinking, "I need an agent!" No you don't. You have enough problems as it is.

8. Repeat Steps 1–6.

Over the weekend, I wrote this up as a proposal for a new book. I rewrote it five or six times before I sent it to Howard. I saw it as a frank and forthright guide to writing a novel, and I was proud of it. I knew Howard had never seen anything like it, and I was excited, anticipating his enthusiasm.

This time I wasn't going to wait for Howard. I put a note on the manuscript that said I would be calling in two days for his comments. I sent the manuscript by Federal Express.

When I called, Howard didn't ask me how things were going or talk over with me the fact that I'd suddenly decided to write a book on writing. He started with this: "Charlotte." That was his standard greeting, this simple declaration of my name. Then came his blunt assessment of what the work needed: "More."

"More?" I said. "What do you mean? More? You mean I should develop the ideas further? Expand upon each stage of the writing process and go into detail about character, plot, dividing the chapters into—"

"Nah," Howard said. "There's already far too much on that."

"So what do you mean by 'more'?"

"When I look at this, the words 'major motion picture' don't come to mind. I don't see the words *low-fat* or *easy* in the title. And I don't see anything in here that tells me that true love and piles of money are waiting for me if I follow the book's instructions. You see, Charlotte, these are some things that would make people want to buy the book. People don't want to read a book that tells them writing is hard work and that they probably won't ever earn any money doing it. You might as well write a book called *Life Is Unfair.* Sure it's true, but we don't want to go out and spend money on a book that tells us that! Nobody wants to buy a book that says writing is a lot of work for very little payoff. Say anything but that! Say it's easy, it's simple. Say anyone can do it, make millions, and be happy."

"But that's not what I—"

"Wait. I wasn't finished."

"Oh. Sorry. Go on," I said, although I didn't really want to hear any more.

"OK. Examples: You have here—where is that? Oh, yes, here, about the first draft: 'It's not good. It's not supposed to be. This is a first draft, not a book.' Then later on, 'Keep writing until you can't stand it anymore.' These are thoughts that do not belong in a book. It may be necessary for every writer to understand these true statements on the very deepest level. But some truths are really better left unspoken, don't you agree? Now. If you can make writing sound *fun* and *good,* then you'd have something that people will want to buy. But if you don't like that idea, if you feel that your *integrity* would be *compromised* by writing that kind of a book, then you're going to need a hook, a gimmick. Writing as a road to reaching a higher spiritual plane, maybe. Or, I don't know, some technique that's different, new, maybe even a little strange but that people will want to try. You want to offer something that will make people *feel better.* Do you see where I'm going with this, Charlotte? What you have here, I mean it's—well, it's bitter. Bitter doesn't sell. Hope sells. Hope is very big. So if you could *delete* the bitter and *insert* some hope in its place, maybe you'd have something. But *this.* I can't do anything with this. I'm sorry. This just does not—"

I said, "It's a book about the *craft* of writing for beginning writers, experienced writers, stuck writers, and would-be writers. This is the thing I know best. You'll never find a more honest, to-the-point handling of—"

"Mm-hm," Howard said.

He didn't get it; I should have known he wouldn't get it. "It's *realistic!*" My voice was starting to squeak with frustration. "People need to *know* this stuff before they get all these *illusions* about success and finding and reaching an audience and—before they end up completely disappointed and desperate for something, anything to—"

"Charlotte, Charlotte, Charlotte, excuse me, but I'm going to have to stop you right there. Let's rewind here. Let's go back fifteen or twenty years. You heard then, I know you did, that writing was hard work and almost impossible to make money at. You probably heard it from a lot of people—other writers, writing teachers, editors, your parents. *Me,* even. I'm right, aren't I? And I'll bet I know what you said to those people who told you that you had chosen a tough road—years of quality work and no recognition. You said, 'Fuck you, you old fart!' Didn't you? Maybe not out loud, but that's what you felt, didn't you? And you went ahead and became a writer anyway! Because you knew that difficulty and profitability were *beside the point.* There were stories you had to tell. Why? Because *you had no choice!* The material is all there. It's in you, and it has to come out! Like it or not, easy or hard, sales or no sales, the stories are inevitable, unstoppable. Now if you want to write about *that,* you might have something I could—oh, sorry, Charlotte, one sec." Howard put me on hold.

I hated when he did that, especially when I was just about to set him straight about something important. I waited several minutes. I was about to hang up when a woman's voice came on. "Who were you holding for?"

"Who was I—well, for Howard. I was holding for Howard. Who is *this?*"

"This is Bethany. I'm Howard's assistant."

"Oh, my lord," I said.

"And you are—?" She waited for me to fill in the blank.

"I'll call back," I said and hung up. "Pretentious jerk," I said through my teeth. *"More,"* I sneered. "Hope, my butt! Like you know the first thing about it, sitting there with your telephone and your, your—*voice.* And your *assistant,* for crying out loud. Some people just really do not get it. Ever. As long as they live!"

I went to my computer. I copied the file for the manuscript onto a Zip disk. I put a sticker on it and wrote *Book About Writing* and the date. Then I dropped it into a box of disks, right behind the unfinished novel about the teacher. This wasn't the first time that Howard had killed a great idea. Lucky for me, I no longer had to worry about ideas not working out or about winning Howard's approval. I was a teacher now. I had a regular job. With benefits. I was finished with all that back-and-forth about what worked and what didn't. And thank goodness. It was satisfying to know that I had made the right choice when I quit. Maybe I got the book idea in the first place just to confirm that I was doing the right thing. And I was. Doing the right thing.

I didn't have to wait long before PRS took over. First there was a tight feeling in my throat, then my eyes filled quickly with tears that almost immediately spilled over and ran down my cheeks. I curled up into a little ball on the couch and planned never to go outside again, never to speak to anyone. Why had I ever tried to write anything? What could I have been thinking? I closed my eyes and planned to stay in this exact position forever. I should add a chapter on PRS, I thought, in some back corner of my brain. But of course, now additional chapters would not be necessary.

17

I was standing in the kitchen in front of the open refrigerator. I was about to reach for some pudding and a container of whipped cream when the doorbell rang. "Oh, great," I said to myself. "Now what?"

It was Dave. Of course it was Dave. Who else would it be?

He held up two big paper bags. "Dinner!" he said.

The nerve of this guy! How did he know I hadn't just eaten a healthy, satisfying meal with a group of my closest friends?

I looked at the bags of food and shook my head. "Not for me," I said.

"For you *and* me," Dave said. He craned his neck around the doorjamb. "I'll just put it on the table." He stepped inside.

"I couldn't possibly," I said. "For one thing, I don't need dinner. And you know, I was just going to wash my—"

He held up one hand. "Don't say wash your hair. Please. And I know you haven't eaten dinner."

"How would you know that?"

"It's too early, for one thing. And for another, your kitchen is too clean."

Twenty minutes later, I was dipping a last chip into the guacamole. The dinner Dave had brought over—burritos, enchiladas, beans, and rice—was enough food for six people. I had eaten too much. I put the chip in my mouth, chewed, swallowed.

"Some of these teachers are downright mean," I was telling Dave. He had asked about my school, the people I worked with. "You wonder how they got into the job in the first place." I put another chip into my mouth.

"Not everybody is in the right job," Dave said.

"Sure, but wouldn't you get out of it if you found that you were mean to the kids? If you realized that there was no compassion in your wizened, shriveled *heart?*"

He didn't say anything, just nodded.

I took another chip, scooped up some guacamole. "I would. I would just do something else. That's easy enough. People do it all the time. Change careers."

"Maybe these teachers were compassionate when they started, but they got burned out. Maybe all the years of being with kids has taken everything out of them until they have nothing left to give."

I put the whole chip in my mouth and chewed, thinking about this possibility. "You might think so. And I guess that could be the case with a few of them. But some young ones already seem closed off. Just no enthusiasm, no ideas, no *empathy* for the kids. Then there are teachers who have been doing it for a couple of *decades,* and they're just as kind and loving and full of energy as they can be. They know each kid inside and out. They're always noticing the details—how this child seems tired after lunch, that one might be farsighted, another one is upset about something at home because his coloring looks different. It's *amazing.*"

"Maybe you're one of those."

I twirled a chip in the guacamole. I wasn't eating it; I was drawing a circle. "I'm not used to being with people all day. I used to work at home. For a long time. At school, you have to talk so much and listen. I didn't realize I would get so sick of the talking. I also hate the meetings and the memos." I dipped the chip into the guacamole. *This is your last one,* I told myself. "I didn't realize how much each kid's differences were going to matter. To really make it work, to be truly effective in the job, you have to take each kid separately."

"Is that possible?"

"Well, *I* don't know how to do it."

"So maybe you're just not cut out for this."

"Thanks for your support," I snapped. "Could we please throw away these chips and guacamole if you're not going to eat any more?"

"I thought you liked them."

"I do. I think I just gained four pounds."

We gathered up the trash and the leftovers. While he was stuffing it into the garbage can, he said, "What did you used to do?"

"I was a writer," I said. As I said it, I wanted to put my head down and close my eyes. "I just sent my agent—my former agent, the agent I used to have back before, when I was a writer—a book. I sent him an idea for a book." I sat down again. "He didn't like it." I put my hands over my face and rubbed my eyes. *I am not going to cry in front of Dave,* I told myself firmly. "It was a book about writing. It should have been really good. You know, I had enough experience to write a few books, a whole series of books, but—"

"Maybe he's wrong."

"He's not. Unfortunately. He's right. He's absolutely right."

"Oh," Dave said softly. "Yeah. I hate when that happens." He didn't say anything for a minute. Not that I was going to change my opinion about him after all this time, but he was pretty understanding about this. Some people don't know what to say when you get a book turned down and they make you feel worse rather than better. They say things like, "Maybe you should take some writing classes," or, "I don't know how you stand the rejection. I mean, over and over again, people telling you that what you do isn't good enough," things like that. Not helpful.

Dave said, "So what kind of books did you used to write?"

"Novels."

"And why did you stop?"

I said, "Because I wasn't making enough money and—" Midsentence, I froze with my mouth open, my two hands palms up in front of me. I had heard myself say this so many times that I thought I might throw up if I said it one more time. I said, "Do you mind if I tell you the absolute truth? I mean, I know you didn't ask for this. But would it be all right with you if I leveled with you completely?"

"Uh, fine." Dave waited.

You know that thing where people confess what's in the depths of their souls to somebody they happen to sit next to on an airplane, somebody they've just met five minutes ago and will probably never see again in their lives? I was about to do something like that. Of course, Dave was not a complete stranger, but as far as my emotional life was concerned, he was about as familiar with me as the kid in the McDonald's drive-through window.

"The reason I stopped writing novels was that I got stuck. I was working on this novel, and I could not find a way to finish it. It was about a teacher. Every day I'd sit down at my desk to write about this teacher and what happened to her. And I'd think, OK, maybe I need a cup of coffee, just to get me going, you know? I'd get up and I'd get the cup of coffee and sit down again. Then I'd write a couple of sentences and just sit there for the longest time. Nothing was happening, so I'd go for a walk to start the flow. By the time I came back it would be lunchtime, you know, so I'd think, after lunch I'll really get going. I needed money, so when I couldn't stand it anymore, I took a freelance editing job. I was thinking I'd work on the book in the morning and the job in the afternoon. Of course, they wanted the work right away, so I decided to finish the work completely, get the money, then have all this free time to work on my book.

"OK, so you know what happened. I finished the project and took on another one. All this time, I had this bad, bad feeling that I couldn't get away from.

"It was like, let's say, you're taking a class in high school. You signed up for it because you just adore this teacher. You get the assignment, the big thing you have to do for the grade, and you know the teacher is going to love yours the best. You're going to turn it in early just to please him, just to make him happy. But somehow you don't seem to get started as soon as you thought you were going to. And now you don't feel as enthusiastic about the project as you thought you would. More time passes and you can't seem to get going. Pretty soon, it's the day the thing is due, and you haven't even started. Now your project is not only not going to be early, it's going to be late! You tell the teacher it will be ready tomorrow. You promise him. The next day you go back and ask for one more day. Then you have to stop going to class to devote all your time to the project. Somehow, though, you feel so bad about not doing it that you *can't* do it. Now you can't go back to class because you can't be in that room with the teacher's huge disappointment at finding out what a worthless loser you are. Suddenly, to your shock and horror, you find that you're failing the class. You've never failed anything before, but the combination of poor attendance and missing work has done it. Before you know it, you're not going to school at all. You're not even going to graduate. You hide out, hoping everyone will forget all about you. You move to another town because you don't want anyone to see you and know how you failed.

"Not finishing the book was like that," I said, looking at him. He opened his mouth to say something, but I went on. "Or it was like, let's say, you borrow all this money, and you can't pay it back and you, or, wait, no—you *stole* this money. You didn't mean to, but it was a lot of money, from someone you love, and you—" I stopped myself. I was getting way too carried away with analogies. "Never mind. I think you get the idea. Anyway, I tell everyone I quit because I wasn't making any money. Of course I really *wasn't* making enough money. So it seems like an acceptable enough reason. I say I needed more to live on. But that wasn't the reason I switched jobs. Money is nothing. My deepest desire in this world was to finish that book. I would have given anything I had just to get the whole story down, fix it up so it was right, make it work, and—" I bit my lower lip and opened my eyes wide, trying not to cry. "I had this character, and I was trying to—I just couldn't—"

Dave blinked and said, "Have you said this to anyone else, about why you stopped writing? Your sister, for instance?"

"No!" I said. "Absolutely not!"

"Your sister's like the favorite teacher in your story, maybe."

"Oh, listen to you! The psychologist!"

He shrugged.

"So," I said. I wiped a hand over each eye. I was OK, just a couple of tears had leaked out, not a major flood. I wiped them off on my shirt. "What about you? What do you do, anyway? Computers or biotech, right?"

Dave shook his head. "I'm a psychologist."

"You're kidding!" I said. "What! You should have told me that before I—that's creepy. You just let me tell my deepest secret without—"

"I'm sorry," he said. "I didn't know it would matter so much. I wasn't listening to you as a psychologist, just as a friend."

"Sure," I said. "What about that thing you said about my sister?"

"Anyone could have—"

"Yeah, right. And why are you home all the time? What are you doing living *here?* In these apartments? Aren't you making big bucks from being sympathetic about people's problems?"

"I'm living here because my house burned down."

I gasped and put my hand over my mouth.

"Remember that big fire last year?"

"Up north when all those houses—"

He nodded.

"Oh, no!" I said. "That must have been awful! You didn't—was there any—I hope nobody—"

"No one was hurt. Is that what you're trying to ask? We'd been evacuated."

We? Suddenly a little jolt went through me, a shock at finding out that Dave could be part of a *we.* It was even more of a shock than the news that he was a psychologist. "And you're not married, and you have no kids because you devoted so much of yourself to your—"

"I'm married. Separated. No kids."

To my surprise, my stomach dropped in disappointment. "Where's your wife?" I blurted out.

"The fire was harder for her than it was for me. She's a doctor. She specializes in infectious diseases. She's working in Africa now. Have you heard of an organization called Doctors Without Borders?"

I nodded, amazed. "The group that a French doctor started, those physicians who go to devastated countries and work for no pay?"

"That's the one," he said.

"She's working for them? That's so—I mean—"

"We were having a crisis in our marriage at the time of the fire. And she felt that all the economic issues involved in HMOs had undermined her purpose as a physician. Doctors Without Borders was something she'd wanted to do for a long time. We had decided to separate anyway. Then the house burned down, and she took off almost immediately."

"I'm sorry. You must be—"

"It was pretty hard for the first couple of months. But to be honest, it's been kind of like a rebirth, in a way," he said, nodding to himself. "I've closed my regular practice to new patients, and I do some volunteer work."

I looked at him, waiting for him to go on. He smiled at me, and at that moment, he looked sort of like a new baby, bald, a little pink, and vulnerable. In high school, when everybody had long hair, I didn't know that Dave's ears stuck out. Now his ears and the lumpy shape of his skull were exposed to the world. For a second, I had an urge to put a blanket over him or something.

"Well," I said. "Gosh. Now my big problem doesn't seem that bad. Writers get stuck sometimes, right? So it happened to me. I mean, it's not as though my house burned down or I'm living in a war-torn country with hardly any doctors. I mean, *geez.* What's my problem anyway?"

"A little perspective never hurts, I guess," he said. "But that doesn't diminish the magnitude of your own—"

"Anyway, thanks for listening to me say all that—." I stood up.

He stood up. Then he took two steps forward and hugged me. I had this sudden vision into the future. I could see what was going to happen as clearly as if I had outlined the plot myself: His wife was not coming back. She was going to get involved with some other doctor, an Italian or a Spaniard, whom she was working with in Africa. Dave and I would become dear friends, leaning on one another through transitional phases in our lives. And even though he had not, at first, appealed to me as a—

The phone rang.

Dave let go of me, and I picked up the phone. It was my sister.

"Oh, Em, can I call you back? I was just—"

"Just quickly, any more kids have to go home today?"

"Two more had lice," I told her.

"Did they check you?" she wanted to know.

"Yeah. I was clear. But I keep scratching my head and worrying." Dave was looking at me. "Anyway, right now I really have to—"

"Olive oil," she said. "Put olive oil all over your hair, then put a shower cap on and sleep in it. The oil smothers them. They spread easily, and they're hard to get rid of."

"Oh, great," I said. "Just what I need. So I have to sleep with all this grease all over my hair in a shower cap? I'll have to wash it about seven times tomorrow before I go to school. Listen, I have to go."

"It's a good conditioner. OK, I just wanted to know what you're doing this weekend."

"I don't know. Why?"

"Come over for dinner Saturday."

"What am I bringing?"

"Salad, dessert, and whatever I need you to pick up at the last minute. OK? See you then."

I hung up. "My sister," I said.

"You have lice?" Dave said. "I mean, in your classroom?"

"Yeah. It's very common. *I* don't have any. Personally. I got checked. This is the fourth round of cases. So we're not out of the woods, yet. I was clear *today,* this *morning,* but what if, since then, one got on me? I keep thinking I feel something creepy." I scratched my scalp. "My sister said to put olive oil all over my scalp."

"Sounds like fun." Dave had discovered another Styrofoam container on the lamp table, and he went to the kitchen to throw it away.

"Thanks for dinner."

"Thanks for joining me. You may like to be alone, but I need people around. I can't stand sitting there listening to myself chew."

"That's a different kind of being alone. I know. Of *course,* I know. Ha! I could write a book!"

Dave laughed. "See you soon."

"See you."

Nothing like a discussion of head lice to put a damper on a romantic moment. I guess we would have to continue that next time. After Dave left, I covered my hair with olive oil. I didn't have a shower cap, so I found a plastic bag from the Gap that worked. It had a drawstring. "Hm," I said, looking at myself in the mirror with a navy blue bag on my head. "One size fits all!" I pulled the string tight and tied a knot. I went to bed and fell asleep almost immediately. It was eight-thirty. Unfortunately, the crackling of the bag kept waking me up all night. At four, I gave up on sleeping, got up, and washed my hair.

18

In the staff room the next day, I was trying not to eat a frosted brownie on a paper plate that someone had left sitting on the table with a sign that said, "Eat this." There were always leftover treats from kids' birthdays that were really hard to resist.

"No," I said out loud to the brownie.

"Excuse me?" said a kindergarten teacher, Phyllis. She had a kind of screechy voice that sounded like a small, angry bird.

"Oh," I said. "I was just trying not to eat that delicious-looking brownie."

"Why not?" said Phyllis glancing over her shoulder at me from the coffee machine. She must have weighed close to 200 pounds, though she was about five four. "I'm sure you've earned it."

"Full of fat and sugar," I said. "Not to mention carbohydrates."

"Oh, come on," said Phyllis. "Life is to enjoy."

I picked up the plate and the fork and started shoveling it into my mouth. It was as good as it looked, gooey and soft with smooth, rich frosting—not too sweet and with just a little bite of chocolate bitterness. There were even big, chunky chocolate chips mixed in.

The lounge was filling up with teachers now. I scraped the last glob of frosting off the paper plate with my finger, then stuck it in my mouth. I folded the paper plate in half and shoved it into the garbage can.

Bernice Fitz walked in with a steaming mug, looked at the table, and glared around the room. "Where's my brownie? Who moved my brownie?"

My face started to burn.

"Uh-oh," said Phyllis's bird voice. She started backing away from me, as if being close to me were dangerous, as if I were emanating radioactivity or something.

I said, "Oh, I'm sorry. I didn't know anyone had claimed it. I thought—"

"Claimed it? It was mine! I brought it from home. Mother baked them, and it was the last one."

"Your mother?" Holy smokes. "I'm sorry. I just thought—There was this sign on it, saying 'Eat this,' which I, wrongly, I see that now, took as an invitation to—"

"Ha! Talk about seeing what you want to see!" said Bernice to her friend Liz Muñoz. She held up the napkin with the writing on it: "Eat this—and you won't live to tell the tale!" The paper plate must have been covering part of it.

"Oh, my gosh," I said. "I sure wouldn't have touched it if I'd known it was *yours.*" Somehow these words came out sounding kind of insulting, though I honestly didn't mean them to.

"I went to take a short phone call and you just snatched my personal food that I brought from home. It's not some crazy free-for-all around here, you know. We respect one another's property!"

"I have apologized several times, Bernice. I don't know what else I can do, short of getting the recipe from your mother and making you a new batch."

"Mother would *never* give out her recipe!"

"Well, you're out of luck then." I pivoted on my heel and walked fast out of the lounge.

In the work room, I tried to swallow away a lump in my throat and this sinking feeling about working in this school. I was experiencing something related to homesickness, longing to go to my apartment, my computer, and sit there alone in dead silence. For a moment, I considered calling Dave and bursting into tears. I even thought about calling Howard before I remembered that I was mad at him. Instead I put paper into the copier. I put my originals on the feeder and pressed Start.

I went back to my portable. I guess when I made this move to a new career, I was thinking about teaching kids to read and not about angry adults yelling at me about brownies. Teaching reading was difficult enough. Having to deal with the other teachers pushed me right over the edge.

I put a math sheet and a baggie of pre-counted lima beans on each desk.

The bell rang, and I went out to get my class. I led them into the room. "Quickly and quietly, boys and girls, please take your seats and listen while I explain what we're going to do. You have ten beans in your bag."

"I don't like beans," one of the Ryans shouted out.

"We are not going to eat the beans. We are using them for math. For each problem, I want you to use beans for counting. Let's say your problem is two plus two. You would take out two beans, then two more." I showed them by very deliberately taking out two of my beans from a baggie. I took out two more.

"Then you'd count your beans. Everybody count these with me, please. One, two, three, four. Wow! OK. Two plus two equals four."

"I knew that!" said Seth. "I already *knew* that!"

"Seth, please!" I said too harshly. "Thank you. Then you write down your answer next to the equals sign. No talking now. I'll come around and help you." I started showing Amanda what to do with her beans.

"Mrs. Dearborn?" said Grace. "I don't—"

"Grace, I'll be right there. I'm going to work with the Grasshoppers, then the Ants—"

"But I don't—"

"Grace? Is it an emergency? Or can you try by yourself until I get there?"

Grace hung her head.

"Thank you. I do appreciate your patience."

"What?" said Patience. "Me?"

"No, Patience. I was talking to Grace. Grace, by the time I get there, you might have already solved the problem yourself. You might surprise yourself."

Grace didn't even pick up her pencil. I moved on to Seth.

"I got it, I got it," Seth said, waving me away.

"But I—" Grace had her hand up again.

"I'm almost there," I said.

I was at Amanda's desk when there was this sound of liquid hitting a hard surface at close range. Grace had just thrown up all over her desk and the two desks on either side of her. Several kids screamed. Most had jumped up out of their seats, either to get away from or to see the vomit. "Ew," said a couple of kids.

I went to Grace. "Boys and girls, I want you to listen to me now. Everyone go to the blue carpet right now. NO TALKING." For once, they didn't talk but hurried right over to the carpet. "Now,

Grace, first we're going to wash your hands and face. Good girl. Right over here. Plenty of soap on your hands. That's it, sweetheart." I wiped her face with a wet paper towel. "Now, can you walk by yourself, sugar pie?" She was woozy, so I put my left arm around her shoulders and held her right hand with my right hand.

"Boys and girls, I need to go next door to Mrs. Thompson for a minute. *Best behavior!*"

"Marilyn," I said from her doorway. "Grace just vomited. I need you to watch my class while I get her to the office."

"Send them over," Marilyn said. "Have them bring whatever they were working on."

Math papers, pencils, and beans in hand, my kids went over to Marilyn's classroom.

I walked Grace to the front office. "I need a custodian right away, please. One of my students just vomited."

"I'm so sorry, Charlotte, he's left for the day," Cindy said. "He was feeling a little under the weather himself. His helper didn't come in today."

"Uh . . ."

"You got it. You're on your own." She shrugged. "Sorry."

"Please call Grace's mother. She needs to go home."

"Will do." She picked up the phone.

"Grace, you're going to lie down in the nurse's office until your mom gets here."

Grace nodded.

I got her settled in the nurse's office. I tucked a blanket around her on the narrow cot. A paper pillowcase crunched under her face, which was completely drained of color. "OK?" I said. Of course, she wasn't.

Grace started to cry.

"Your mom is going to take you home, honey. I know you feel bad. Soon you'll be in your own bed." I patted her skinny shoulder and pulled a wastebasket close to the cot. "If you think you're going to throw up again, just lean over and use this, OK?"

At the reception desk, I said, "Is there anyone who can sit with Grace until someone comes for her?"

"Ha!" said Cindy the receptionist. "If you'll answer the phones!"

"I hate to leave her in there all alone," I said. "I've got to clean up the vomit and get my class—"

But Cindy was answering the phone. "Corona Vista Elementary! Good morning! This is Mrs. Roland. How may I help you?"

I went to the custodian's room for supplies: paper towels, sawdust, a mop and bucket, air freshener. I had this heavy feeling, as though I were carrying a tremendous invisible load on my back, my shoulders, even my head. The room was little more than a large closet. It had no windows. I leaned against the wall for a minute, while I gathered the strength I needed to go back to my room. I was tempted to turn out the light, close the door, and sit there in pitch darkness until everyone went home. Instead, I gathered supplies and headed back to the pool of barf that waited for me in Room 14.

"You had to clean it up *yourself?*" my sister said on the phone that night. "One custodian for the whole school all day?"

"Two. But the other one had a family emergency and is out all week."

"Good thing you've had experience with my kids' barf. Can you imagine how it would have been if you were a novice?"

"Even worse than it was, probably. The governor should be a little more worried about the custodian-to-student ratio, if you ask me. Ever since class-size reduction, there's also been a reduction in services, and it just—"

"My kids' school is the same way. What about you? You feel all right?"

"So far, so good."

I didn't start vomiting until about four-thirty the next morning. This was the first time I had been sick since I started teaching, so I had to think about what I was supposed to do. I called the district office and left a message on the tape. Then I threw up again and lay down on the bathroom floor. Nice and cold. I woke up there an hour later, freezing and covered with sweat. I threw up again and then after a short rest on the floor, crawled to my bed, climbed up, and got in. Then I had a terrible, urgent desire for water. I wasn't sure if I could walk to a faucet. Now I was hot and sweating. I stood up, reeling a minute, steadying myself on my bedside table. I went to the kitchen, got a glass, filled it with water, drank, threw up.

At seven, Emily called. "You're sick," she announced.

"Yeah."

"I knew it. I'll get the kids to school, and then I'll be over."

I was asleep when Emily got there, but she had a key. She opened the windows, straightened up, put ginger ale in a glass with ice cubes.

"We were going to type their new stories on the computer today," I said without opening my eyes.

"The sub will do it. Or if she's lame, you can do it tomorrow. Or Monday. Did you have a parent coming in?"

"Seth's mom."

"Is it in your lesson plan?"

"I'm not that good at, you know, writing stuff down. I mean, I *plan* and everything, but I don't always—Can you get me the phone, so I can talk to my sub? And I need my address book, so I can cancel Dylan for today."

"Call Seth's mom, while you're at it. Do you have her number?"

"I'll get it from Cindy."

I made all the calls, then started worrying. "The sub sounded flaky. I hope they don't get too wild."

My sister said, "They probably will, but that's part of the deal, you know."

There was a knock on the door. Emily looked at me. I turned over. She went to the door.

I could hear Dave's voice from the bedroom. "I saw your car. I was worried. Are you sick?"

"I'm Emily," I heard my sister say. "Charlotte's twin sister. It's OK, a lot of people mix us up. One time my husband even—oh, you don't want to hear all that. She's got stomach flu."

"Dave," Dave said. "I live down there. Can I do anything?"

"Nah," Emily said. "Just a stomach bug."

I was mentally sending Emily a message: DON'T LET HIM IN. I must look awful, and I probably even smelled bad.

"Come on in," Emily said.

When he was at the bedroom door, I held up one hand. "I'm OK," I said.

"Sure?" said Dave.

I nodded

"OK. I'm going to work for a few hours. You can page me, if you want anything, groceries or whatever."

"No, really," I said. "I'm fine. My sister's here, and—"

"I'll check on you tonight."

"Thanks," Emily said. "That would be great, because I've got three kids, and they'll be home by then." She showed him out.

"Charlotte," she whispered when she came back in. "Why didn't you tell me."

"Tell you what?"

"That things were, you know, *progressing* with you and Dave!"

I closed my eyes. "You're imagining things. He's married. His wife is in Africa." I fell asleep.

Dylan called. I had been asleep when the phone rang. Emily was gone. "I have all these math problems!" he said. "How come you're not *here?*"

I said, "I have the stomach flu, Dylan. I called your mother. I thought you would stay in Aftercare today."

"Nobody told me!"

"So you're home by yourself?"

"Yeah."

"You wouldn't want me near you. I promise. Are there any neighbors you can—"

"I stay by myself all the time. But I don't *get* these problems," he whined. "They're division, and I don't *get* division."

"Division is the opposite of multiplication. You just—"

"Everyone keeps *saying* that! I'm telling you, I don't get it!"

"Dylan, would you listen to me for just a minute? On your desk is a multiplication table."

"I'm doing DIVISION! Didn't I just say that?"

I didn't reply right away. I had never met a child who spoke to adults this way, so I didn't always know what to do. I remembered what his parents were like and that he was home by himself, and I tried to be understanding.

"Dylan, I will work with you, as long as you're polite to me. Do you understand that? I know division is hard for you, but it will get easier. Now, I want you to apologize, then maybe I can help you over the phone."

"Sorry," he said quickly and without any sincerity.

"Try again," I said. "And I want to hear what you're sorry for."

There was a barely audible grunt of annoyance. "I'm sorry I yelled. And was rude. *OK?*"

"I accept your apology. Now. Are you at your desk?"

"Yeah."

"Tell me what the first problem is."

"OK. There's a six outside the little thingy and then there's a forty-eight inside."

"So, I want you to read that, 'Forty-eight divided by six.' What you're going to do is divide the number forty-eight into six equal parts, right? Does any of this ring a bell?"

"No."

"Try this. Six times something is forty-eight. Do you know what that number is?"

"Six?"

"Six times what is forty-eight?"

"Times six. I just *said* that."

"Look at the multiplication table I gave you. Find forty-eight. Now find a six on the left side. Got that? Now go straight up above the forty-eight and you'll find the answer."

There was a long pause. "Eight?"

"You got it. Write that down on top of the bracket. Got that? We're going to do four more problems, then I want you to do some on your own."

We did the four problems. He did the next one by himself and got it right. Then he did two more and got them both wrong. I closed my eyes and said, "Let's try something else. Remember those buttons we were working with last time?"

"Yeah."

"Get those out, please. I want you to count out seventy-two buttons, divide them into groups of eight. You may put the phone down while you do it."

"OK, hold on."

I fell asleep while he was dividing the buttons. Then he said, "OK, I did it. But what does that have to do with—"

"How many groups are there?"

There was a pause while he counted. "Nine."

"That's your answer."

"Oh."

"Say it to me. 'Seventy-two divided by' . . . Come on, Dylan."

"Seventy-two divided by eight is nine."

Somehow we made it through the rest of the problems.

"Now I have to make a poster about the book I read."

"When is that due?"

"Monday."

"OK, let's work on that next time. What else?"

"Reading test on the last two chapters of *Island of the Blue Dolphins.*"

"Did you bring home your work sheets?"

"Yeah."

"I want you to reread those chapters and answer the questions again. *Write out* your answers and don't look at what you wrote last time until you're finished."

"OK." I could hear him rummaging in his backpack.

"Dylan, I'm going to hang up now, and you're going to do the reading by yourself."

"That's not going to work!"

"Dylan, remember what we talked about at the beginning of this phone call?"

"Right, but I mean—"

"You can do this. Call me when you've finished reading the chapters, and we'll go over the questions together."

"No. I'm not doing it!"

"Dylan."

Quietly, he repeated, "I'm not doing it."

"OK."

Long pause. "My dad isn't going to like this."

"Dylan, I won't be able to force you to do this. I'm sorry I'm sick and I can't be there. Now if you choose not to do your homework, you'll have Mrs. Fitz and your test score to deal with."

"I could read it out loud to you on the phone," he said on the verge of tears.

"Is that what you want to do?"

"Yeah."

I didn't want to do this. But if a child says he'll read out loud to you, it's very hard tell him not to, no matter how much you want to pull up the covers and close your eyes. "Fine," I said. "Go ahead and read me those chapters. I'm all ears."

I lay on my side and listened to the last two chapters of the book. He would know if I fell asleep because he would hear the change in my breathing. And he wouldn't hear me say, "Start that sentence again. Now, what does that mean?" Every once in a while, when I felt myself drifting off, I sat up and drank some ginger ale. By the time we finished going over the questions, the ginger ale was gone, and it was dark outside.

"OK, that's it," Dylan said. "I have to go now."

"Are your parents home?" I said.

"Yeah, I just heard the garage door."

"Good," I said. "Dylan, I want you to go over those questions and answers one more time before you go to sleep tonight."

"Bye," he said.

I didn't throw up anymore, but I didn't want to stand up or move, either. "Good," I thought, "I'll lose some weight."

At eight, there was a soft knock on the door. I stood up in my dark bedroom and went out to the living room to open it.

Dave was standing there. "I called a couple of times, but your line was busy. Soup," he said, holding up a paper bag.

"No," I said. "I can't." I stepped back so he could get in.

I shuffled back to my bed, while he opened drawers and cupboards in the kitchen. My hair was dirty and uncombed, and I was wearing a pair of old pajamas that I was sure made me look even fatter than I was. But I still felt too sick to care very much. I got back in bed. After a minute or two, Dave came into the bedroom with a bowl and a spoon.

I held up my hands. "No, thank you."

"It's just broth," he said. "One spoonful."

I sat up and ate a few spoonfuls. "Good. Mm. You didn't have to do this." I scooped up some more. I finished half of it and handed him the bowl. "Thank you." I lay down again and closed my eyes. "I bet you're good with your patients."

"We call them 'clients.' Yeah, this is my best skill, too, serving broth from a deli. It's how I built my reputation."

I heard him wash the bowl in the kitchen. I thought he was going to leave then, but he came back into the bedroom. "Charlotte, I have to tell you something. I've read all your books."

"You have?"

"Yes," he said.

"Well," I said, "you're probably the only one in the world, beside my sister. My mother, maybe."

"We went to high school together—you probably don't remember—and I read each book as soon as it came out."

"I remember. Of course I remember. I just didn't want to say anything in case you didn't remember."

"Oh. Same here. So. Well. I'm glad we got that out of the way."

I stayed home another day, which I spent on the couch sipping water. Saturday morning, I took a shower, got dressed, and ate some plain toast. I felt OK, a little shaky maybe, but not bad.

There was a knock, and I knew it would be Dave. Now, instead of holding still and staying silent and hoping for him to go away, I found I was hurrying to open the door.

Dave was wearing a ratty sweatshirt that had faded from navy to purple, a pair of shorts, and the same sandals he had on the day he ran into my car. No wonder I was surprised to find out that he was a psychologist. "All better?" he said.

"I think so."

"I'm going to get a donut and some coffee to take to the beach. Want to come?"

"A donut? I don't think I—"

"Yeah, you're right. Maybe you better—"

"I'll come with you, though."

"Good."

Without Dave telling me, I knew the donut place he was thinking of. It was VG's in Cardiff. I'd known people who had moved away from here who made annual pilgrimages from the north or the east primarily for these donuts.

We went in Dave's car, which was an old brown Nissan, sort of like the car I had replaced. There was a winter sky, dark gray and not sure whether it wanted to be fog or rain. Dave turned the wipers on a couple of times to wipe away dots of moisture, but then turned them right off again. The donut place was full of people, families mostly, it seemed to me, parents around my age with young kids or even teenagers. But then, that's the way the world always looks to me, as if everybody else has a spouse and kids. I wondered if that was the way Dave felt. Then I realized that to the other people in line for donuts, Dave and I would seem to be a couple. And I didn't mind too much that they would think that.

I got some tea with sugar, and Dave got a couple of maple bars, some donut holes, and a coffee. Some people can just eat and eat and never gain any weight. We drove a block to the beach to a wet rock in the fog. Halfway through my tea, I felt I might be able to manage the donut hole Dave offered me. "I don't want to start barfing again," I said, taking it cautiously between my thumb and forefinger. I took a little nibble.

"The vomiting with these viruses usually lasts only about the first six hours or so. You were probably over that day before yesterday."

I thought about this. "You're right. I was." I ate the donut hole. "How did you know that? You're a psychologist, not a doctor." Dave shrugged. Then I drank some tea and ate two more donut holes. "I think I'm over it," I said.

"You look better," Dave told me, peering at my face. "As a matter of fact, you look better every time I look at you."

"Thank you," I said. "So do you." It just slipped out. He laughed.

19

I went back to school Monday. I wore a pair of olive cargo pants with a pink sweatshirt. I tied a floppy pink chiffon scarf around my hair and knotted it at the side. I thought maybe the pink color would cancel out my sick pallor. I added a pair of dangling troll-doll earrings with fuschia hair. Those ought to perk up my look.

The topic of the staff meeting on that morning was homework. I had strong feelings on this subject, so I would have to try to keep quiet today. The principal was talking about last year's standardized test scores. Apparently a school district nearby had done better than ours. "So you want to present very real consequences for failure to turn in homework assignments on time. This is a serious issue. We are training responsible students, who need to be held accountable for their work from first grade on. Feel free to take away recess from the student who doesn't live up to expectations. Use that detention. That's what it's there for."

There was a sinking feeling in my stomach. Just be quiet, Charlotte, ignore this.

"We have a reputation to build here," he went on. "Those math and reading scores need to be higher."

"Excuse me," I said. Everyone turned to look at me. "I'm just wondering, what does detention for late homework have to do with math scores? It seems to me that the emphasis ought to be on what we do in the classroom, not what the kids do on their own at home. Maybe there are some things we could cut out here at school to make more time for math or reading or in-class writing assignments."

"Mm-hmm," he said. "Thank you, Charlotte. If you feel you're wasting time in the classroom, then certainly, you ought to change that." He went on to talk about something else. "Now, next week, we're all going to have to—"

"Excuse me. Again. Sorry," I said. I couldn't let this go, even though I knew I was going to get myself in trouble. "It's just—I'm thinking there's time we spend on things other than reading and doing math that we could—for instance, videos and coloring isn't the best use of—"

The media teacher straightened up. "Now wait a minute! When I have the kids color those bookmarks, it helps their fine motor skills. And the videos I show tie in with books!"

"No, I mean, gosh, I didn't mean to criticize *you,* of course. It was just an example of, I mean, if you want to improve reading scores, certainly you should spend a lot of time reading. Same for math. Right? And if we get it done here at school, then there's really no need to load them down with homework. It was just an example of how—" A lot of teachers had turned around to glare at me. "Sorry, it was a bad example, never mind." I slid lower in my chair.

"She's right, you know." It was Rick, who was sitting on the other side of the room.

I put my hand up to tell him to stop, forget it, never mind, but he wasn't looking at me.

"I've read several studies that demonstrate that loading elementary kids with homework is not only not helpful, it can be *detrimental.*"

The principal paused, pursed his lips. "Maybe you two would like to share those findings with the district office. May I go on?"

I could tell Marilyn was trying not to look at me. She would have a word with me later.

Sure enough, ten minutes later, as I was getting ready to bring my class in, Marilyn came into my room. "Charlotte, listen," she said, "you're going to have to stop doing that."

"Hm?" I said innocently, erasing my already clean board. "Doing what?"

"Don't voice your opinion at every single meeting. Let *him* run the show and do what you want in your own classroom. That's the beauty of it. It's your own little world in here. And your days will be a lot more enjoyable for you if all those other teachers like you."

"Right," I said. "I know. I see what you're saying."

"Good, because I just don't know how you're—"

"I get it," I said, cutting her off. "Excuse me, I have to go get my class."

For the rest of that day and the next, I stayed out of the teachers' lounge. I ate my snack and lunch in my classroom, while my kids were out. I came in early Friday, at about six, to do my photocopying and laminating, and to use the paper cutter in the work room. But even though I didn't see the other teachers that much, I still had a bad feeling about my job, a creeping despair, a growing fear that I could not make this work.

Friday afternoon, my heart lightened a lot, especially once the bell rang at 2:30. I took my bus riders to their lines and waved to my walkers and their parents. "Have a great weekend!" I kept saying.

As soon as my kids were all gone, I straightened my room quickly, turned off the computer, and switched out the lights. I grabbed my purse and my bag of work for over the weekend, locked my door, and headed for the parking lot.

In the car, on the way home, I was thinking, Maybe it's going to be all right. Human beings are very adaptive. I can learn to fit in. I just have to practice. These things take time. What did I expect, that everything would fall into place immediately? That's ridiculous. Really, I'm doing fine, considering I have a brand-new job and I'm working with people I hardly know. Marilyn's my friend. She seems a little gruff and judgmental sometimes, but that's just her manner. She likes me, really she does. And one good friend is really all you need. Once those other teachers get to know me, they'll like me. We'll get really close. Before you know it, we'll be doing stuff together on the weekends and chatting together during breaks. It will be great. I'm a nice person. Good sense of humor. Loyal friend. I have nothing to worry about.

I pulled into my parking space at my apartment building. I was setting the parking break when I saw Dave coming down the steps of the building. There was someone with him, a woman. I didn't think it was anyone who lived in our building. I had a sinking feeling in my stomach then. I plastered a smile across my face and got out of my car. "Hi," Dave called from across the parking lot. "I want you to meet somebody."

I wanted to run upstairs into my apartment, go inside, and slam the door, but I didn't. I walked over to them.

"This is my wife, Kathy," Dave said.

"What a surprise!" I said.

"Nice to meet you," she said, shaking hands. Hers was small, bony, and cool. She smiled at me. She was smaller than I would have thought. I guess I pictured someone big and strong going to Africa to take care of people. She was slight and pretty. She had dark blue eyes and worry lines across her forehead and between her pale brows.

"Dave told me you lived here," she said. "Small world. You're his favorite author."

Again novel writing seemed small and unimportant compared to what she did. "I don't do that anymore," I said. "I'm a first-grade teacher. I teach children to read. And do math. And develop—"

"He told me." She smiled at me. "That's great!"

"Kathy decided to come back until after the holidays."

"Wonderful!" I said. "Hey, I've got to get going. It's so nice meeting you. Have a terrific weekend!"

Hope is a funny thing, I thought. You hardly know you have any until it's swept away and you feel your insides shred with its loss. Before I had even made it upstairs to my front door, a few tears had already spilled down my cheeks. I put the key in the lock and bit my lip and tried to stop the tears at least until I was inside. I went straight to the bathroom for tissues.

As I was blowing my nose and sopping up tears, this thought came into my head: *Three months into it, her new life was falling short of expectations.* I tried to think where this sentence was from. Did I make that up just now, or had I heard it or read it somewhere? Maybe it was from a book. I couldn't place it. I wiped more tears that had started to pour down my cheeks. I threw the tissue away and took two more.

Twice over the weekend, I ran into Dave and Kathy. Saturday I saw them zoom into the parking lot on bikes. Dave looked all sweaty and happy. I managed a wave but no words as I hurried to my car on my way to Emily's. Sunday they were coming up the stairs as I was going down. Kathy was carrying a bag from the donut place. I could smell the donuts from several yards away.

"Want to join us for donuts, Charlotte?" Dave said. "I got some donut holes for you."

"Thanks," I said, "but I can't."

"Come on. Please?"

"Really, no thank you," I said, and I rushed to my car, as if someone were expecting me, as if I had somewhere important to go.

Monday morning, as I was waking up, a feeling of dread weighed me down, cold, damp, and heavy as an old tarp left out all night in heavy fog. I didn't want to open my eyes, choose my clothes, and go to my job. When I pictured the staff room and the other teachers' grim disapproval of me, I thought I would rather do almost anything else than go there. Then I had this thought:

> *Desperate for guidance and camaraderie, she turned to her colleagues for advice.*

These words came into my head fully composed, as if I were reading them, as if I had memorized them from something. What was that sentence from? It sounded like something from a novel. What novel? I certainly didn't remember reading it anywhere. Still, it seemed to come from something I knew well. Was it something I'd read somewhere, or maybe a narrated film I'd seen? I couldn't place this sentence either. As I was brushing my teeth, I kept repeating it to myself: . . . *she turned to her colleagues for advice.* I still couldn't place that sentence. I thought about my own colleagues, and the way they could freeze you out at a meeting or in the lounge. I had never turned to my teacher colleagues for advice because some of them had been so disapproving and unfriendly that I was afraid of them. It would be nice to have colleagues who would help you. Too bad I couldn't ask mine for help.

Could I?

Could I even bring myself to admit to them how I was struggling? Could I confide in them and ask for their advice? I stopped brushing and thought about this for a second. It would be embarrassing to tell people that I didn't know what I was doing. But feeling embarrassed certainly couldn't be any more miserable than feeling like an incompetent failure. What could it hurt? The other teachers might really be able to tell me something that I didn't know. It was worth a try.

I stood in front of my closet to choose my clothes. I didn't exactly feel hopeful, but at least I had a purpose for today. I took out a pair of black leggings, a T-shirt, a long shirt, and a pair of hiking boots. In San Diego, there aren't many days cool enough to wear hiking boots, so I tried to take advantage of this time of year as much as possible. I tied a floppy flowered scarf around my head to keep my hair back and put on a pair of dangling book earrings. Quickly I ate some cereal and drank some orange juice, found my bag of corrected spelling books, and left for school.

The morning was the usual struggle, me yelling and trying to teach a lesson, while the kids talked and squabbled among themselves. I kept looking at my watch. If you think recess is an oasis of free time to kids, to me it had become the focus of my entire being. Over and over, I pictured the way I was going to sprint out of this room, the minute, no, the second, the bell rang. Finally it did.

As soon as all my kids had run out the door to the blacktop, I went straight over to Bernice's room. If I was going to do this, I might as well try the scariest, meanest teacher in the whole place. I was eating a Power Bar on the way. My thinking was that if I ate something full of healthy ingredients, I wouldn't be as hungry, that I wouldn't be tempted to eat so much junk all day.

"I hope she's there," I whispered to myself in the hall. "Oh please, oh please, oh please be there!"

"Talking to yourself again, Charlotte?" It was the music teacher.

I laughed as though this were funny.

Bernice was just stepping out through her door about to bustle off somewhere. "Wait!" I called from ten yards away. "Hold on!"

She looked at me, startled.

"I wanted to talk to you."

"OK," she said, looking down at me over her half glasses as though I were a mental patient begging for more medication before my next scheduled dose.

"I wondered if you could give me some advice." I was at her door, standing next to her now, out of breath from walking so fast. She stood there, looking at me, waiting for more. "I need help, and I thought, I don't know, maybe, could you help me?"

She sighed. There was probably something she really wanted to do, like go to the bathroom or sit down with her friends for a minute and commiserate about behavior problems. Instead, she said, "Come in." She pushed her door open again, and I went in.

I closed the door. Bernice sat down at her desk. I pulled a student chair over and sat on it. Because the chair was so low, I was looking up at her. She folded her arms across her round stomach. She was wearing a peach-colored pants suit and running shoes. She had bunions that hurt her if she wore the wrong shoes. Her lipstick matched her outfit, I noticed. "Advice on what? What's the problem?"

"On teaching. I'm terrible at it, absolutely hopeless. My class is unruly and disobedient. And they're not getting any of the lessons, because I can't get them to pipe down long enough to hear anything I say!" I noticed I was holding a clump of my hair on each side, as if to demonstrate that I was ready to tear it out.

Bernice nodded. "Go on."

"That's it. So, I thought, you've got a lot of experience, and I was hoping, you know, that you might be able to help me, tell me what to do, tell me how to do this better."

"I see." She pressed her lips together.

"So can you?"

"I can try. But we've only got a few minutes now."

I might have known. You level with someone, completely humble yourself, and they don't have time for you.

Bernice said, "Why don't you come to dinner tomorrow night, and we'll talk about it?"

"Oh! Thanks!" I said. "I *really* appreciate that. It will help. I just know it will!" I touched her forearm. I almost wanted to hug her, but Bernice wasn't inviting any further contact. In fact, she got up and started walking toward the door. I followed her.

She nodded. "Sure," she said and opened the door to let me out.

"Really!" I said. "Thanks!"

Bernice actually smiled at me then. She said, "Don't worry. It's probably not as bad as you think."

Or it might be far worse, I was going to say, but Rick walked by then eating an apple on his way back to his room. "Oh, hi, Charlotte," he said. "I was thinking we could get our classes together again soon. What do you think? Maybe in December, we could do some kind of holiday activity."

"Sure," I said. "Good idea." Maybe mine would learn to behave by then. I was going to say thank you again to Bernice, but she was halfway down the hall by now, on her way to something she had to do before her class came back.

* * *

I was following Bernice home. At the moment, we were just exiting our third freeway. It was dark, and we had been driving for fifty minutes. She does this twice a day, I kept thinking. How does she stand it? We got off on a busy street where there were a lot of fast-food places. We drove east for several miles, then turned north, drove a minute or two more, then went east again. We turned off on a small road called Calle Ruiz, then again on another road whose name I didn't see. We drove straight uphill for a while, then turned off onto a small lane called Acacia. "No Outlet," a sign informed me as I parked. The house was down a steep driveway and seemed too small for five children, but maybe it went back farther than I could see from here. Two boys were playing basketball in the driveway.

"Here we are!" Bernice said.

"Wow!" I said. "That's a long drive to do twice a day."

"You get used to it. This is my son Jeff," she said. A boy who was a lot taller than I was came over to shake my hand. "And this is his brother Jack. Jeff is in tenth grade. Jack is in eighth. Boys, this is Miss Dearborn."

"Charlotte," I said.

"Nice to meet you, Miss Dearborn," said Jack.

"Nice to meet you, Miss Dearborn," said Jeff.

"Charlotte," I said. "Really. Call me Charlotte. Nice to meet you both."

"Give me the homework update," Bernice said to the boys.

"Did it," said Jack.

"In progress," said Jeff, not looking at her.

"Jack, I'd like to see your work. Jeff, go back in and finish. You can play when it's all done."

Jeff groaned. "I can't work all the time, you know. I'm a *kid.* I've got to have some fun!"

Bernice said, "The sooner you get going, the sooner you'll be finished."

"If I hear that one more time . . ." said Jeff.

"I wish I didn't have to keep *saying* it," Bernice said sharply.

The two boys went inside. We followed, but as they went right to the bedrooms, we went left to the kitchen. The refrigerator was covered with magnets. One had a cartoon of a woman with her hair standing up straight, glasses askew, a stack of papers and books toppling off her desk. "Is it time for recess yet?" it said at the bottom.

From another room came the sound of the television, Oprah wrapping up the day's program. "Girls!" Bernice shouted. "Homework?"

"Mom's home!" someone hissed. The TV was silent.

"Hi, Mom. How was your day?" Three girls walked into the tiny kitchen, which was suddenly crowded.

"Fine, thank you," Bernice said. "Girls, this is Miss Dearborn."

"Charlotte," I said. "Just plain old Charlotte is fine." I shook hands with each of them.

"This is Jennifer. This is Julia. And this is Jill."

"Wow," I said. "I'm going to have trouble with all the J's. I just know it."

"No, you're not," Bernice said firmly. "You're a teacher. We learn names fast. The oldest has the longest name, Jennifer; the youngest has the shortest name, Jill; and Julia is right in the middle on both age and name length."

"Got it," I said.

"Girls, if you've finished your homework, I'd like to see it. If not, go do it. Right now." The girls left the kitchen.

Bernice took a gigantic casserole dish out of the refrigerator and put it in the oven. The temperature dial was already set to 350. "It's Jennifer's job to turn on the oven fifteen minutes before I get home," Bernice explained. "So it will be hot."

"What a system!" I said. "What can I do to help?"

"Nothing. It's all done. I do most of my cooking on the weekends." She pulled something wrapped in foil from the freezer.

"You sure are organized! How did you figure all this out?"

"Out of sheer necessity. My husband was a firefighter. He was killed in a fire here in town. Jill, our youngest, was just a baby. I wasn't working. I'd taught a couple of years before the kids, but I hadn't worked in a long time. At first, I just fell apart. I could not cope with the loss of this man. I had counted on him for absolutely everything. I don't think I got out of my nightgown more than a couple of times during the first two months. My mother and our neighbors fed my kids. I could hardly get it together to go to the store. Every time I thought about the number of lives I was now responsible for, I sort of folded in on myself and either collapsed into sobs or lay down and went to sleep."

"What happened?" I wanted to know. "What changed?"

"The refrigerator did it!" she said, and she tipped her head back and laughed. "One day I looked into the refrigerator, and the milk was bad. There was a stinky old watermelon with white stuff growing on it. Jelly was smeared on the shelves. There were old take-out containers in there. In about one second, I went from being a depressed slob to being hyperactive and organized. I got a big garbage bag and threw all that old stuff away. I cleaned all the shelves with ammonia. I took a shower, got dressed, went to the grocery store. I organized that fridge like you would not believe. I had plastic boxes for lunch foods, snacks, fruits, and so on. I was downright mean about putting things away in the right places. That was my first step. Then I started on the kids' rooms. Plastic boxes for everything—sweatshirts, socks, pencils, stuffed animals. Oh, it was a sight to behold, let me tell you! The next month, I started subbing. When Jill was old enough for preschool, I went back to teaching full-time. Having five kids and no husband got me organized real quick!" She laughed again.

"I guess it would," I said. "Wow. You've had a lot to handle."

"That's right," she said. "But it's been a good learning experience. I don't take any"—she lowered her voice to a whisper—"crap here *or* in my classroom. I have a system for everything, and I follow it. I'll be right back. The salad's in the other fridge."

She went out a back door. I looked at the front of the fridge some more. There was a grocery list that had been printed on the computer with several items circled. There was a practice schedule for the piano on a plastic board that had each of the kids' names on it. A grease pencil dangled from a string. I checked who had practiced today: Jack, Jennifer, and Jill.

Jack came in now with his homework. He was so tall he made the refrigerator look small.

"Your mom's in the garage," I told him.

"Oh. You the new first-grade teacher?"

"Yes, I am," I said. "I've been having a hard time with my class. I asked your mother for help, and she's going to help me figure out how to do things better."

Jack rolled his eyes. "Good *luck,*" he said.

Before I had a chance to ask him what he meant, Bernice was back. "Let's see that homework."

Jack handed over his work. Bernice put on the glasses that were dangling around her neck and leafed through the papers, making an occasional comment. "More detail on these two answers. Where are the rest of these problems? Oh, here. This one's hard to read. Is this all you had to do for Spanish? Then it ought to be neater. Just fix all that up, please, and I'll look at it again."

Jack left the room, shoulders drooping wearily. Bernice took her glasses off.

"You check their work every night? A lot of kids would have a hard time with that." I knew my sister didn't do this. She helped them with the things they couldn't figure out themselves, but otherwise she left them alone. If she tried to insist that they do something over, she'd be in for a fight.

"A lot of kids wouldn't be happy with what I do when their grades slip, either."

"What's that?"

"Give them extra homework for the next grading period and make them stay in their rooms and do it after school and on weekends."

"That's, well, gosh," I said, "that's pretty severe."

"Life is tough. The sooner they face that and learn to work hard, the better off they'll be. And it works," Bernice said. "They get good grades."

Julia came in. "I don't get these," she said to her mother. "And don't yell at me."

"Fractions?" Bernice put her glasses on again and looked over the paper. "We went over this last night."

"I still don't get it."

"Did you ask Jennifer or Jack?"

"They said they had too much homework."

"Tell Jennifer I said that if you don't have this by dinnertime, she won't get to watch TV this week."

"Great, Mom. Now she's going to hate me."

"No, she'll hate *me.* Now scoot." Julia left the room. "I try to get them to help each other as much as possible. It benefits the teacher even more than the learner."

I said, "I'd be terrible at this. I really would. You should see me in the classroom. I never know what to do."

"What's your main problem area?"

"Classroom control. And teaching. The room is noisy. The kids talk all the time. They interrupt each other and me—"

"Don't let them get away with that!" Bernice snapped, wagging her finger at me.

"I tell them not to, but it doesn't—"

"Scare them! They should be afraid of you! Above all, don't be *nice* or they'll walk all over you! Be mean! If they don't listen, then send them to the office. Be tough. Be firm. Let them know you're in charge!"

"If I did that, half of them would be in the office all the time. They'd miss everything."

"That's where you're wrong. Do that a few times, to a couple of your worst kids, and you'll see they'll all get the message. What kind of discipline system are you using now?"

"Uh . . . well, I was . . . I guess I expect them to behave. If they don't, I kind of, well, talk to them about it."

"No, no, no," she said, shaking her head. "Wrong. Here's what you should do. When I taught first grade, I had clothespins with each of their names on them. They start out in the morning clipped to a smiley face. If they do something wrong, move the clip to a sad face. If they do something else, move it again to a picture of a clock, which means a time-out. Next it goes to a picture of an envelope, which means you're writing a note to their parents. If the bad behavior doesn't stop, I put the clothespin in a drawer, out of sight, and send the kid to the principal's office."

"Oh," I said. "And what do I do when they do something well?"

"What?"

I got flustered, embarrassed. I'd said something stupid again. "You know, do you have something to—say, you know, maybe a reward for good behavior?"

She looked at me for a long moment, as if wondering if I were slow-witted, or as if maybe she should start over from the beginning. "Sometimes I say, 'Good job,' " she told me. "That should be plenty. Most of these kids get entirely too much in the reward department, if you know what I mean. Ever been to one of their houses?"

"I see." I nodded.

One of the boys set the table, while another poured the drinks. There was a chart for whose turn it was to do everything, including cleaning the bathrooms, vacuuming, and dusting; doing laundry; and mowing the lawn. I had to stare at the charts for a long time before I could figure out what happened if the kids didn't do what they were supposed to. It was weeding on Saturday. Apparently it worked because Bernice had a neat house and well-behaved children who did their homework.

Dinner was lasagna, salad, and garlic bread. During the meal, Bernice told me that she cooked two casseroles on Saturday and two on Sunday. She washed three heads of lettuce, tore it up, and packed it in plastic bags. "Those bags of prepared salad you see in the store are way overpriced," she told me fiercely. Friday nights she made hamburgers on the barbecue, and she gave one of the kids money to go to the McDonald's at the end of the street for french fries. Saturdays they had homemade pizza. Sunday was spaghetti night. "That's my food system," she said.

After dinner, while Julia and Jeff were doing the dishes, Bernice took me to the garage, where she had some teaching supplies that she wasn't using. She was going to give me these. She got a big shopping bag with handles from a very neat collection of them. Her shopping bags were arranged by size on hooks in the garage. Bernice dug through a set of clear plastic bins full of teaching materials and handed me things like a bag of clothespins to write my students' names on and clip to something to show who was in trouble. "Thank you, Bernice," I said. "Great. Super. Thanks a lot."

"You also need a signal that everybody should stop what they're doing and listen to you. I use a bell. But, oh, look at this—perfect!"

She handed me a buzzer, the kind you sometimes see at a meat counter in a grocery store. I pressed it. It rang so loudly that I made myself jump. "Oh, my goodness!" I said. "That's horrible!"

Bernice smiled. "Gets their attention."

She gave me two whole bags full of stuff—flash cards and behavior charts and even a book on classroom discipline and, of course, the buzzer. "Thank you so much!" I said. "It's so nice of you to help me out like this."

"Glad to do it. You've just got to learn how to be firm, be tough, and not let them get away with anything."

"Right," I said. "And thanks again for dinner. It was great meeting your kids. Tell them good-bye for me, will you?"

"Sure will," she said. "You drive carefully now."

The next day the two Ryans got into a fight. I separated them. "All right," I said loudly and firmly. "That's it! I would like you two boys to march right down to Mr. Dean's office this minute. Your behavior is absolutely unacceptable! Now!" I was being tough. Bernice would approve. As they left the room, I called the front desk and told the receptionist to expect them.

Almost immediately I started to feel guilty. I should have been the one to go to the office. I was the one in charge, and I kept allowing these things to happen. I worried that the principal would be too hard on the boys. He might call their parents and bring about some kind of severe punishment at home. Really, it was my fault. If I didn't have this entire class to worry about, I would have gone down to the office myself and walked them back to the room. I would have hugged them and said, "Don't do it again, OK? Be nice to each other."

The two Ryans were back within twenty minutes. They didn't seem even the slightest bit upset.

I took them both aside. "Boys, did Mr. Dean talk to you about why it is wrong to push and hit?"

The boys shook their heads.

"He didn't?" I said. "Oh. Well, did he tell you to apologize to each other?"

They shook their heads again.

"He didn't? What did you talk about, then?"

"We sat down for a long, long time, but he didn't come."

"So you never saw Mr. Dean."

They shook their heads. "So who told you to come back?"

"Mrs. Roland."

"What did she say?"

"She said, 'I need those chairs, boys. Get back to class.' "

"OK," I said. "Now, I want you to listen to me. Everybody in this classroom has to be safe all the time. Do you understand that? I cannot have you in this room if you're going to hit or push. Got that?" The boys nodded solemnly. "Also, I expect you to treat each other with kindness and respect. I want you to shake hands and apologize to one another."

"Sorry," they said in unison. One boy put out his right hand, and the other put out his left. Briefly, they held hands. They looked at me.

"Fine. Now, I don't want this to happen ever again. *Ever.* You may go back to your seats now."

As I was finishing, the noise level in the room was reaching a crescendo. "All right!" I yelled. "You have work to do!" The kids barely acknowledged me.

I pressed Bernice's buzzer. I jumped and so did a lot of the class. Six kids ran to the door. Amanda clapped her hands three times. "Fire drill, boys and girls," she announced. "Line up quickly and quietly!"

"No, no, no," I said, waving my hands. "Back to your seats, everybody. This is my new attention buzzer, not a fire drill. Amanda, what did I tell you about being the teacher? Will you please try to remember that? Thank you." Patience was in tears. "What's the matter, Patience?"

"That noise scared me! I want to go home!" I had to hug Patience a long time to get her settled down. While I was busy calming Patience, the two Ryans got into another fight. When lunchtime finally came, we had hardly completed any of the work I had planned for the day.

20

I stopped by Brooke's classroom after school. Her class seemed to be doing really well. In our first-grade meetings, she was always showing us long stories that her class members had written. Maybe she could give me some help.

I knocked. "Come on in!" she called. She was standing on a chair, hanging up paintings. She was wearing a denim jumper with a white T-shirt under it. She had blonde hair that she styled with electric rollers every morning. She could have been a model for Teacher Barbie. "Hi, Charlotte. Good thing you're here. Could you hand me that bag of clothespins on my desk? Thanks. How are things?"

I gave her the clothespins. "Not great," I said. "Honestly, I'm having a hard time with my class. I was hoping you could give me some advice."

"Sure. What's the problem?"

"Lots of things. Some of the kids aren't reading. Some of them are really not getting even the most basic number concepts.

They're noisy and don't listen. I don't know what I'm doing wrong."

"OK. I have two words for you: *Use parents!* Let's start with the nonreaders." She jumped down off the chair and went to her file cabinet. She pulled out a thick packet of photocopied pages. Then she went to the bookshelf and took out a set of books. "Ask the parents of each nonreader to come in. Tell them their kid isn't performing up to grade level. Tell them to do this stuff every night at home."

"Really? But, I mean, aren't I supposed to be the one to—"

"If they don't want to do it or if they say they don't have time, just say that the kid might have to be retained. That always gets them where they live."

"I don't want that kind of worry hanging over them. I mean, I just wanted to maybe try to restructure—"

"Hold it. I'm not done. For the kids who need math help," she said, pulling open another drawer, "use these manipulatives and these packets. Here. I have another set." She handed me a lot of Ziploc bags filled with connectable plastic counting pieces in different colors. "Same thing as with reading. Call in the parent and send packets home with all the kids who need help."

"I see, but what about—"

"And let me tell you what else I do. If you have some kids who are a little slower getting work done, get a parent or two to volunteer every day. Set up a corner where they can work with kids, getting them caught up with daily work. Set up a reading corner for a parent to work individually with kids who need reading help and a math corner. Lots of the moms and some of the dads really love this. One of my dads this year is a pilot, and I have him come in for an hour a day whenever he's not flying."

"But what are the other kids doing while these kids are getting help? Won't they miss important lessons? And doesn't it get noisy for the other kids when they're trying to get work done?"

She looked at me blankly. "In my room, we sometimes have five or six things going on at once. They have to learn to *focus.*"

"Sure, but I don't know if my kids would ever—"

"I put on a little music while they work, and they're fine. They do great. And whatever they don't get done at school gets added to their homework. They know that. They expect it."

"Gee, I don't know. Five or six activities and music? I have quite a few who have trouble working quietly without talking to each other. It seems like if I had even more going on in the room, they'd probably—"

"Kids talking to each other is not a bad thing! The more they help each other, the better. Some of my kids collaborate all the time. I encourage that!"

"I thought the goal was to get them all working independently."

"Another important skill is to be able to find help when you need it. Looks like you're working on that yourself!" She smiled at me. She even had blue eye shadow like an old-fashioned Barbie.

I nodded. "OK, well, thanks. You've given me a lot to think about."

"Sure, Charlotte. Any time. The first year is always tough."

"Thanks. I was starting to feel that I was the only one who didn't take to this naturally."

"My mother and grandmother were both teachers. My older sister is a teacher. I sort of already knew what to do before I got here."

"You must feel really comfortable in the classroom."

"Oh, yeah." She nodded.

"Thanks again."

"No problem."

I went home. I could not see myself calling in a bunch of parents or sending more work home with the kids. This would only make things worse, I felt sure. But I didn't know what else to do.

Looking at the problem from a different angle, a simple startling solution came to her. This sentence popped into my head as I tossed my keys onto my desk. What did it mean?

Was I giving myself advice now? And what problem was I supposed to look at from a new angle? My teaching, probably. But just thinking about it again made my shoulders sag. Pick something smaller, I thought. There were a lot of smaller problems to choose from. I could try looking at Seth's reading problems from a new angle. I'd already tried every approach I could think of—flash cards, practice with me, practice with his mother, practice with other kids. He didn't even seem to want to look at the books. What hadn't I tried? I'll *be* Seth, I thought, Seth reading a book. I picked up a magazine, opened it, and sat down on the couch. I looked at the letters inside. Then I put my head on my hand and looked out the window. I looked at the magazine again, then at the ceiling. I read a sentence and put one hand over my eyes. *Oh, dear,* I thought, *oh no!* How could I have overlooked something so obvious! I should have tried being Seth a long, long time ago, the first day of school!

Over the weekend, I went to Emily's for dinner. As we were washing the dishes, I told her about these sentences I kept hearing in my head. "It's as if my brain is writing a novel without me."

"So, what's it about?" Emily wanted to know.

"Emily, you know I don't talk about projects before I've finished two drafts!"

Emily looked at me. "It's not a project, Charlotte. You said you heard some sentences in your head. What project? You gave up writing!"

"Yeah, I know. I just don't feel like talking about it, that's all."

"Who brought it up?" Emily said, looking at me in the most offended way.

I couldn't say, "I didn't know that I didn't want to talk about it until I started talking about it. I think it's about me! It's a story about me struggling in my new career." For one thing, that wasn't much of a plot, and for another, I had spent many years insisting that my fiction was not autobiographical. I didn't want her to laugh, chuckle, or even smile slightly at the obvious irony in that. But most of all, I didn't want to discuss how badly things were going for me at school. Once I got started, I wouldn't be able to stop. Details and stories about every single kid in my class would come pouring out of me in an endless flood. I'd be in tears within a few minutes, and I wouldn't be able to stop. Emily would have to send the kids upstairs to watch TV while we both faced up to the terrible mistake I'd made deciding to become a teacher. Emily would feel that she had to somehow rescue me from my job and my own miserable mess. I'd feel guilty unloading it on her. The whole time, I'd be scrambling to find a way to convince her that it wasn't really as bad as I'd just made it seem. So it was better, really, not to talk about it at all, but to just try to find some way to get through it without doing too much damage to the kids in the process.

"How's Dave, by the way?" Emily asked, trying to change the subject.

"Dave? Oh, Dave. Well, he—I haven't seen him in a while. His wife is back from Africa, and they're—"

"His wife! You're kidding. You must have been completely—"

"What?" I said. "I told you he was married. Anyway," I said, "about that other thing, it doesn't happen that often. The sentences." Before she got a chance to ask any more questions, I said, "Ever hear of a kid who was farsighted, I mean who needed reading glasses but could see distance just fine?"

"Sure," she said. "Two kids on this street have that. Trouble is, schools and pediatricians only test for nearsightedness. You have to take them to an eye doctor for reading glasses. Why?"

"A kid in my class is really having a hard time with reading. While I'm working with him, he looks at the ceiling, he closes his eyes, he looks out the window. I think it's hurting his eyes to focus on the print. It seems like he needs reading glasses."

"That is incredibly perceptive!" my sister said. "I bet you're the best teacher that school has ever had!"

"Hardly," I said. Time to change the subject again. I held up a wineglass. "I'm going to wash these by hand."

21

It was December, and I wasn't doing any better with my class. For a day, I'd try Bernice's tough love method, but by the time I went home I found it hard to like myself. Then a couple of times I called in parents to work with children who were behind, but as I expected, the extra activity in the room made it harder for the rest of the class to focus; the child who was getting help in one area fell behind in whatever we were working on while the parent was there.

One morning my class was doing math when there was a knock on the door. I opened it, and there was Rick with his entire class of sixth-graders. I suddenly remembered we'd made an appointment. I gasped and put a hand over my mouth. My face and ears burned. I said, "Did we plan to make candles today?"

Rick said, "Did I get the day wrong?"

"No, *I* goofed," I said. At that moment, I realized that Rick was exactly the kind of teacher I wanted to be: The kids loved him, and he was always in charge. Right now, his class was lined up outside, patiently waiting to come in. Meanwhile, in the few seconds that my back was turned, Seth had knocked over a whole jar of counting beans, Amanda and Patience had started arguing over a hair clip, and at least three other children were plaintively calling my name.

I put my hand into the pocket of my overalls and pulled out a scrap of wrinkled paper, today's lesson plan torn from my desk diary. "Gosh! I don't know how I—We have a first-grade safety assembly in five minutes!" I said to Rick. "I'm *really* sorry!"

"No problem," Rick said. "We'll reschedule." Sudden changes at the last minute did not derail Rick the way they did me. He led his class back to their room.

"Boys and girls!" I said to my class. "Line up for assembly! Now! Hurry! No, put down your beans first! OK, let's go."

While a real-live firefighter demonstrated how to stop, drop, and roll, I worried again about what to do about my teaching. I was always reading about disillusioned people leaving careers and starting over—surgeons who quit medicine to make quilts or lawyers who left their high-powered firms to run bed-and-breakfasts. After the switch, these people always said they had never been happier. I had taken comfort in the belief that if I gave up my dream to do something else, at least my new job would be easier than my old one. Finding out that it wasn't felt like falling for somebody's mean joke.

After school, I went to Rick's sixth-grade classroom. He was redoing a bulletin board: a snowman border around the students' essays about December family traditions.

I said, "I'm really sorry about this morning."

"No problem," Rick said. "My class got a little more time to prepare for their social studies test. I'm sure they were grateful."

"I don't think I'm ever going to get the hang of this."

Maybe Rick heard the slight tremble in my voice, because he stopped to look at me.

I said, "My kids are all over the place. They talk all the time. They don't do what I tell them. They're getting a lousy deal for their first-grade year. I'm no good at teaching."

"You can't say that," said Rick.

I straightened, a spark of hope lighting in my chest. Maybe someone believed in me, even if I didn't believe in myself.

Rick pinned up the next essay. "It's only December, too soon to know."

I said, "The other first-grade teachers don't seem to have the kind of problems I do. And some are almost twenty years younger than I am!"

"Age has nothing to do with it, of course." He twisted in a push pin.

"I just want to know how everybody else does it," I said. "I just want to be in on the secret of how to get kids to listen and learn." I folded my arms and waited as though I would not leave the room until I got the information I was after.

"Hm . . ." He thought a minute. "Have you ever been in a play? Teaching is like acting. You choose what parts of your personality you're going to let the kids see." I waited. He aligned an essay but didn't go on.

"I've never been in a play," I said.

"OK, you're always yourself—there's no getting away from that—but you kind of let some parts take over, and other parts retreat into the background. You know what I mean?"

"No, I *don't,*" I said. "That's the problem. All you guys keep telling me these different—"

"I'll give you an example," Rick said, calmly cutting off my complaint. "Today during math, one of my kids was playing with some beeping electronic toy. I did the heartbroken-father thing."

"What's that?"

He gave me a look—hurt, sad, let down—and something clenched within me, as if I had disappointed him irrevocably. "Like that," he said, flashing a smile before turning back to his board. "You don't want to make a big deal about something like that or the kid gets a lot of attention, and *you* look like a jerk. Without a word from me, the boy walked up and handed over the toy."

"You're kidding, right?" I said. "You don't honestly mean that every teacher but me has a stockpile of effective *looks* to use at any moment?"

Rick considered. "It's not just looks. Sure, what *comes across* is looks, voice, body language, sure, all that external stuff. But its *source*"—Rick tapped his temple with his index finger—"is what you're thinking."

"Are you saying that I could get a roomful of rambunctious first-graders to sit down, be quiet, and pay attention if I looked at them the right way, if I had the right *thoughts?*"

Rick looked at me. "No? You don't think so?"

I shook my head. "Most of the time, they don't look at me *or* listen to me. I don't think you realize what I'm up against. They're *first*-graders!"

"I see," Rick said. "And here I am up in sixth grade, so I guess I don't—"

"Of course you don't! Your students are almost twelve years old!" I said.

"Some already are." Rick nodded. "Practically a different species!"

"There must be something else I can try, besides *acting!*"

"There *must* be," Rick agreed, picking up another essay. "Think back to September," Rick said. "Haven't things settled a little bit since then?"

"No," I said. "Every day is hard. Really, really hard."

"Oh," he said, startled. He thought a minute. "You know, it throws me every time you do that. Most people, you know, lie about how well they're doing." Before he spoke again, he pinned up two more student papers. "There are people who are just really horrible at teaching," he said.

"Oh, great! That makes me feel just—"

"I may be wrong, but I don't think they're the ones who worry about it all the time, who volunteer to tutor after school, who—"

"Yeah," I said, "and that's another kid I can't seem to—"

"Is there something outside of school that you just love to do? Sometimes I get my best ideas about teaching when I'm not thinking about teaching."

"I don't see how not—"

He wasn't going to let me interrupt him now. "Personally, I love to surf. Sometimes you get these transcendent moments. You know? There's the board, the water, and you. When it works, when it's right, there's that wave holding you up, and it's as if you have no choice but to be carried upright on top of this force of moving energy. You feel this peaceful, this perfectly harmonious, I don't know, *balance.* It's as if this is what you were born to do and here you are doing it. Now. For those few moments on that board on that wave, everything is just right: Life is perfect. You can't think about anything else but the water, the wave, your board, staying up. There just isn't room in your brain to wonder about how your life's going or what else you can do for that kid in your class who really should be reading better or that wrong thing you said in the last staff meeting."

"Those are exactly the things I worry about!" I blurted out.

"Everyone does," he said, as if this were obvious. "But not while surfing! And this is the weird part. Sometimes a solution to the very problem you're not thinking about seems to pop into your brain while it's off duty." He shook his head in wonder, then seemed to remind himself that I was still there. "Is there anything that *you* love doing?"

"Me?" I said. "Sure, I guess so."

"What?" He looked at me. I realized that the conversation couldn't continue until I told him what it was.

"Oh. Well. Making up stories," I said quietly. "It's nothing like surfing, of course, but I love making up stories. Loved, I mean. I don't do it anymore."

"Why not?"

"I couldn't make a living at it, and I—"

"Oh," he said, swiping the air with his hand. "A living. Well. Money. Heck, money is nothing. Now, teaching is what I was born to do. I actually get homesick for the classroom during vacations. But do you know what I do every summer?"

I shook my head. "Surf?"

"I'm a bartender at the racetrack. I've done it for years."

"Really?"

"Yep. I've got two girls in high school. They're expensive. But I wouldn't quit teaching because the salary isn't enough. Because teaching is what I *am.* I don't do it for the money."

"Hm," I said. "So surfing is the thing that gives you solutions."

"Usually," he said. "It's just something you might want to try. Not that you have to try surfing, necessarily. I just mean, you know, try *not* trying so hard."

"I'll try," I said. "Not to. I mean, I'll try not to try." He laughed. "So do you have any other suggestions?"

Rick had turned back to his bulletin board. Over his shoulder, he said, "For behavior problems, you mean?"

"And for getting them to follow directions and just, you know, anything to help my *teaching!* I want this to work! I want to be good at it. I *have* to be! I've got twenty kids who need to learn reading and math, maybe the most necessary skills for their whole lives! They're counting on *me,* and I'm not coming through for them!" I threw my hands up and let them slap down against my thighs. When he didn't answer right away, my voice got higher and more insistent. "I want to go in there *tomorrow* and have them pay attention, behave, and *learn something!*" I was dangerously close to tears. "What should I *do?*"

There was a long pause during which we were both embarrassed by my outburst. "Every teacher gets frustrated sometimes," Rick said quietly. "Really. Every single one. If there were any fail-proof tricks to keeping order and motivating kids, believe me, I'd have told you months ago."

I exhaled and couldn't think what to say next.

He looked straight into my eyes and didn't look away. His steady gaze caused sparks of attraction to shoot through me. Suddenly, it seemed that our almost nonexistent relationship was about to blossom. You just never know when something like this is going to happen, I thought.

"OK, well, I guess I'll figure something out," I said. Then when he kept looking at me, I said, "Maybe you could come over for dinner sometime."

Rick started to answer, "Thanks, I—"

"How about tonight? I promise my cooking is better than my teaching!" I smiled, but I could still feel the threat of tears prickling behind my eyes.

"I appreciate the invitation," Rick said quickly. "But between school and my girls, I'm pretty busy. Too busy, really. Sometimes I wish I—"

"Sure. I understand." I turned quickly and headed out the door.

"Hang in there, Charlotte," he called after me.

"Yeah, thanks," I said.

I was getting everything wrong in this place. Too late, I realized what Rick's look meant. He was just letting me know that he sympathized, even if he couldn't help me. What was I thinking? Whatever I did in this school seemed to make my situation worse.

At home that evening, I picked up the *TV Guide.* I looked at the listings for all the movie channels. I wanted to see something old and black and white in which the main character, a single woman, sank into the dark, cold depths of despair. I wanted to watch how, through a combination of hard work, native intelligence, and some lucky breaks, she resurfaced into warmth, light, and love by the end of the film. But there wasn't anything like that on TV tonight. This was my favorite kind of story, the kind I had tried for in my own novels.

For me, the first draft had always been the hardest part, developing a group of characters, trying out various personal histories and experimenting with different problems for them. For a long time, it would appear that I wasn't getting anywhere. Then after many difficult, bad days, usually when I was about to give up, my characters suddenly seemed to develop lives of their own. Something as simple as the invention of a quirky gesture, a particular way of speaking, or a small physical flaw could be a turning point. Seemingly subtle adjustments to a character would cause a chain reaction of changes in the other characters as well as the plot. All the bits and pieces that, until this point, had seemed unrelated scraps would become one big, complex picture, a 1,000-piece puzzle magically rattling into a unified whole.

Once that key bit of information revealed itself, dialogue among my characters came to me almost as easily as if I were eavesdropping on a conversation. My own plot surprised me with unexpected turns. I almost started to think of the characters as real. At the grocery store, I'd reach for a flavored coffee that one of my characters liked. I'd want to tell one that her favorite band was coming to town. I'd have to remind myself that I'd made these people up. When I finally got to that point, writing the story hardly seemed like work.

The last novel I'd worked on before I quit writing hadn't reached the stage of sprouting legs and walking by itself. I had stopped writing it before I got that far. With the main character of that abandoned book, Janet Greenhill, the teacher, I had been shooting for a modern Jane Eyre, a solitary and plain woman, composed and self-possessed and with deep passion and a defiant spirit. I knew the outer details of her life, where she lived, what she did for a living, a bit about her early life. But I had not found my way into her inner life, her own dreams and thoughts, the things she wore, her early memories, the unexpected turns her life would take as soon as I got all the details right.

So far, my first year of teaching felt exactly like a first draft—awkward, painful hard work with no payoff in sight. If I could just phone Miss Greenhill for advice, she would know how to get through to my unruly, uncooperative class. Unfortunately, she was a figment of my imagination. See what I mean about my characters starting to seem real?

If she *were* real, Miss Greenhill would have a radically different approach to teaching. To begin with, she would use a different seating plan, and she would never allow several groups simultaneously rotating to various activities around the room, the way I was supposed to. Instead, she'd have everyone working on the same task at the same time. Rather than raising her voice and getting frazzled when the children misbehaved, she'd *lower* her voice, compelling them to listen. Unlike me, she would never teach in overalls and T-shirts. Instead, she would wear dresses and skirts, neat, plain ones, the kind of thing you and I couldn't find in stores if we tried. But, of course, Janet Greenhill wasn't real.

As I thought about my character, I heard another one of those disconnected sentences in my head, the ones that sounded as if they came out of a book:

> *Frustrated with the results of applying others' strategies, she was forced to reinvent herself.*

I liked the sound of that, the idea of someone reinventing herself, but who was she in the first place?

I went to my desk, opened my notebook, and took a pen from the jar. Across the top of the blank page I wrote the date. Underneath that, I wrote all the sentences that had recently popped into my head out of nowhere:

- *Three months into it, her new life was falling short of expectations.*
- *Desperate for guidance and camaraderie, she turned to her colleagues for advice.*
- *Frustrated with the results of applying others' strategies, she was forced to reinvent herself.*
- *Soon her former role models were following her example.*

That last one just came to me as I wrote. I looked over what I'd written. What was this? Where were these sentences from? What came to mind was the character I had been thinking about, the teacher from my novel. It seemed that Janet Greenhill, my character from the novel I didn't finish, was trying to reach out and write my life. I turned the page of my notebook. I would continue and see what else she had to say. This had been one of my methods for generating new material when working on a novel. I would write a monologue in the voice of a particular character, sometimes leading myself into new areas of the book that I hadn't thought of yet. I wrote:

Introduction

My name is Janet Greenhill. Officially I have been teaching school for forty-three years. By my own count, it has been much longer.

Until the age of seven, I was schooled in the state of Kansas. I was the only child of a university-educated lawyer and his young wife, Frances. (She was only seventeen when they married.) I don't remember much about my father, as he died of influenza at age thirty. Two years later, my mother remarried an adventurous farmer who wanted to try his luck farther west. I was six and kept a journal of our trip to our new home. My mother was, by the time of our departure, pregnant again, and I wanted to be able to one day recount our journey to my younger brother or sister. This simple journal marks my first early consciousness of myself as instructor to those who would come after me. My stepfather purchased land in the Central Valley in the state of California. As our mother was often unwell and there was no schoolhouse in the region, the schooling of my four younger half-sisters and four younger half-brothers fell to me. My few years of schooling in Kansas and my mother's tutelage after our arrival in California served as the basis of my early training. (Later I was to return to Kansas to receive a university degree and formal teacher's training.) At thirteen I began to teach my brother Edward, six, my sisters Mary, five, and Elizabeth, four, to recognize letters, write, and read as appropriate for their ages.

Books were scarce for my young pupils. When my stepfather

delivered a ream of newsprint to our little schoolroom, purchased on a supply-buying trip, I took it upon myself to write history and story books for each child. My guides were the set of my mother's high school books brought from Kansas. This practice has served me well. I am now the author of seven reading books used in the California public schools as well as two state histories, one for fourth-graders and one for high-school freshmen. I have spoken in our own state capitol building about matters of concern to both teachers and students as well as before the United States Congress. I have advised three presidents on education. As I look back over my lifetime of work, nothing has been more rewarding than watching a child thought to be dull or difficult transform into a reader or a young mathematician, much in the way a seemingly ugly, dry, brown cocoon will, under the right circumstances, open to reveal a bright, multi-colored butterfly. Surprise!

My brother Edward went on to study economics at the University of London. Frederick, who came after Elizabeth, is now a doctor in the city of San Francisco. Stephen is a lawyer in that fine city, and young Everett, once the baby of the family, now manages the financial accounts of several large California ranches. Three of the girls, Laura, Rebecca, and Patricia, became teachers like myself. Elizabeth has been employed as a nurse and has also published a volume of poetry. I could not be more proud of their accomplishments.

The purpose of this small volume is to instruct young women who are beginning teachers in the primary grades and those who may be challenged by uncooperative students.

The classroom should be cheerful but uncluttered, with a minimum of decoration to distract the young mind.

Classroom rules should be simple and clear, stated in the

positive (that is, composed so as to leave out the words no *and* not*) and four or fewer in number. Here is an example of classroom rules that have worked nicely for me in a variety of schools.*

1. Treat everyone in this room kindly.

2. Speak only when called upon.

3. Finish your work.

Enforcement is a matter of rewarding the student who follows these rules with praise. In my experience, punishment is best omitted from the classroom.

Desks and chairs should be placed in neat, even rows facing the blackboard. Desks should be at a distance that impedes frequent student-to-student communication but does not hamper paper passing. Seat quiet workers at the heads of rows between their more vociferous counterparts. The front of the room is equally important for those whose behavior needs a constant watchful eye as well as those who consistently demonstrate quiet competence. The competent student is often ignored. Such an error can be as destructive to the good student as neglecting to teach a child to read.

Tailor all class activities so that they focus the child's attention on what is to be done next, and nothing else. All work should be completed in the classroom. Between the dismissal bell and the first bell the following morning, students' time should belong to themselves and their families. In the elementary grades, homework is necessary only for the teacher who has tried to pack too many activities into the day or who fails to motivate her students to complete their assignments. Instead of burdening students with uncompleted seat work, in this case it is the teacher who should take time in the evening to review and revise her practices so that they increase classroom productivity. A quiet, orderly classroom can achieve an astounding amount during the school hours.

When group chemistry is such that a class has difficulty applying itself to its purpose, small rewards will bring about renewed dedication and motivation. A chart may be helpful for tracking and celebrating student achievements and as a motivator for those who enjoy public acclaim. You will find that when classroom harmony is achieved, and only when it is achieved, students will perform to the full extent of their potential. The converse is also true: Discord in the classroom will result in a lapse in the group's progress. No group of children, however badly behaved or seemingly lacking in effort or intelligence, is beyond the reach of a good teacher with a loving heart.

Occasionally a child may slip behind the others. Allow this child some extra time with you after school or at recess. If you present this opportunity correctly, he or she will view this activity as a reward. Praise his or her every effort. While this may be the child you like least, soon your feelings will blossom into affection and approval. At exactly the same time you begin to feel your heart warming, the child will begin to retain his or her sums or letter sounds, or begin to read stories unaided from start to finish. Both of you will be rewarded for your efforts at precisely the same moment.

Like your classroom, female teachers' clothing should be plain and simple. In my long years of experience, I have found that the following colors will serve teachers best: the color of wet sand, the deep green of the ocean on a cloudy day, the white of a chicken's egg, the pale blue of a robin's egg, and the dark blue of the summer sky after the sun has entirely disappeared from the horizon. These colors, by reminding us of natural tones of the earth, will serve to calm and center your students. Hues that should be avoided include red, yellow, violet, and black. Patterns and textured fabric are best left out of the classroom entirely. A teacher's hair should, at all times, be kept back away from the face in a style that does not vary from morning to afternoon or from one day to the next. It is best to find a style in which the hair is held firmly in place by means of combs or other fasteners and from which there is no possibility of loose strands to distract either teacher or students. Once a hairstyle is chosen, it should remain invariable for the entire school year. Jewelry, it should be obvious by now, has no place in the classroom.

Because of the strenuous nature of the teacher's work, diet is an important factor in maintaining both physical stamina and a stable mood. A teacher's three daily meals should contain a careful balance of protein, starch, and fruits and vegetables. These meals should be of sufficient quantity to sustain high energy throughout the long work day. At the same time, teachers should make every effort not to overeat, which will lead to mental and physical sluggishness. To maintain an even temper, teachers should restrict their consumption of sweet desserts to no more than one per day, this to be enjoyed at home after school hours. While providing momentary pleasure, candies and rich desserts can contribute to unnecessary outbursts of impatience and temper. Especially in the lower grades, a teacher will occasionally find that fatigue is nearly overwhelming. Chances are, your class is feeling equally tired. An immediate session of vigorous exercise is the cure. Take a brisk walk around the school grounds. Jump in place 100 times in the classroom, chanting in unison material you are working on (an opportunity for counting, spelling, or addition practice as necessary!).

In the voice of Janet Greenhill, I wrote *A Young Teacher's Handbook.* When it was finished, I could see the way it would have been published in about 1935. It would have a dull green cover, and it would have been about sixteen pages long. I knew I could type it into my computer with very few changes. I bet I could even index Janet Greenhill's handbook and then later look up a problem, say, *addition, difficulty learning,* and the book would tell me what to do. This little book told me a lot about my main character, who, to my complete relief, wasn't me, after all, but a character I'd invented purely for the purposes of fiction.

You might be wondering where all this was coming from. Or, to put it another way, if I knew enough about teaching to write a little instruction manual, why didn't I just apply that knowledge to my class? Why bother with all the writing? This is tricky to explain. I didn't know *anything* about teaching. You've seen that. But Janet Greenhill, my character, did. And I had created her completely enough so that now she almost had a life of her own. Having her speak out like this was not even surprising. In fact, it seemed the most natural thing in the world. It happened every time I'd created a character—not right away, of course, but as soon as I had developed enough details about him or her. What was harder for me to understand is why I didn't let her speak out months earlier. But stories develop on their own schedules.

I put my pen down and closed my notebook. I stood in front of my closet and pulled out a blue dress, a hand-me-down from my mother ten or fifteen years before. I had never worn it because it was too plain; I didn't feel like myself in it. I hooked the hanger over the top of the door. I rummaged around until I found a pair of black pumps. I changed into the dress and shoes and redid my hair. With a couple of clips, I pulled it all back from my face and up off my neck. When I looked in the mirror, it seemed that Janet Greenhill was inside me looking out. "Take your seats quickly and quietly," I told an invisible class in a voice much lower than usual, "and start work at once." *At once,* I had said, using a Janet Greenhill phrase completely unconsciously.

When I was a writer, I had to explain over and over again that my fiction was *not* based on my life. People never believed me. No one ever asked me if my life was based on my fiction.

22

Early the next morning when I arrived at school in the blue dress, my hair pulled back, Cindy Roland, the receptionist looked up and said, "Is it Eleanor Roosevelt's birthday or something?"

As soon as I got to my room, I moved the desks. I lined them up, all facing the same way. Three feet of space separated the rows. The two most difficult boys, Seth and Ryan J., were at the heads of the second and fourth rows, with Rosie, who was quiet, obedient, and attentive, between them. There she would be a stabilizing influence without being overlooked.

I spent fifteen minutes pulling decorations off my bulletin boards and removing the mobiles I had dangling from the acoustic ceiling tiles. All of this fit nicely into a cardboard box that I stored at the bottom of the metal cupboard at the back of the room.

I passed out plastic bags of dried lima beans for each child along with a photocopied sheet of addition and subtraction problems. The first bell rang just as I finished. Quickly, I pinned up a chart with all my students' names and dropped a box of adhesive-backed stars into my dress pocket.

I went outside to where my class waited in line. The children stared at me; some of their mouths dropped open in surprise. "Boys and girls," I said. They had to stand still and strain to hear my low, measured voice. "I will be giving stars to those of you who go into our room quietly, find your new seats, and start working. I'll give you lots of chances to earn stars this morning. If you have five stars before lunchtime, you will earn something from my prize bag." I held up a cloth shopping bag.

Grace and Patience, at the front of the line, mimed locking their lips and throwing away the key. Seth did his best to snap to attention, arching backward, his hands stiff at his sides.

There was hardly a sound during math. The children watched as I stuck stars next to each of their names during the first ten minutes of class. When everyone had finished the math, I said, "Now, quietly take out your journals." I looked around the room, awarding stars as the children followed directions.

As soon as everyone was ready, I said, "Here is our opening sentence for today." I went to the board in the front of the room. I wrote, "December is a month of surprises." I didn't make this up; the whole district used the same writing book. I picked up my pointer. "Let's all read this sentence together." I pointed to each word in turn, as the children read the words in unison. "Perfect," I said. "Copy this sentence in your journals and then continue with at least five more complete sentences of your own."

"I can't think of anything!" Seth shouted, setting off several others.

"How do you spell 'Hanukkah'?"

"Can we write about something else?"

The day before, I would have shouted above the noise for them to be quiet and listen. Today I recalled a sentence from *A Young Teacher's Handbook*: *"To command student attention after control has been lost, a teacher's calm silence will bring order to a room far more quickly than loud, angry admonitions."* I stood still and silent at the front of the room, looking at them, waiting. The talking gradually subsided until all the children were looking up at me. I found that this was what I expected of them; I was not even surprised. I said, "Those of you who follow the Writing Rules will earn another star." On the spot, I pared down the eight steps from the writing book I'd recently thrown away. I used only two:

1. Get started.

2. Keep going.

I looked at what I had written. In four words, I had summed up everything I knew about how to complete a writing project. I used the pointer to guide the class through reading the rules aloud.

"Get started!" they chanted. "Keep going!"

"Good," I said, "No more questions." I brushed the chalk from my hands.

Just before lunch, I announced, "Boys and girls, each one of you has earned five stars." My chest filled with pride. I smiled at them, and they smiled back without a word. On their way out of the room, one by one, the children dipped into my bag to pull out an eraser shaped like an animal. They behaved as though I were handing out diamonds and rubies, instead of molded latex, and I knew that the changes I'd made were permanent.

I was eating lunch at my desk when Marilyn walked in and took a shocked step backward. "Whoa! *I* went to school in rooms arranged this way. What did you do with your decorations? Make sure you change it back before anyone else sees it!"

"I'm leaving it this way," I said.

Marilyn gasped. "Your seating plan doesn't follow district policy! You're supposed to group your desks in *cooperative clusters!*"

"Some district policies are impractical," I said crisply, surprised at my own conviction.

Marilyn stared at me. She spotted my star chart. "What's *this?* I hope you're not giving out prizes! Once you start that, there's no end to it." She folded her arms and looked me over. Today she was wearing a denim vest with red plaid presents around the bottom and Christmas-tree buttons down the front. "How come you're dressed like that?" she asked me accusingly. "Oh, I get it. A book character!"

"Yes," I said, wondering how she'd guessed.

"I hope you're not reading *Sarah, Plain and Tall* to them. That's fourth grade."

After school, I rang the doorbell, and Dylan let me in. "What are you—how come you're—Come in."

"Thank you," I said. My heels made a muted clopping sound on the tile floor.

Dylan and I sat down in the study. "As I mentioned last time, today I'll be testing you on the multiplication tables."

Dylan's face burned a deep pink, and he looked at the floor. This was new. Usually when he hadn't studied, he whined about all the other things he'd had to do that had prevented him from doing the assignment. Or he complained that the assignment was too hard.

I went through the multiplication flash cards quickly. He was confident through fives. When it was clear that he didn't know any of the higher ones, I stopped.

"Well done, Dylan. You know everything up through the fives. I'll test you again next time. If you know the multiplication facts through the eights, I'll have a prize for you." For a second, I worried that he would say, "No, thanks."

But Dylan didn't say that. He said, "You will?"

"Yes, I will."

"What prize?"

"I can't tell you that," I said quietly.

He looked at me for a long moment. "I'll try, Miss Dearborn. I promise I'll try."

I'd never heard him say he'd try anything before, and I don't think I ever heard him make a promise, either. I was not surprised to hear it now, though. For once, I had a clear impression of the true Dylan, not the whining, manipulative child that I had been nagging and cajoling three times a week for the last couple of months. This Dylan was sincere and hard-working. He wanted to do well. I looked into his deep brown eyes and said, "I know you will do your best, Dylan, and I'm looking forward to seeing the results." A tentative little smile flickered across his lips.

A couple of days later, I was wearing another blue dress. This one was the color of the sky on a cold winter day. It was one of several that I had bought at a church thrift store. All the dresses were too big, but I had taken them in, one per night for the past three nights. Like a paragraph describing a defining detail about a character, the right dress was key to my classroom persona.

In the work room, I was writing comments on students' papers. I printed a single sentence across the top of each paper: "Amanda, these are excellent sentences.—Miss Dearborn"; "Seth, your handwriting is improving every day.—Miss Dearborn"; "Patience, this is your best spelling test yet.—Miss Dearborn."

Bernice walked by on her way to the copier and looked over my shoulder. "Run out of stickers? I've got thousands you can have."

I looked up. "No, thank you," I said. I didn't use stickers anymore. If I just affixed a smiley face or stuck a happy apple at the top of each paper, how would they know I'd even read it?

"Oh," Bernice said, somewhat taken aback. "OK. Well. You write a comment on *each* paper? That's going to get old real fast. And it's going to take you forever to get their work back to them."

"Not really," I said. "If I do it as soon as they've turned the work in, I'm able to keep up with it easily."

Liz walked in. "Is that green construction paper in yet? Oh, great! I need this today." She took a packet of paper from a cupboard.

Bernice was quiet, reading what I wrote on one of Rosie's papers. "Look at this, Liz. Look how she marks her papers."

Liz came over to look. "Every paper? You write on each one? I bet they love that. But aren't you going to burn out on that pretty quick?" She shifted her paper to the other arm.

Over my head, Bernice commented to Liz, "It's extra reading practice for the kids to get all these comments."

"It is," Liz agreed. "They need that in first grade."

"I'll bet they think it's like getting mail," Bernice went on. "Reading all the notes on their papers. Additional reading practice is a benefit in any grade. And they feel their teacher is really paying attention to what they're doing."

"The parents would like it, too, I imagine. I'm going to try it on my kids," Liz said. "I'll see what happens with the spelling sentences they just gave me.

"I'll try it too," Bernice said. "I just got a bunch of math packets back."

Liz said, "We'll let you know if it helps."

"I'll be looking forward to that," I said.

"I think you're on to something here," said Bernice. "At first, I just thought, 'What a lot of busywork! She's just making it hard for herself.' But now I see how this could be very good for the kids. Oh, nice shoes, Miss Dearborn!" Since I'd started dressing differently, the other teachers had begun calling me Miss Dearborn. "Are they comfortable?"

"Thank you. Quite comfortable, yes." I was wearing a pair of navy suede shoes with low heels. They had thin leather laces and a high vamp that came right up to the top of my instep. I had bought them just the week before at an expensive specialty shoe store that carried wide shoes, insertable arch supports, and homely flat shoes with thick crepe soles for beleaguered feet required to keep marching. I didn't have a reason to go into that store, but for some reason, I did. I wasn't sure what feature of my new shoes was orthopedic, but I didn't think they'd be affordable. It turned out that they were a clearance item, which made them about the same price as a pair of the most basic sneakers. The one remaining pair happened to be my size, so I bought them.

Lately this was the kind of luck I was having; solutions appeared almost before I realized I had a problem. Until I saw this pair of shoes, I hadn't given a moment's thought to the fact that my feet had been aching nonstop since I started teaching. The way I was getting these lucky accidents kept reminding me of a story falling into place. After I finally got hold of my character, suddenly, out of the blue, dialogue popped into my head. All I had to do was write it down. Or several strands of plot that I hadn't been able to relate to one another seemed to tie themselves together perfectly. As I sat there in the teachers' work room, I realized that this was the kind of experience that I'd left out of my proposal for the book on writing. Imagine that! I thought.

And this was the very best part. This was the reason for writing in the first place, the magical, transcendental part that made writing worthwhile, the big payoff, when everything finally worked out, when I finally had no choice but to let the story out. I wrote for that feeling of absolute harmony. Now that I thought about it, this was probably the same feeling Rick got from a good day of surfing.

"Now, what kind of pen is that you're using?" Liz wanted to know, taking a seat at the table.

"Pardon?" It took me a second to get myself back into the conversation. "Oh, it's just a fountain pen."

"I haven't seen one of those in years," Liz said. "This reminds me of my grandmother! May I try it? Look at that! It has such a smooth flow! Where did you get that?"

"Just, you know, Office Depot or someplace," I said and shrugged.

"I'm going right down there today after school and get one. Your penmanship is excellent, Miss Dearborn," Liz said.

"Thank you."

"You have beautiful handwriting," Bernice agreed. "Where did you go to school?"

I almost said Kansas. I wondered if actors ever had this experience of their characters' lives spilling over into their own.

"Let me see." Bernice leaned over to have a better look at my handwriting.

I had already put my students' papers away, so I opened the notebook I carried with me to give her a look at a sample of my writing. In the middle of the page were the words, *"Soon her former role models were following her example."*

"Pretty," Bernice said. Picking up my pen, she copied the way I did the uppercase *S* on a piece of scrap paper.

I looked at the clock. In two minutes, the bell would ring.

Bernice handed me my pen. I capped it, closed my notebook, and put everything into my bag, another serendipitous find. At a garage sale down the street from my apartment last weekend, a man was selling a fabric-covered portfolio. It looked like old-fashioned sofa upholstery, intertwining flowers in muted colors. I went straight to it, picked it up, and paid the price he was asking, which was three dollars. The man shook his head. "You just never know what people are going to want. Here I'm sitting all morning with this good-as-new back massager." He held up a fat, five-fingered wand with an electric cord. "I can't *give* it away."

Now the bell rang, and Liz said, "Man your battle stations!"

"See you, Miss Dearborn," Bernice said.

On the way back to my classroom, I passed Rick as he was hurrying down the hall.

He stopped, turned around, and looked at me. "Miss Dearborn?"

"Yes, Mr. Barnstable?"

"Um," he said. Now that he had my attention, he seemed to have forgotten what he was going to say. "Oh, yes! Could we reschedule our candle-making activity?" He tried to straighten the papers he was carrying and somehow lost his hold of them, dropping the whole pile on the floor. "Whoops!" he said and sank to his knees to pick up the pile.

"Certainly," I said, crouching to gather some of the papers near my feet. "Let me check my schedule." I stood up and handed him the papers I'd gathered from the floor. I took out a small leather diary from my bag. "We're free Friday at eleven for half an hour. Are you available then?"

"Yeah, OK, good." He nodded. "I'll, yeah—that will work. Perfect."

"See you Friday morning, then," I said, returning the diary to my bag.

"Thanks. Book reports," he said, as if he needed to explain the papers he was carrying. "Have a nice day, Miss Dearborn."

"And the same to you, Mr. Barnstable." I turned to go to my class, who were lined up outside, waiting for me.

Dylan was working his way through a set of multiplication flash cards. He had paused at seven times eight.

"I know it! Wait!" he said squinting. He held up his hands. "Don't tell me! Fifty-six!"

"Excellent," I said. The next one was nine times six.

"Fifty-four!" he said, snapping his fingers.

"Well done!" I put the card in the "Correct" pile. The next one was nine times eight.

"Seventy-two!" he shouted.

"Right again," I said.

He made it through the whole stack and missed only three problems. At the end, I gave him a second chance on the ones he'd missed. This time he got all three. "Dylan, I'm very impressed," I said. I handed him a package of Red Vines. "All yours."

His hands closed around it as if it were a bar of gold bullion. "Thank you, Miss Dearborn," he whispered hoarsely, awed by his own performance.

"How did you learn all those, Dylan?" I asked. "You didn't know them last time I was here."

"I stayed up late and practiced," he said, smiling.

"You did very well. Let's move on to reading."

"I did the reading while I was waiting for you. Now I just have the questions."

This was the first time he'd started his homework without being told to. "Wonderful, Dylan!" I said. "You are just full of excellent surprises today." He smiled at me. "We'll be finished in no time. Let's get started on those questions."

He didn't need me for the questions. He knew the answers, or he knew where to look them up. I sat there for half an hour, watching him write and saying, "Perfect. Great. Good. Well done!"

Again, it was just like in writing a novel when a slight adjustment in one character brings out previously unseen qualities in others, resulting in significant and unexpected changes in the course of events. Sometimes you just have to abandon your original plot outline altogether as more interesting and satisfying developments come to you, seemingly out of the blue.

Friday morning as my class put away their reading books, I looked up to see Rick in the doorway. He was just standing still and staring at me, as if he'd forgotten why he came. I said, "Boys and girls, Mr. Barnstable and his class have arrived. We're going to make holiday gifts for our parents. Each of you will have a sixth-grader to help you with your project."

Rick's students carried their chairs inside and put them down next to the first-grade desks. While I gave the students tissue paper and gift tags, Rick passed out triangles of beeswax and string. But he was oddly clumsy and disorganized today. He dropped a piece of wax on the floor and accidentally stepped on it. "I have an extra," I said, as he tried to scrape red wax off the floor with a plastic ruler.

Rick explained how to make a beeswax candle, a project he said he'd done every year since he started teaching. He left out a few steps, though, and had to start the directions over a couple of times. A few weeks ago, I would have worried that one of my kids would call out rudely during his long, unusually halting explanation, making me look bad. But since I'd been applying the rules of *A Young Teacher's Handbook,* a deep calm flowed through me. There was not a single interruption.

"OK, that's it," Rick concluded and leaned against the chalk tray, knocking a box of new chalk to the floor. He bent to pick it up, and I saw that he now had a line of white dust across his backside. As the children turned to their projects, Rick handed me the chalk box, every stick now broken, and whispered, "Pretty dress."

My heart raced and my skin grew warm as I imagined that some of the students might have seen his fingers brushing gently against mine or heard him compliment my appearance. I walked quickly to the back of the room, where I pretended to help two students straighten their wicks.

I dreamed I was moving. I was standing in a garage filled with stuff, all kinds of old belongings that I'd somehow saved over a long period of time and that I'd need to sort through piece by piece, deciding what to keep and what to give away. I felt so overwhelmed about doing anything at all that I backed out, turned off the light, and closed the door. But then I was in the house, which was also piled with old furniture and clothes and books. How was I ever going to cope with this much stuff? I woke up and couldn't go back to sleep. I decided that this was like the anxiety dreams I used to have when I was beginning a novel. I knew what I would tell my students in such a situation.

1. Start.

2. Keep going.

Next I thought about the process of learning a new skill, say, reading, speaking a new language, or ice skating:

1. Start.

2. Keep going.

I thought about learning to play the piano and, for that matter, *teaching* someone to read or doing a fourth-grade social-studies project.

1. Start.

2. Keep going.

The strategies for assembling a photo album, walking across a continent, climbing to the top of Mount Everest all seemed to fit into the model. I added two more classroom rules that I used to keep my students focused.

3. Keep your eyes on your own work.

4. Stay in your seat until the bell rings.

The phrase "A Simplified System for Achieving Your Goals" came to me. I went to my computer and typed my idea. Two hours later, I closed the file. "Do you want to save changes to 'How to Write a Novel?' " the machine asked me. I clicked OK. But after I'd quit, I changed the title of the document to "How to Accomplish Anything You Want." The title had too many letters, so I cut it down to "How to Accomplish Anything." Then to simplify it even more, I dropped the "How to," reducing the title to "Accomplish Anything." On the manuscript, I would add the subtitle "A Simple System for Achieving Your Goals."

It would be a short book. I saw it as a small, slim paperback with a nostalgic cover. It could be positioned with gift books, journals, and calendars. The next day I printed out the manuscript. Without even so much as a cover letter, I put it into an envelope and addressed it to Howard.

Almost as soon as I'd dropped the manuscript into the outgoing mail slot at the post office, I forgot about it. There was so much to do before the vacation. I wanted my class to finish two more spelling units and complete one more math packet before the holidays started. And I wanted to have every bit of their work corrected and returned for the children to show to their parents.

Every day now I went to school early. I spent my breaks in the work room, instead of the lounge. It was quieter there, and as no food was allowed, I didn't have to keep explaining that I wasn't on a diet. After writing Janet Greenhill's *A Young Teacher's Handbook,* I'd completely lost the desire for cupcakes, brownies, and butter-flavored microwave popcorn. For breakfast, I ate a bowl of oatmeal with milk and raisins, and drank a glass of orange juice. At recess, I usually had a banana. Lunch was a sandwich and an apple. Without much thought or effort, I noticed I had started to lose weight.

23

One morning, I was just about to leave for school when the phone rang. "Hello?" I said.

"Charlotte," a voice declared.

It took me a couple of seconds to recognize the voice. I had been so focused on my class and their journals that it was hard to think about something completely unrelated. "Oh, Howard," I said. "It's early!" Howard never called me before nine, my time. Over the years, you get used to a person's telephone habits. He must be in town or having some kind of crisis.

"It's OK. I'm up and everything. I just—"

"Big," he said.

"What?" I said.

"This is big. Really big," he repeated.

"What is?" I said. "What's big?"

"*What* is big? Are you being coy with me? The new work, your *manuscript* is big."

"Oh, that," I said. "You read it? I'm sorry. I apologize for that.

Just toss that. I don't know what gets into me sometimes. You know, I'm teaching first grade, you know, six-year-olds, and I'm with these little kids all day, and I guess I—"

"Stop. Listen to me," he said. "Are you listening?"

"Yes, Howard," I said.

"This. Is. Huge."

"What—no, I—"

"Charlotte, this is it, your escape route. This is your ticket out. Or in, depending on your perspective. It's your entrée into the big numbers. Big advance. Big control. Big sales. This. Is. It. You're on your way. Now, I have to admit that there have been times in the past when I questioned our—"

"Howard?" I interrupted him.

"What, babe? What is it, my love?"

"I'm glad you're happy with, with something I've done. I appreciate that. Really. I do. But, you know, now that I've had a chance to think this over, I don't want to go through with the process of submitting this to publishers. Forget it. OK? Forget I sent you the book. You can send it back. Or better yet, just dump it. I don't think I want to see that again. It's just sort of this—well, a kind of—I wrote it as sort of a note to myself, let's say. I really shouldn't have let anyone else see it."

There was a long silence. Then Howard turned away from the phone and snapped at someone, "Tell him I'm on the phone with a client and I'll call him back!" To me, he said, softly, gently, "What is this about, Charlotte?"

I thought a minute. "I no longer have the stomach for the process. I want to drop it. And, really, this book is nothing. You know, like those pocket so-called 'inspirational' books they have by the cashier's counter in bookstores, the ones with the pretty covers that say what everybody knows already? Nothing. There's nothing to it."

"Charlotte. Listen to me. Are you listening?"

"Yes, Howard. What?"

"Two things. First. Those little books that you dismiss with such scorn, those books *sell. Lots* of copies. That's why they get that nice spot near the cash register. You with me here? That's what those charming covers are all about. People like them, they pick them up to hold them. They open those little books and find something they want to read. They're already standing in front of the cash register with their wallets open, so—You see how that works? Two. This is good. I mean, the actual work, the, you know, what it says. It's good."

" 'Start' and 'keep going' is good? Howard, no. Come on. You're kidding. Are you kidding? Sometimes it would really help if I could see your face. Like right now I'd like to see your expression, because I can't tell if you're serious."

"Charlotte, you're making me a little crazy here. You should know that I am absolutely sincere about this!"

"Oh." I had to think about this a minute. "But I think people know enough to start and keep going. I mean, I think they can figure out that the way to—"

"*You* may know it already. Even *I* may know it already. But there are a lot of people out there who would like a sweet little book to carry around that will tell them, urge them to *start, keep going.* They'd like to have the reassurance of that, the encouragement, the gentle, loving push in the right direction. You've got all these people out there in the world not doing that thing, that one special thing, that they were put on this earth to do. And here it is, for $2.95, or hell, let's go for it, $4.95, you're giving them the two things they need to go ahead with that."

"I am?" I said. "And what two things are those?"

"You—you really have no idea, do you? All right, then, I'll tell you. The two things they need are *permission* to try and *discipline* to follow through." With an urgency that I'd rarely heard in his voice, he whispered, "There's something simple and deeply lovely, something truly *good* about this message." He seemed to choke up at the last part of that sentence. I tried to make myself believe that maybe it was just phlegm or a stifled burp, but I had been talking to this man for a good portion of my adult life, and, honest to God, it sounded as though Howard was moved to tears about *Accomplish Anything.*

"Howard?" I said. I didn't quite know what to do here. This had never happened before. "Howard, are you OK? Is there anything going on with you that—"

"Charlotte," he stated. "I'm an agent. I'm not an artist, and I don't think I've ever pretended to have any talent or taste. But there are some things I *know.* You know how I know? I get this humming in the back of my neck and it spreads down my spine and up into my skull. I'm hearing it now, Charlotte. Mmmmmmmmm. Right this minute. It's so loud and insistent, I'm surprised you can't hear it yourself, through the phone. Listen to me. Are you listening?"

"Yes, Howard. I'm listening."

"Here's what the humming is telling me: This. Will. Sell."

I didn't hear any humming, but I could hear him bang his fist against a file cabinet for emphasis on each word. "Well, gee," I said. "Food for thought. Yeah. Sure is. Can I get back to you on this?"

"*I'm* supposed to say that!" he barked. "What do *you* have to get back to me about? You wrote a book. I can sell it. What's to think about? This is what we do! We're going to auction with this one, Char."

"Char? You never called me Char before."

"Excuse me. Please forgive that lapse. I should be calling the author of this beautiful work 'Miss Dearborn.' " He took a breath. "Miss Dearborn, I would be honored to have the privilege of offering this book at auction."

"*Auction*? You're thinking auction on this? Geez, Howard, I don't know. None of my other books ever got—"

"Charlotte!" he snapped. "What's the matter with you? You wrote something good! You've elevated your own smallness until it has huge, magnificent resonance. For God's sake, I just want to take it out there and get some money for you. That's my job! I take the product of your incredible talent and hard work, I journey out into the ugly and dangerous marketplace for you, I do battle with the terrifying forces of competition and limited vision, and I return with money. *Your* money. Think about it for twenty-four hours, if you want to, but then I'm going for it. I don't care what you say. I haven't had anything this good in—well, in too long." He banged the phone down.

I called my sister. "Howard's lost it. He's nuts. No sense of humor. It's awful. I haven't talked to him often enough lately to know what's going on, so I really don't know what it's about. Maybe someone died. Or maybe he's going through some sort of mid-life catastrophe or something. I think he's about mid-life range. Of course, I've never *seen* him, but I've always thought—I hope he's not sick or something."

"What happened? What did he do?"

"I sent him this little manuscript—I left one for you at the house. It was in an envelope on the coffee table You were on the phone, and I forgot to tell you. Anyway, I should have just thrown it away. It was this trifling thing that I just whipped out. You know those inspirational—"

"Wait. I read it already. I was going to call you tonight."

"Oh, so you know that it was just a—"

"I love it. I was waiting for the boys in the car after school. I started reading it, and it seemed like this rude interruption when the kids got into the car. I read some more at basketball practice. I couldn't stop. I had to order pizza for dinner so I could finish it. That little book just blew me away. It's *good.* I cried. It made me want to change my whole life. Charlotte, I'm selling the store! That's not all. There's more. I figured out my new career! I've decided. You know how I've always wanted to—"

"Emily?" I said.

"What?"

"You're selling the store? Just like that?"

"It's not just like that. I should have done it a long time ago. And I wouldn't have done it at all if it weren't for *Accomplish Anything.* I love this little book. It's changed my life! When it's published, I'm going to give copies to everyone I know. Hey, maybe I'll just start handing it out to strangers, people I don't even—"

"You can't be saying what I think you're saying. We're supposed to agree on everything."

"Sorry. But I'm telling you I could photocopy the manuscript, staple it together, and sell it as is. You're too close to the material to see it clearly."

I didn't say anything. I felt as though any minute someone was going to jump out of my closet and say, "April Fool!"

"I love it," my sister said. "I think other people will too. I know they will. It's very simple."

"Of course it's *simple,*" I said. "There's nothing to it!" Maybe I was dreaming. That was it. I was going to wake up any minute and find myself in bed or on the couch with the TV on. "Em, I'd be embarrassed to have my name on that book."

"Make up a pseudonym."

"I can't do that! I can't—" I stopped and considered.

"Sure you could. You could make it a man's name, like the Brontës did."

"No, I wouldn't want to do that."

"OK," she said. "You keep your own initials, but just make up a fake—How about Carol Dunlap, something like that?"

"Honestly, Emily, do you think Howard can really sell it?"

"I do. Are you kidding? *Yes.*"

"Oh, my god," I said. "Oh, my god."

"Yeah," my sister said. "No kidding."

True to his word, Howard called me back exactly twenty-four hours after our last conversation. "I've got three editors who want to see this right away and two others I'm going to talk to as soon as I have your go-ahead. Bethany is making copies right now."

"I want to use a pseudonym," I said. "You didn't tell anyone I was the author, did you?"

"No, no, no. I didn't want to give them too much yet. A pseudonym! That's brilliant! Real genius. Yes. Perfect! It's a fresh start. You won't have your old sales record dragging you down. Sometimes it's better to be an unknown, to just explode onto the scene out of nowhere. No expectations. I'm very excited about this, Char."

"Call me Carol."

"Carol?"

"Carol Dunlap. My sister made it up. It's my pseudonym."

"Hm. I don't like the Carol. Can we jazz that up a little? How about Carly? Candy? Chrystal?"

"Those don't sound real. Christine, then?"

"Christine Dunlap. Now the Dunlap is falling flat for me."

"Hold on. Hold on. I have it!" I said. "It's Janet Greenhill."

"OK," Howard said slowly. "Yes, I like that. Good. Down to earth, simple, sounds like a character from an old English novel. Then again, it sounds real. A new author appears on the horizon. Now, look. I'm thinking series here. So, work with me on this.

We can follow up this one with other 'Janet Greenhill' titles, but not right away. If you think of something, go ahead and write it, but we'll sit on it for a while. Let's not give them too much right now. You're with me on this, right, Char?"

"Sure, How."

"*Charlotte.* Sorry. What comes over me? But, no, I'm serious. Listen to me. Are you listening?"

"I'm listening."

"This book will change everything. Everything. I'm telling you: Through. The. Roof. Now, I'm going to present it as the work of a first-grade teacher. *A First-grade Teacher's Guide to Life.* Something like that. You like it? It makes you think of this simple, no-nonsense, uncluttered approach to solving problems. But I want you to like this. I want *you* to be happy."

"Sure," I said. "I'm happy. Whatever. Now what happens if they want to meet Janet Greenhill or send her on tour or something?"

"Can you just let me handle this one step at a time? Can you trust me that much, believe that I know what I'm doing? I have been selling books for a long time, and I do know this part. Also, just as a personal challenge, I'm going to try to withhold paperback rights for now. Then when the book takes off, we'll have something else to sell."

"Can you do that?"

"Not easily. Not the way we used to. But I'm going to give it my best shot," he said. "God damn it, I *believe* in this book. I'm going to give it everything I have. I'm making it my own personal cause."

Suddenly it hit me that I had been talking to Howard all these years, that he was as close to me as any three-dimensional person in my life. We had been through so much together over my work. I said, "Howard, I want to thank you for all you've done for me all these years. I believe it's common knowledge, I mean it's a well-known fact, at least I hope everyone realizes, that, that I love you with all my heart and all my soul." I paused, exhaled. "I just wanted to say that. I just wanted you to know."

Howard cleared his throat. "Thank you, Charlotte. I'm very fond of you, too. Now, was that it? Were you done? Because I've got one of those other editors on another line."

"Oh. Yeah, I guess," I said. "That's all."

Howard sold the book in forty-eight hours. Five editors fought over it. One of them didn't even have time to read the thing before he jumped in with his bid. Janet Greenhill got more money for this slim, simple volume than I'd gotten for all my previous books put together and all their combined royalties to date. If she had wanted to spend her advance, she could have bought a four-bedroom house with a nice view in the neighborhood where the kids in my class lived and still have enough money left over to live on for a year. I mean she could have paid cash for the house. Of course, she wouldn't do that. She wasn't the type.

The last day before the winter vacation, some of the mothers brought cupcakes for the class. While the children ate, I opened the presents they had brought me. Seth's gift was a basket of bath products, my third of the day. This one was peppermint-scented, a holiday touch. "It smells like candy canes!" he shouted.

A few weeks ago, I had worried that Seth would never learn to sit at a desk for more than a three-minute stretch, let alone memorize the short vowel sounds. But just this morning, he had read the class three jokes out of a book I had given him as a reward for a week of good behavior, his glasses slightly crooked on his nose. As I held Seth's gift, I had a tight, clawing feeling in the middle of my chest: love. I hugged him and inhaled his familiar scent: sweat, pencils, peanut butter. Without warning, my eyes filled with tears. I said, "Thank you for your gift, Seth!"

After the last bell, I packed my presents into a shopping bag and locked my room. I congratulated myself on getting out of school promptly. None of my students had missed the bus or forgotten a sweatshirt.

Instead of going home, I went downtown to a movie theater that was showing a series of films based on classic novels. I had tickets for the entire series, my reward to myself for all my hard work at school. Today was the first one, *Jane Eyre,* the 1944 version with Orson Welles and Joan Fontaine. The theater was surprisingly full for the time of day. While I waited, I took out an old copy of the novel that I'd had since high school. Shortly before the film, a man's voice said, "Excuse me? Is that seat taken?"

"No," I said, taking my jacket off the arm of the chair next to me.

"Miss Dearborn?"

I looked up. It was Rick.

"What a coincidence!" he said. His hair was windblown, and he was slightly out of breath. "Well, it's not really. I wanted to talk to you after school, but you were already in your car and—well, so, I followed you, then I couldn't find a parking space! I had to run to get here before—" With a sigh, he sank into the empty seat.

I nodded, wondering if I was going to speak at all.

He looked at me. With the tip of his index finger, he tentatively touched the edge of my sleeve at my wrist. "Velvet?"

I nodded. Today my dress was sea-green with fabric-covered buttons from its ankle-length hem all the way to its high mandarin collar.

Rick cleared his throat. He said, "A few weeks ago, when you came by my room, you asked me to—" He took a deep breath and then exhaled. "I wanted you to know I'm not *that* busy. I don't know why I—So, after the movie, I was thinking, if you want, I mean if you don't have any other—we could—" There was a pause that went on and on, as if he had no idea what words to use next.

As I mentioned, changes in one character often trigger unexpected transitions in others. It's a ripple effect, one seemingly small alteration affecting first what is closest to it and then creating movement in ever-widening circles until nothing is left as it was.

"—have dinner?" he finished finally.

Quietly, I said, "There's something I've been meaning to tell you." Honestly, this was the first I'd heard of it myself. "You're the reason I came to Corona Vista Elementary. The more I've gotten to know you, the more I want to be with you." I didn't know I was going to say this; it just came out.

The theater lights suddenly dimmed, so that for a few seconds, we were in complete darkness. In that suspended moment, he took my hand in both of his and kissed my open palm.

Once you've established your character, when you've found that critical, defining detail, you just have to get out of the way and watch what she does.

24

I didn't change anything right away, just kept going to work every day, teaching. I supervised the building of Dylan's model California mission, San Juan Capistrano. At the beginning of the project, I had a brainstorm and got him together with Emily's son Ted, who had to make the San Luis Rey mission. The two boys hit it off, working hard in Emily's garage for several weeks.

When the check came in for my advance, I did buy a pair of incredibly expensive walking shoes (over $100!) to wear to school and new seat covers for my car. I got very generous birthday gifts for my niece and nephews.

There are hard-working, talented writers producing perfectly beautiful jewels in the dark underground cave of fiction. Unfortunately, because the light of the marketplace fails to shine on the fruits of their labor and bring them up to the surface, these authors get diddly for their efforts. It makes you sick, doesn't it?

Accomplish Anything was chosen as a Book-of-the-Month Club Main Selection. I started getting royalties before you could say *New York Times* best-seller list, which it entered right away in a high position and stuck. When I thought people had finally had enough of the book, Howard sold the paperback rights, and I got more money.

My novels languished for a while. Then I wrote an article about Janet Greenhill for a big women's magazine. In that article, I included a summer reading list, the author's favorite books. Janet Greenhill said that Charlotte Dearborn was one of the most underrated novelists of our time. My fiction sales improved dramatically. Before you knew it, I was getting manuscripts in the mail from writers who until recently had had bigger names than mine, asking for *my* endorsement. And I don't think it was any coincidence that I won two awards that year and that I was asked to sit on a couple of important panels and judge a national fiction competition. Sometimes all it takes is the support of one important author to make all the difference between struggle and success.

Two weeks after Howard sold *Accomplish Anything,* my sister sold her store. She said she had always wanted to teach. This was news to me. Not kids, she said, she'd always wanted to teach adults. She told me that my little book had made her finally realize that it was important to do that one thing that you felt you were born to do. (I want to make it very clear here that I do not take credit for urging people to live their dreams. I did not say that anywhere in the book. I've looked; it's not there. But it turns out, people saw it there anyway and credited my book for inspiring them to do exactly what they'd always dreamed of doing.) The publisher was giving Howard a hard time about promotion, so I suggested it to my sister. She loved the idea. Emily went to work immediately as Janet Greenhill. She got a good haircut and a lot of nice new clothes, all of which I paid for, of course. She taught a series of *Accomplish Anything* workshops. I wrote scripts for motivational audio tapes, and Emily recorded them. She was much more successful with this than she ever was with the store.

Janet Greenhill got a lot of fan mail. I was a little jealous, but I answered it for her. I believe that if someone takes the time to write to an author, the author should have the grace and good manners to write back. I practiced a signature for Janet Greenhill, straightforward and clear, but with a certain distinctive, old-fashioned style.

I did make it through my first year of teaching, but I didn't stay for a second. I put the experience to good use, though, in the novel I'd started before I thought I had to give up. The book turned out differently than I planned, much better, actually. It wasn't anything like *Jane Eyre,* after all. It was about a grade-school teacher who, in mid-life, finds unexpected success and fulfillment by publishing her notebooks. *A Young Teacher's Handbook* was a little chunk of the book and gave me a toehold, something to hang on to in the early days of my rewrites.

Rick and I are now working on a book together, a guide to writing for children and teenagers about how to use real-life experiences as a basis for fiction. At first, I was reluctant to collaborate with him. We've been married less than a year, and I was worried about mixing our work and personal lives. But after I'd thought it over, I realized that if I were completely honest, it would be hard to find a clear dividing line between the two. Sometimes I still help Dylan with homework, for example, but he also goes to the beach with us, Rick's daughters, and Emily's kids.

All of these developments were unexpected, but they shouldn't have been. Life is like writing a novel: You set off in a certain direction and then end up somewhere else altogether. Upon your arrival at the surprise destination, you think, "If only I'd known then what I know now, this is where I would have been going in the first place. This is where I belong."